Pieces & Stems

Stories By
Stephen O'Rourke

ISBN: 978-0-615-54300-0

We are tied to each other,
just as the messenger is to him
to whom the message is addressed . . .
If a game is being played with you,
it is not less so with me.

FRANZ KAFKA

For Beatriz and Evan . . .

Contents

The Curse
of the
White Squirrel

My name is Bogswell, Dr. Jonathan Bogswell. I am Chief Psychiatrist at Beeswax Hospital, Port St. Blackie, New Water. I have been Chief Psychiatrist at Beeswax Hospital for a couple of years. Prior to arriving at Beeswax, I had tenure at Mt. Ursus Hospital, also in New Water, for thirteen years. Over these past fifteen years, I've written a number of papers that have been printed in well-respected medical journals and have earned the respect and admiration of my colleagues in the field. I mention my credits here in the beginning of this story in advance so that the reader will understand that by no means am I a novice to the medical profession. I also want to qualify that hitherto, I have never exploited the revered doctor-patient privilege by breaching the confidence of any individual under my own care. Indeed, it is with regret that I find I must do so here by discussing the details of one Steveann Gooding. I only do so because as a patient of mine, Steveann, more than any other individual that I have ever treated, impacted my

1

own life in a way that should be a lesson to all medical physicians, and especially those practicing psychiatry. It is the reason that I have submitted this story to the *New York Journal of Medicine*.

I first heard the name Steveann Gooding on the first day of April, 2001. I recall it was a beautiful spring morning. There was a gentle breeze that rustled the leaves of the oak trees near my home, the birds were singing and children were laughing (there is a schoolyard right near Beeswax). Everywhere I looked I saw the world renewing itself. I remember having a sense that I was on top of the world as I stepped out of my Lamborghini in the hospital parking lot. I had a feeling that there was nothing I couldn't do if I set my mind to it. I also recall feeling very good about my place in the world as a physician. Knowing that I was of salutary importance to my fellow man on the very basic level of mental health, made me feel at harmony with the world and of indispensable value. Needless to say, I was in a good mood and more than confident of my abilities as I arrived at my office that morning. I slipped into my white lab coat and began the routine of my duties with an inimitable vim and vigor. The first thing I did was return a few of the phone messages left on my answering machine and secondly I perused some papers concerning a patient I was to meet later that day. The woman suffered a severe nervous breakdown and her family was less than optimistic about her ever recovering. They were considering committing her to a mental institution and I was perceived as being her last hope for rehabilitation.

At that point in time, Steveann was living with her Aunt and Uncle. They were her only family. Steveann had been thrown out of her own home for not paying the bills and had nowhere else to turn. What precipitated her losing the house was her fear of leaving the house. Steveann had been afraid of a white squirrel that supposedly lived on her porch. No one else had ever seen this white squirrel but that made the squirrel no less a reality to Steveann. It was because of this phantom that she'd lost her job and with it her ability to fend for herself independently. It seems she did not go outside of the house even for the most basic necessities like food and health aids. Fearing for her welfare, her Aunt and Uncle gradually assumed the responsibility of providing her with these necessities. Steveann accepted their gifts but would only do so through a window located in the back of the house. This window was the only one in the house that Steveann would open fully because she said it was, "just high enough to prevent the white squirrel from getting in." Steveann was also paranoid that the squirrel might spring at her from one of the tree branches in the yard. There were a lot of trees and all of the other windows happened to be located near or at least not far from these trees. Steveann argued this point as a reason for caution. Opening the door for others to come into the house had never been an option. Steveann considered such a proposal, "an unnecessary risk." This paranoia had affected her so severely that she reportedly did not sleep at night, fearing that if the squirrel did somehow gain entry she would be caught in a vulnerable position. For the same reason she did not like to be 'distracted' on the telephone for too long.

According to the notes available to me, once Steveann had gone to live with her Aunt and Uncle, she did show some signs of improvement. For instance, she reportedly stopped seeing the white squirrel, she started to sleep again and on nice days even ventured outside to help her Aunt with the gardening in the yard. This was quite a development for a woman who only a month before refused to even step foot out of her own house. Steveann's Aunt and Uncle attributed this improvement to the fact that Steveann had been removed from the troubling environment of her 'lonely home life.' They assumed that by bringing her to live with them they had put Steveann on the road to recovery. Unfortunately, this proved to not be the case. It was only a matter of weeks before Steveann began to talk of the 'white squirrel's return.' What brought this fear of hers to the surface again is unknown. What is known is that Steveann began to take out books on squirrels from the local library, ostensibly to better understand the demon that she expected to encounter again. Steveann also occupied an inordinate amount of time furthering her research with the Internet. As if that were not enough, she took it upon herself to contact many prominent geneticists around the country to find out if a white squirrel was possible as an aberration in nature. She was told by one of these geneticists that white squirrels were not only possible, but did in fact already exist in nature. This was just enough to push her to the brink. Steveann confided to her Aunt that she'd been hoping to have confirmation that a white squirrel could not actually exist, even if that meant she was demented. She considered it a small price to pay for the reassurance of knowing she could never be attacked by 'such an abominable creature.'

Having read all of this research on Steveann and having had the opportunity to meet with her family later that same morning, I had a pretty good idea of what to expect from her. As a psychiatrist, I had seen this type of patient many times before. I expected to meet a woman lacking good reason, nervous in demeanor and defensive about the choices she had made leading up to her debacle. To my great surprise, I found instead a rational creature, well composed and dare I say even charming; a woman who seemed to recognize and even regret the extent to which she 'cowered' from her problems, instead of facing them. But I wasn't quite sure whether or not to believe her. Individuals suffering from diseases of the mind are usually not able to cure themselves without at least some medical assistance. I suspected that Steveann held onto the reality of her delusions as vigilantly as ever, but recognized in advance the futility of trying to sell them to me as her appointed physician. At the same time, I suspected that she wanted to spare herself the untold aggravation of arguing her own sanity. Furthermore, I suspected that she had only agreed to meet me in an attempt to placate her family's concerns. I've seen this kind of game played before in my experience. In the end, such charades are revealed for what they are. Individuals suffering from delusions of this magnitude cannot conceal their infirmity from the eye of a trained physician. Yet it seemed that no matter how hard I tried I could not get Steveann to discuss her thoughts on the white squirrel with a convincing expression of honesty. She spoke as if the white squirrel and all that it had wrought were another's concern or a distant faded memory that no longer bore relevance. It took much concentrated effort before I finally hit upon a therapeutic approach. I asked her to talk about the day that she first encountered the white squirrel. To my delight, she gave a narrative that seemed to be forthright and not at all lacking in subjective detail. It was as if I was there with Steveann on that first day she encountered the demon that had wrecked her life.

It was snowing that morning with a calm and quiet of a winter's day when all of the children are at school and the neighbors at work. Steveann had called her office and told them that she would not be coming in. She wanted to spare herself the long messy commute into the city and did so by telling her boss that she was feeling under the weather. She spent the rest of the morning quietly waiting for the postman. Steveann had been expecting some important documents, so when she saw the mail truck stop in front of her house and then saw the postman shove some envelopes into her mailbox, she became excited. Steveann quickly put her coat on and ran down to the curb, leaving her door unlocked. When she got to the mailbox and opened it, she was somewhat surprised to see that it was empty. But beyond a little disappointment she didn't give it another thought. She shrugged it off thinking she must have been mistaken about what she had seen and decided to go back into the house. On her way up the front lawn, Steveann was startled by something that moved in front of her. She could not quite discern exactly what it was because whatever it was it blended in perfectly with the white of the snow on the ground. All that she could definitely make out were two small eyes that reminded her of watermelon pits, but then gradually as she continued to stare she made out the shape of an animal with a fluffy tail. What drew her attention to this tail was a jerky, sudden movement. It was at that moment, as Steveann studied the animal, that she realized it was blocking her path back to the house. As Steveann decided her next move (she was afraid to walk past this creature or around it), she finally guessed what it might actually be. It looked like a squirrel or some other rodent. The animal remained very still and did not move, until Steveann attempted to frighten it away by stomping her foot. Steveann was startled by its reaction. The white squirrel repositioned itself so as to block her path to the house more completely. That betrayed an intelligence that Steveann had not expected to encounter. Lacking the wherewithal to do much else, she rolled a snowball and threw it at the animal. The squirrel moved, but only just enough to dodge the snowball. Steveann was exasperated. She looked at her watch. It was 11:25. Her favorite television game show was about to start but unless she could circumnavigate her way around the animal there was an even chance that she might miss the program entirely. The thought frustrated her patience to its absolute limit. Steveann hissed and cursed at the squirrel, she stomped her foot and threw another snowball. But it didn't seem to make a difference. The squirrel was as obstinate as she was. Just when she thought it would never move again, the squirrel surprised her. It climbed the porch steps and waited by the door, wagging its tail like a playful puppy. It was at this point, that Steveann could fully see the form of the white squirrel against the background of the red brick steps. She tried to recall if squirrels hibernated in the winter. She thought she remembered learning in school that they did. But if that was the case, 'Why wasn't this squirrel hibernating?' she asked herself. Was this white squirrel a freak of nature? Possibly it wasn't a squirrel at all but only looked like one. Steveann continued to stare at the animal and the animal continued to stare back. It was like the white squirrel was mocking her with its stare, daring her to cross it and challenge its resolve. Steveann thought to do that very thing by stepping right over it to get into the house. But in a follow up thought she wondered if the squirrel would bite her. What if it was rabid? Steveann was again at a loss. She remembered the back door but just as soon remembered that she hadn't the key. Steveann made up her mind to go around back and find a way in, somehow. She removed a pin from her hair and walked around to the back of the house. She climbed the steps of the porch and stuck the hairpin into the lock. After about ten minutes of tinkering around with the hairpin, she knew it was not going to deliver the results she had hoped for. Her frustration mounted when she heard the phone ringing inside of the house. The thought occurred to her, what if it was someone from work checking up on her? If she'd called in sick, they would certainly wonder why she wasn't answering the phone when they called. She sighed as she noticed the snow starting to fall a little heavier. She could see the layers of snow adding up on the ground. Steveann felt her head and was surprised to see how wet it was. She cursed herself for not putting a proper hat on before she left the house. All at once, she made up her mind to break the glass windowpane of the door and unlock the latch with her hand. But Steveann's bright idea proved itself harder to execute than to conceive. Steveann was not a big fisted woman, nor was she strong enough to deliver a blow powerful enough to break the door's window. She did not let any of that stop her though. Steveann banged at the door repeatedly, because it made her feel better. She was just about to give up and seek the help of her neighbors when she saw out of the corner of her eye the little black eyes of the white squirrel in the snow. It had been watching her; Steveann wondered for how long. As she stared at the animal and it at her, eye to eye, she wondered if it had any comprehension of the aggravation it had caused her. Indeed, she wondered if the animal relished the aggravation it had caused her. Suddenly, a thought dawned on Steveann. If the white squirrel was in the backyard with her that meant that the front door was unguarded and she did not waste a second racing down the steps of the back porch and around the corner of the house back to the path that led to the front door. Steveann ran up the porch steps excitedly. She heard a mad laugh escape her lips as she opened the front door and felt the warmth of her home again. She could not believe that she was inside of the house! Steveann had an overwhelming sense of victory over the white squirrel as she turned to close the door but it was then that she realized the shortcomings of her haughty conceit. The squirrel was half way in the door, practically inside of the house itself! Steveann screamed and kicked the animal as she opened the door again more fully in an effort to oust it from the premises. In a flash, she had succeeded where others with slower reflexes might have failed. If her timing had been just a fraction of a second off, the white squirrel would have been in the house, causing unimaginable damage and potentially posing a health risk, according to Steveann. As a psychiatrist, I called her entire fantasy into question. As you will see, it knew no limits. For instance, Steveann told me that from that day onward the white squirrel never left her front porch. She went so far as to declare that the white squirrel would still be on her front porch had the bank not foreclosed on her house and forced her out. In a Socratic effort to help Steveann draw her own rational conclusions, I asked her if her Aunt and Uncle had ever seen the white squirrel for themselves, either during the time she was a self-imposed exile in her own home or later after she had moved in with them. What Steveann told me was a jolting surprise. She said that her family never saw the white squirrel for themselves until after she had moved in with them. If this was true, and I suspected it wasn't, it meant that Steveann's Aunt and Uncle had been less than forthcoming with me about their own delusions. But mass hallucination is not as easy to believe in as are the lying habits of a desperate (and potentially deranged) woman. Especially when the testimonial is from that desperate (and potentially deranged) woman herself. Nevertheless, I allowed her to continue, hoping she would betray her sophistry and reason for it in some respect. Steveann then added that her Aunt and Uncle believed her to be cursed. Furthermore, they believed she'd passed the curse onto them. I interrupted her only briefly to find out how she believed the curse passed on. Steveann said she had passed on the curse of the white squirrel merely by telling the story of her encounter with it. Steveann also said that her Aunt and Uncle were now seeking to rid themselves of the curse by passing it onto someone else, someone that they did not know or care about. Steveann confided to me that that person was none other than myself, 'the good doctor.'

Of course, all of this sounded perfectly ridiculous. But the story as told by Steveann did offer an explanation for her quiet and reserved demeanor. If she honestly believed what she told me, that meant she believed herself cured of *The Curse of the White Squirrel*. No doubt, this conclusion conflicted with what her Aunt and Uncle told me. To remind the reader, Steveann's Aunt and Uncle claimed she had certain expectations of encountering the demon again. And while I did not altogether dismiss the possibility that they'd lied to me, I found it much harder to accept Steveann's insinuation that they were cold, calculating liars that sought my counsel only as a pretense to pass on their curse to me. Steveann explained that her Aunt and Uncle had calculated their plan carefully. They wanted to pass the curse on to a Good Samaritan that would never suspect their malicious intent. A psychiatrist was a logical choice because a psychiatrist would embrace the challenge of the curse as an opportunity of his profession.

Honestly, I wanted to laugh out loud. It was only my professional ethics that prevented me from doing so and it was that same ethical frame of mind that directed me to listen and to nod and to politely ask Steveann follow up questions that I knew could only lead to even more ludicrous answers. Trying to find a weakness in her story, I asked Steveann what she thought the origin of the curse was. Where did she think it came from? Predictably enough, she told me that she couldn't be sure. However, she did offer what she called her Auntie Moira's explanation:

"Auntie believes the curse came from the mysterious postman on that fateful day. Remember I saw the postman just before I saw the squirrel. Also recall, that when I looked in the mailbox it appeared as though nothing was inside. But Auntie Moira says that there was indeed something inside of the mailbox on that day. I just couldn't see what it was. And although this *something* was invisible to me, I did feel its presence soon enough. Auntie Moira called this *something* the equivalent of a chain letter. I am, of course, speaking of the curse. It was passed onto me that day and I inadvertently passed it on, albeit unwittingly, to my dear Aunt and Uncle."

Steveann went on to say that she felt very much ashamed she was helping her Aunt and Uncle to pass the curse onto me. She said that she only agreed to be a party to their plan because she wanted to free her only family from the burden that had already caused them much grief. She solemnly added, "And besides it's about time someone else had to deal with all of this evil. In time, Doctor, you too will perhaps be fortunate enough to rid yourself of this pernicious curse. Meanwhile, you will have the opportunity to know my story first hand and to appreciate my burden as your own."

Those were Steveann's last words to me on the subject. Soon afterwards, our session came to a close and I never did get to see her again. I was prevented from treating her (or anyone else) for reasons of health, or ill health. Looking back, I can honestly say that not solving *The Curse of the White Squirrel* is probably the greatest regret of my career. The fact remains that my regret on the entire matter probably further aggravated my health to an irreversible, hopelessly moribund extent. Days go by and I wonder if I will ever be capable of leaving the house. It has been many months since my first and last meeting with Steveann Gooding and still my health is far, far from normal. As for Steveann, her Aunt and Uncle, I have since learned that they moved to Hawaii. I receive postcards from them every now and again that send their regards and thanks. They tell me they are well and 'owe it all to the good doctor'. These postcards are forwarded from my office at the hospital, courtesy of the Post Office. In summary, I would like to conclude this case history for *the Journal* with one final comment. Today, I spend much of my free time dwelling on the subject of the white squirrel. I would rather not say why. It pains me to do so, as a psychiatrist. It is sufficient enough to say that if I could have one last word with Steveann and her family on the subject, I would remind them that *in order to survive a squirrel needs a steady supply of nuts.*

Two Dead Ends

Mr. Snowden drifted down the dreary avenue, as might a moving camera, recording the events around him with objective repose. He was unemotional and seemingly disinterested in anyone that might care to notice him. But no one noticed him. The dark solitary figures that passed him on the avenue were too concerned with their own worlds to care about his. The rain continued to fall and the gloom mirrored Snowden's mood. He held his photo album tight between his underarm and his body so that he could keep both hands free. The hands were in his trench coat pockets. He looked down at his leather shoes drenched from the many puddles he had walked through. His mind was on the photo album and Snowden was glad he had remembered to wrap it in a plastic bag to protect it from the weather. It was too bad that he forgot his umbrella, however. Well, life wasn't perfect nor was his mind.

He was disappointed and more than a little puzzled that his uncle did not keep their appointment to meet. It was after all, the reason that Snowden had dragged the photo album out of his closet and into the rain. Uncle Flex had wished to see the old pictures and reminisce about the old days when he was a young man and his nephew a young boy. In those days Aunt Fugg was still alive. She had been like a mother to Snowden and he often missed her, as did his uncle. Where could his uncle be? Snowden asked himself. He could not have been at home. Who refuses to answer the door to a favorite nephew, especially when that nephew has pressed the doorbell no less than thirty-three times? It was so unlike Uncle Flex to make an appointment and not keep it. Perhaps something came up. Perhaps the new puppy died and Uncle Flex had to bury its remains in the backyard with the other ones. Perhaps that was why Uncle Flex didn't hear the doorbell. Snowden briefly entertained the thought of turning back toward his uncle's house with the idea in mind that his uncle might still be digging in the yard. And he might have turned back had he not seen out of the corner of his eye a pub called The Next Stop. Snowden suddenly had the urge to drown his sorrows in some lager. Having a few pints in the pub would also allow him the excellent opportunity to dry off and look through his old photo album. He was feeling so nostalgic and he loved to think about the past while steadily inebriating himself.

Snowden opened the door of the pub and stepped out of the cold and into the warm and inviting environs that would be the setting for his mind's greatest test. The place was practically empty. Eight of the ten eyes in the pub gazed up to meet him, interrupting one dart game and one conversation. Those same eyes returned to their original business once Snowden's average countenance had been measured. Snowden went over and stood by the bar. He temporarily rested his photo album on his intended chair, while he relieved himself of his drenched raincoat. The raincoat he draped around the back of the chair. Because of its length and the disproportionately short height of the chair, the raincoat draped onto the floor. Snowden examined the raincoat briefly and decided in short order that he didn't care if it were dirtied. Another time and another place, he might have been more meticulous. It seemed too trivial to care about tonight, as did everything but his photo album. He picked the plastic bag that contained the album up off the chair and sat down. As he adjusted himself, he pulled the album out of the bag and placed it on the table. The bag he crumpled into a ball and shoved into one of the raincoat pockets at his side. The bartender came over and asked Snowden what he wanted to drink. Snowden asked the man what he had on tap and when he heard the name of his favorite lager, he ordered a pint.

Snowden turned the first few leaves of his album. He beamed remembering the beach on a warm summer afternoon of his youth. There he was, surrounded by his family. He accounted for his younger brother and sister, so very young; his Uncle Flex, who looked rugged in those days and Aunt Fugg, who cut a beautiful figure herself then. As Snowden studied the photograph he realized, as if for the first time, just how beautiful his aunt was. The man on the next blanket over was blatantly staring at her cleavage! And this man's own family was totally oblivious to his prurient interest. Each of their faces was directed at the shoreline. Snowden could only make out the profile of the man's son (or the individual who he figured to be the man's son). Snowden wondered who these people were and what their story was. Certainly the son (about eight or nine years old in the photo) was about his own age now. What did the man do for a living now? Was he even alive?

His thoughts were briefly interrupted by the brusque bartender who placed the pint of lager that he ordered right next to the photo album. Snowden reached down into his pocket and pulled out a five-dollar bill, which he handed over to the man. He thanked him and told him to keep the change. Snowden grabbed the pint, cold to touch and brought it to his lips. He gulped down about a quarter of the glass and brought it to rest on the bar again. Suddenly a gust of wind blew through the place as the door opened and yet another lonesome traveler stepped into the midst of The Next Stop Pub.

Snowden returned his attention to the photo album. There were several other pictures from that day at the beach. And in every one taken, his oldest brother was absent. He remembered that was because Bramo always liked to play the photographer. Funny the way life fulfills fantasy. Now his oldest brother was a photographer for *Invisible* magazine. Snowden felt the presence of another beside him. It was the stranger who had just walked in and he was taking the chair next to him at the bar. Ordinarily, Snowden wouldn't have cared but it seemed odd to him that the stranger would choose that particular chair, when there were so many other available chairs to choose from. They were the only ones at the bar, after all. Everyone else was standing around or at a table. Snowden thought that if he were the stranger, he would prefer to take a chair down at the other end of the bar where no one else was and where there was more elbowroom. 'What was the big idea?' he wondered.

The bartender was drying his wet hands with a towel and he addressed the stranger. The stranger told the bartender that he wanted the same lager that Snowden was having. That raised Snowden's eyebrow and he turned to the stranger to make sure he heard him right. At that point, the stranger stared at Snowden for a second and then down at the bar and said, "Could use a pint of lager right about now. Or maybe I should get an Irish coffee?" he asked himself. Snowden returned his attention to the photo album and said nothing. There were some photographs from a day spent at a carnival when he was ten and in one of those photographs, a man standing beside his aunt in the crowd was wearing the same type of hat that he noticed the stranger at the bar wearing. It was white with a black brim that held a red feather. The stranger had never taken it off his head. Snowden took a double take. He was particularly taken by the hat's red feather. It was quite a coincidence in both instances. He looked at the photo album again and then at the stranger beside him who noticed Snowden's subtle observation and remarked, "Oh the hat? It's my father's, you know."

He took it off his head and placed it on the next chair over. "I hope no one sits on it. It means a lot to me. By the way, my name's Boggler . . . " Snowden raised an eyebrow again. *Boggler* sounded like a surname. Snowden did not feel obliged to share his surname with a perfect stranger and so said, "Nice to meet you," and that was all.

Boggler giggled. "You're looking at a photo album in a pub?"

"What of it? " Snowden remarked picking up his glass to drink. He swallowed. "It's none of your business, anyway."

"I'm sorry," said Boggler, "You're absolutely right. It is none of my business." The bartender brought Boggler his lager and Boggler handed him a five-dollar bill. "Keep the change," he said.

Snowden turned the page. There was another photograph of the man with the white hat and black brim. The red feather was not visible. Snowden figured it would be on the other side of the hat. It was the first time that Snowden had ever noticed the man with the hat in this particular photograph. The prominent people were his aunt and uncle, younger brother, sister and himself. Bramo had taken this photograph too. Snowden had seen it a million times. His uncle had it framed in his living room. It was again from that day at the carnival.

"I'm sentimental myself," said Boggler. "I have photo albums of my own. I look at them from time to time. So many sweet memories, cherished relics of a bygone age."

Snowden looked over at Boggler and was startled to see Boggler smiling at him. "That hat of yours is very interesting," he commented. "A man in one of my photos is wearing the exact same type of hat. Wherever did you buy it?"

"I told you. It's my father's," Boggler replied. "Funny, I thought it was a one of a kind hat." The stranger took a sip of his lager and smiled again at Snowden. "Show me the picture you're talking about."

Snowden was taken aback by what he perceived an intrusive nature, but he shared the album with Boggler. He recognized this man as somehow being key to answering the conundrum that had arisen in his mind. At the very least, Snowden hoped to receive from Boggler an acknowledgement of the strange coincidence discovered.

"Well, what do you know about that?" Boggler laughed. "I'll be god damned. Do you know who that man is in your photo? That's my father, and there's my mother right next to him! My parents are in the background of your photograph. Isn't that funny—and I'm there too! You can't see me too good, but I'm there, must be. There I am. I'm right behind this crazy looking lady with the wig and the blue dress. She's blocking me out of the photo."

Snowden winced. "That *crazy looking lady* is my mother."

"Huh? Oh sorry," said Boggler. He pulled the photo album closer. "Gosh, I remember this day so well. I hadn't thought about it in years but these photos bring it all back so clear. Say, do you realize how unlikely something like this is? Of us meeting like this? The hat in this photo is the exact same hat that I have here." Boggler turned around and reached for the hat and held it up to Snowden. "Do you realize how incredible this is, how unbelievable this situation is?" He laughed incredulously and pointed at the photo. "My father and mother took me to that carnival for my birthday. What was the name? Oh yeah. This was at Font's Point, wasn't it?"

"Yeah, that's right," Snowden nodded, amazed.

Boggler finished his thought. "They took me there for my . . . ninth birthday—that was it—my ninth birthday. And then right after they took me home and there was a big surprise party. My grandparents were waiting and my friends. Gosh, I'll never forget it. I think I do have some photos from the party laying around somewhere." Boggler had a far away look. "But not the carnival. I don't remember taking photos at the carnival." He laughed out loud. "Oh man. This is just so crazy." Boggler looked at the photographs and turned the pages. "I'll have to tell my wife about this. She'll never believe me." He shook his head. "Oh my God! Here I am again. Is this you here?"

"That's me alright," Snowden acknowledged.

"Well, this is me right behind you!" Boggler exclaimed. "Where was this taken? It looks like a roller rink."

"Yeah that was at the roller rink," Snowden answered. "I think I was in the eighth grade there. And you think that's you standing behind me?"

"That's me. I can't believe it, but it is!" Boggler boasted. "That was at Rollerworld, right?"

Snowden took a sip of his lager. "You got the name right again. That's Rollerworld all right." Snowden didn't know what to believe, but he obliged Boggler by looking at the photograph. The boy standing behind him in the photo could have been Boggler but it could just as easily have been any other little boy.

"That's you?" Snowden asked. For a second he couldn't believe how indulging he sounded. 'You think that's you?" he asked again.

Boggler nodded and took a swig from his pint of lager. "That's me, man. That's me." He waxed reflective. "That must be twenty-four years ago! How do you like that one? Man, I can't wait to tell my wife about all of this."

Snowden wondered if the stranger had been humoring him about the hat. Certainly that made the most sense. The stranger was probably making up all the rest for fun. His claims were too preposterous to believe. He realized that he did not know this Boggler person at all. He couldn't even be sure if Boggler was the man's real name. Perhaps this stranger was a complete nut and the proverbial coincidence of the hats nothing more than just that. Such were Snowden's thoughts as Boggler turned the pages of the photo album and recognized himself again and again in one photo after another, at age nine, thirteen and twenty-one. Indeed, there did seem to be a consistency of appearance in the characters that Boggler pointed out as himself. The boy in the background of one photograph taken at the beach could have been the same boy at the carnival eating cotton candy in another and the teenager laughing with his friends at a roller rink in another. But there was no way to tell.

When Snowden examined the situation mathematically however, he could not escape the law of probability that reasoned such coincidences were unlikely to occur repeatedly. Nevertheless, the two men could still share a few pints of lager, a few laughs and some indulgent talk. It was a cold, rainy night and each had something to share with the other; whether or not that something was truth is a matter of speculation. Most valuably, Snowden walked away from the experience with a thought that would stay with him for the rest of his days: some events in a man's life are not meant for his limited comprehension. Such events transcend a man's experience as well as his range of understanding. At best, they can only be appreciated as unsolvable puzzles.

Snowden went home that night to his wife, Malla, a little drunk but greatly enlightened. The next morning he told her the story of the stranger who kept appearing in the background of his photographs. The story amused and entertained Malla Snowden like no other she'd ever heard before. In fact, Malla was so taken with her husband's story that she decided to write a short narrative about it. She had the idea to enter the story into a writing contest and she was sure she could win. Unfortunately, when she actually sat down to write the narrative not long afterward, she found she could not recall the stranger's name. Snowden had only mentioned the name to her once and when Malla asked him for the name again, he told her that he had forgotten it. Malla suspected that he did know the name, but for superstitious reasons was refusing to name it. When pressed,

Snowden told his wife that the name did not matter because the story itself did not matter. He told her that the story would mean nothing without an arbitrary interpretation of his encounter with the stranger and such an interpretation would be unfair to the reader. He then encouraged Malla to write about something else entirely. Snowden's objections to the short story did not discourage his wife. Malla decided to write the narrative using a pseudonym as a substitute for the stranger's name.

In the end, however, Malla did not need to use a pseudonym. Because of an automobile accident involving her husband and another driver, the stranger's name was restored to her memory. As fate would have it, Mr. Snowden was killed in a head on collision with another automobile at a dangerous intersection not far from their home. His obituary column in the local newspaper that same week was printed beside the name of the other man that had died in the collision. That man's name was Boggler. Apparently, fate had decided the paths of the two men would not cross again. It was a fantastic ending for Malla's short story. She couldn't have thought of a more fitting ending had she tried. One could even say that the narrative had written itself. The award-winning short story brought Malla Snowden fame and fortune and even though she didn't have her husband to share the fame and fortune with, she still managed to have a good time. Not long after the narrative was made into a movie of the week, a reporter asked Malla what it felt like to be a widow and a heralded writer in the same short breath. Malla answered, "Some events in a person's life are not meant for their limited comprehension. Such events transcend a person's experience as well as their range of understanding. At best, they can only be appreciated as unsolvable puzzles."

The Doublecross

This is the story of a man named Sned. I am Sned and this is my story. Since I am true to my story, the story is true and so I can say as much. I can also say that it is my job (and not just in this story) to guard a heap of dung. That is what I do with most of my time in this world. But it is not what I do for most of my time in this story. I only guard the dung in the beginning of the story because of its relevance to later events. I guard the dung heap for the Elders of the State and they pay me well to do so. I live in a place that can best be described as a farm producing community and it is a competitive one at that. Since most of the community is comprised of farmers, they often employ the most ruthless means of outdoing their neighbors in terms of quantity and quality of output. Naturally, these farmers all want the best dung for their soil. The best dung comes from the State, but not all of the farmers can afford it. After all, it is the product of prize-winning lamb and oxen. These animals are especially bred and fed by the State to manufacture a superior product. It is my job to guard this product against the pilfering of desperate farmers who haven't the means to pay for it. Needless to say, many of these same farmers have lamb and oxen of their own and have easy access to the dung of those animals. But that dung is inferior to that of the State's supply. The State knows it and the farmers know it. This difference is attributable to genetic engineering and nutrition specialists who know best how to manufacture cutting edge dung.

Through the years I've guarded the dung heap in the company of one other man. This man's name is Con. It is Con's job to sell the dung of the State to those farmers who are privileged enough to afford its price. These farmers are privileged enough to afford the best dung for their crops reciprocally because they sell the most crops and they sell the most crops because they grow the best crops and they grow the best crops because they use the best dung. In this respect, my village has what some outsiders might call a class structure. Occasionally there are farmers who break from it, but for the most part the system is inviolable. It is very difficult for farmers who have traditionally sold the worst crops to rise above their lot in life. In order to do so, they would have to fall into money or find a way to steal from the State's dung supply. But the latter is impossible as long as I am doing my job properly.

One member of the farming community who is a friend of the State is a farmer named Yelch. Yelch is one of the most distinguished members of the community for a number of reasons. He has been recognized for selling extraordinarily delicious vegetables and for having the most beautiful hair ever seen on a man or woman anywhere. The most distinguishing aspect about Yelch, however, is his lack of hands. Both of his arms end abruptly at the wrist. No one can say if Yelch was born this way or if he lost his hands due to an unfortunate accident. A rumor has persisted that Yelch had his hands chopped off as punishment for stealing something as a boy; some have said a smutty magazine. But there has never been substantiation of this claim.

Con and I have spent a great deal of time debating the inconsistency of Yelch having beautiful hair and yet not having the hands to style it. We have spoken to a number of his neighbors who come from the Jackal's Well where Yelch is known to live and not one of these neighbors has ever seen anyone but Yelch go in or out of Yelch's dwelling. This is why Con has maintained that Yelch is somehow able to style his hair on his own. How I cannot begin to guess. It is my position that Yelch has somebody else living in the shack with him, unseen and unheard but nevertheless on hand. In my debates with Con, I have insisted that this person is Yelch's hairstylist (and maybe even his lover). Con has continually ridiculed me for saying this; "especially that part about the lover," as he is so fond of retorting. I say, that if one were possible then the other is as equally possible. Why couldn't the man have a hairstylist who was also his lover? Stranger things have happened in this world.

Of course, it is entirely reasonable to assume that Yelch has naturally beautiful hair and does not need to have it styled by his own efforts or anyone else's, as Con has maintained. I must, however, make one counterpoint. If it is possible for Yelch to have naturally beautiful hair (always immaculately preserved no matter the weather or the degree of tossing and turning taken through the course of a night), then it is just as possible for Yelch to have a woman or a man living with him. And in exchange for food, water and a place to sleep, this individual serves his master as hairstylist and love slave . . . I will not digress on this love matter too much. It is merely a fancy of mine.

Anyway, Con and I decided to settle this long-standing argument over a bet of three thousand shekels. It was a nice even number but all the same an odd number considering where it came from—namely, Con. It was a lot of money any way that I thought about it. Three thousand shekels were all that I owned in this world. I did not waste any time agreeing to the bet, however, partly out of arrogance and partly out of greed. Con and I discussed the situation. One of us would have to break into Yelch's home in the middle of the night. That person would then wait in Yelch's house until morning, to confirm: a) what Yelch's hair looked like when he awoke. b) that the coiffure we have seen Yelch sporting is not a wig—an idea that Con has proposed. c) that no one is hidden on the premises who might be able to style Yelch's do. The one aspect of the bet that Con and I were not able to immediately solve was which one of us would be the one to sneak into Yelch's home during the night. After all, we could not both go. One of us had to remain behind in order to guard the dung heap. The only satisfactory solution to this dilemma agreeable to the both of us was to flip a coin. We would have drawn straws but neither of us knew where we could get one to cut up on such short notice. And the whole rock breaks scissors thing I always found too conducive to defeat. I cannot close a fist to symbolize a rock because of an old war injury. In the end, the coin toss decided that I would be the lucky one to break into Yelch's home. I considered this to be the more fortunate of potential outcomes, only because I knew that I would know the truth of the conundrum for myself and would not have to trust Con's word. Once more, even if I learned that Yelch did not have assistance in styling his hair, I would still have the advantage of being able to tell Con the contrary (if I chose to be deceptive and wanted to ensure for myself the three thousand shekels). But this optimism was cut short when Con informed me that in order to win the three thousand shekels, not only would I have to see that Yelch had a hairstylist hidden in his shack but I would also need to bring proof of this to Con. I asked him what kind of proof would be satisfactory and it was then that he handed me a camera. He said that if I didn't bring him a photograph of a hairstylist actually combing Yelch's hair by morning, he would assume I had verified that no one else was living in the house with Yelch. Furthermore, Con added that if he saw Yelch later in the day with his usual good looks, he would know that Yelch styled his own hair and that I owed him three thousand shekels. I checked to make sure that that there was film inside the camera and then reminded Con that it was his responsibility to close the gate around the dung heap and to stand guard until morning when I returned. I told him where I kept a cot in the guardhouse and also explained my evening routine of setting up the cot before the dung heap. Because the gates would be closed he could rest, but he was not to leave the dung heap unattended. This would be my first night away from the dung heap in twenty years. I hoped that all would go well for Con in my absence. If the Elders of the State discovered my neglect of duty, I could be court marshaled. But I felt that leaving my post was worth the risk. I had the chance to make a year's salary in one eventful night.

I said goodbye to Con and headed off toward the Jackal's Well. On my way, I thought about a lot of things. But every single one of those thoughts had to do with Yelch. I thought about how awkward it was greeting him day after day; about the absence of a handshake between us when he would approach with a wan smile and wayward eyes each morning; how I would perfunctorily reach into the wicker basket that he had around his neck to take the money that I knew was inside; how I never bothered to count that money because I trusted him implicitly; how I would always give him an extra piece of dung above and beyond his allotment for no other reason than that I liked him; how he would broaden his smile when he knew I had given him that one extra piece of dung. These were the small pleasures in life. I felt good for granting Yelch that extra piece of dung and he felt good for accepting it. Now, I was about to breach the trust and the friendship Yelch and I had cultivated. I was about to sell that bond away for three thousand shekels. Was it worth it? Of course it was worth it.

Yelch's home looked like a big stone box with crags for windows and it had a boulder placed in front of the entrance instead of a door. The challenge for me would be moving that boulder without waking the occupants of the home (notice I said occupants) or their neighbors. I surprised myself as I do whenever a feat of strength is required and I've managed to meet the challenge. I did not move the boulder as quietly as I would have liked to, however. Reason being, the boulder required such force to be moved that I overcompensated by exerting what little resources I had too quickly. The end result was that the boulder rolled away from Yelch's home and over an adjacent precipice. It landed on a barn below and killed several horses and a cow as I learned days later. The hideous sound that resulted from my folly was not to be believed. Thankfully it was short lived. For several minutes that felt like hours, I was afraid to move. I was silent like a church mouse, as if my silence could somehow contain the neighbors that I imagined awakened from their sleep. Perhaps it was my hope that if no further sound were made they would forget the horrible thunder that had disturbed them, like it had been a bad dream or a hallucination. I remained motionless for what seemed like an eternity; as if my catatonic state could protect me from those same neighbors if they did come out of their homes to investigate the noise and the destruction that I alone was responsible for.

But my worries were unfounded. All along the hillside where I stood, nothing stirred and no sound could be heard but for the racket of crickets. If I had awakened Yelch's neighbors, there was no indication of it. If I had awakened Yelch there was no indication of that either. I went forward with my plan to enter the house. I was wary on my first step into the darkness of Yelch's home, but with each subsequent step gained a confidence that I did not think myself capable of. At a certain point, it was no longer a question of sustaining that confidence, but containing it within reasonable bounds. I was quite cocky as I moved about untrammeled. Trespassing was a violation of a man's privacy and while I felt every bit the criminal, I also felt every bit the clever fellow. After all, here I was in Yelch's humble abode, about to answer the riddle that had been the source of a light-hearted rancor between Con and I and I had done it most stealthily. All that I could think about was Con's face when I showed him the fateful photograph. How I wanted to get him so bad for good. We were friends in a sense but competitors in another. We both knew that the day would come when only one of us would have his moment in the sun and that the ultimate question of who was the better man was intrinsically related to the lesser question of who styled Yelch's hair (if indeed, it was anyone). The money was merely the cherry on the sundae, but it was a tasty one at that.

I was trying to ascertain which room of the house I was in and to get a feel for the place when my hands came across something furry and soft. It was a cat and it meowed when I squeezed it. I pet the little pussy and it responded by rubbing its hindquarters against my legs as it walked across my sandal. The tail kind of curled around my calf. It was a pleasurable sensation to have against my naked leg and I thought to beckon the cat to come again but was reminded of my calling and decided better of it. This was no time for fun and games. I found a narrow passageway out of that first room and made my way into what I soon found out was the kitchen. I took a seat on the linoleum floor and decided to wait there until daylight when I could see better. I was hesitant to do any additional exploring because I did not want to risk the potential of calling attention to myself as an intruder. The only fear that I had as I sat there on the linoleum was the possibility that someone in the home might be the type to snack in the middle of the night. I would surely be discovered that way and would blow the chance of catching the household by surprise, as I wanted to do with my camera the next morning. I thought about my own snacking habits then and hoped them an aberration of the norm. My mind wandered to the stash of goodies that I had waiting for me back at the guardhouse. I started wondering if Con could be a midnight explorer. There was a big bag of chocolate chips, a box of devil dogs and a half filled bag of cheese doodles left at risk in my own refrigerator.

I tried to make myself comfortable on the kitchen floor, alternating various positions. After a while I finally found one conducive to comfort: the fetal position. I probably fell asleep sucking my thumb, wishing I was back in my mother's womb, with no knowledge of the evil world I was about to be born into (a game I often played to help me fall asleep). In my slumber, I dreamed that a tall, bald, naked transsexual was standing over me taking photographs as I lay there at his feet on the linoleum. And when I awoke and saw the first glimpse of daylight sieving through the venetian blinds of the kitchen windows, I realized that a tall, bald, naked transsexual was standing over me taking photographs as I lay there at his feet on the linoleum. My eyes widened and I stirred as I recognized this weird being (half man/half woman) from my dream. "Who are you?" I inquired, attempting to stand. "Shouldn't I be asking you that same question?" the transsexual responded. He had a husky, sultry voice and yelled down the hall for Yelch. The transsexual told Yelch to call the police.

Yelch came into the kitchen wearing a baby blue nightgown. I was completely shocked to see what a mess his hair was. My first impulse was to reach for my camera, but when I looked around I saw that it was no longer at my side. It was then that I realized that the transsexual was holding my camera. To think that he had wasted much of the film in that camera photographing me! Exasperated, is the word I would use to describe my reaction to all of this. Because unless I had a photograph of Yelch with messy hair standing next to this naked transsexual, Con was never going to believe a word of what I said I saw. He would see Yelch later with beautiful hair and would assume, as he said he would in the absence of a photograph proving to the contrary, that Yelch styled his own hair without the assistance of anyone and despite the fact that he had no hands. How impossible!

Yelch was staring at me. He said nothing, scratching his head with his handless arm as if he was trying to decide what to do. I attempted to explain away this embarrassing situation with a tall tale. I told Yelch that I had gone into town last night with the intent of blowing off some steam and that in the process I had surpassed my limit. With too many drinks in me, I lost all sense of direction on my way back to the dung heap. "So you decided to sleep here?" he concluded, predicting the outcome of my deceitful story. "I didn't know it was your home, Yelch," I told him. The transsexual laughed at me. Searching Yelch's eyes for a trace of sympathy, I found something else that worried me. It was disdain. Yelch told the transsexual, whom he called Krull, not to call the police. Hearing that, I breathed a sigh of relief. But this relief did not last for long.

When Krull pressed Yelch for a reason not to call the police, Yelch responded not with the anticipated explanation that he and I were old friends and that my transgression could be forgiven. Instead, he told Krull that he had expected this happen. He said that he'd been bragging to 'the salesman down at the dung heap' about the security of their home, how a new boulder had been placed in front of the entrance and that it would prove a formidable impasse to burglars. He said that the salesman ventured to say that no home was impervious to burglary and that he could prove it by getting this fellow (and Yelch pointed at me) to break into their home. Of course, I was mortified to hear this. I could never sufficiently relate the feelings of inadequacy and foolishness that plagued me at that moment. I felt an overwhelming urge to interrupt Yelch but just as I was about to he said something else of great interest. First, he lauded Krull for taking the camera away from me and then he said that he risked losing the bet that he made with Con (an amount of six thousand shekels) if I ever escaped with pictures proving I had been in their home. Again, I felt the need to interrupt Yelch but was compelled to listen as he worried another thought: what if I escaped without pictures but could still describe the details of their home? Would that not prove that I had been in their home anyway? At this point, I knew I would have to reassure them both that I would never oblige Con with such testimony. I opened my mouth so that they would know that I was not in league with Con and had, in fact, been tricked into playing his pawn. They listened politely but passively. The whole time that I implored their commiseration, I had the distinct sense that they did not believe me. Perhaps they thought I was telling them another tall tale. This thought frustrated me to no end, as did their reaction. They simply continued their discussion of what to do with me, as if it had never been interrupted. Yelch was very concerned about not only losing the six thousand shekels he had expected to get from Con but of losing six thousand shekels of his own. He told Krull that they would have to put the house up for mortgage in the event of such a disastrous outcome. He told him that he thought it best to do away with me completely so as not to risk losing so much.

At first I laughed at this. I could not take the proposition of their murdering me seriously. The entire situation was ridiculous. But as I studied their phlegmatic faces and saw the coldness of their eyes, I realized more fully the circumstances that I was in. I had unwittingly placed myself into a very dangerous position. My impulse was to run, but the prospect scared me. Krull was a giant. Would this only provoke him to carry out Yelch's suggestion? Maybe there was still a chance of negotiating my release, without a threat of violence. I wavered before them, staring down the hall to the next room where I remembered the entrance being. That was where I came in and that was where I would have to leave. A decision was called for on my part while I still had the upper hand. In a flash I ran past them both and was surprised at the ease by which I made my escape. The deciding factor for my run was Yelch's query of Krull on the whereabouts of the cannabis rope. Of the two, only Krull ran outside after me. He flew on the wings of Mercury and his hotfoot was my impetus to fly that much faster. I am sure that my speed transcended all records and that at that moment I was the fastest animal on the planet. I accomplished this goal with the vision of being tied up, raped and suffering a long demise as the alternative of my fate. I ran as far as my legs could take me, over hills and through valleys, across lakes and mountains. I ran for days on end, supplied by an enigmatic energy that was determined to ensure my survival. I only stopped running when I had arrived at a place that had no trace (as far as the eye could see) of humanity and civilization. It was my decision not only to leave behind my village and the only life that I'd ever known, but all contact with human kind. I had no trust for others of my species with but one exception. That exception was my mother and I could not cohabit with her without jeopardizing her safety. I was by now a marked man, not only marked by Krull and Yelch for extinction and by Con for extortion but more importantly by the State for leaving my assigned post. Surely, I would face jail time for such a neglect of duty. And if the Elders of the State ever gained knowledge of my other crimes, namely breaking and entering, trespassing and waging illegal bets, I could face the worst case scenario: a death sentence. There was nothing left for me to do but hide from the world and I found a choice cave to do so in. It was there in that cave that I resolved to live out the rest of my days thinking about what I had done. I had no contact left with the outside world after I destroyed my cellular phone. I used it one last time to call my mother and say goodbye. She barely understood what it was I was trying to tell her. She was beside herself, sobbing about her brother's farm; how it had been destroyed by a boulder that rolled off of an adjacent cliff. She cared more about my silly Uncle's dead farm animals than she did me. It served me right. I've searched myself for meaning in all of this, thinking that perhaps somewhere there is a lesson to be learned. And I've concluded that there are many lessons to be learned. The hard part is determining which of those lessons is the most important. Is it that a man should not neglect his duty? That he should respect and not violate the privacy of others? Or is it not more apt to conclude: NEVER TRUST ANYONE WITH THE NAME CON.

The Case
of the
Missing Writer

The name's Serop. I'm a detective. I operate in San Francisco, mainly. My office is on Nob Hill. My first case outside of the Bay Area first fell in my lap a couple of weeks ago. I had a call from a woman by the name of Zuplez. She said her husband had gone missing. I told her to drop by the office to go over the details with me. In hindsight, I wish I'd paid a call at her address. It might have saved me a whole lot of aggravation and you'll learn why soon enough. Mrs. Zuplez knocked on my door about five minutes after I hung up the phone with her. I knew she'd called me from a pay phone and knew she'd done so around the corner because I could hear the distinctive chimes of the church bell that I hear every afternoon, in stereo. So it was no surprise to hear that same voice outside my door so quickly, knocking at the opaque inset glass and announcing her arrival like it was some miraculous event. I could make out a perfect bell shape shadow through the glass and I admired it for half a second before I told her to come in. What I saw when the door opened left me speechless. Mrs. Zuplez bore a striking resemblance to a high school teacher that I had an adolescent crush on twenty years ago. She looked almost exactly like Ms. Red Lids, my English teacher from 12th Grade. Her specialty was creative writing, tight sweaters and long legs. Red Lids was a nickname. All the kids called her that because she dolled her eye-lids up with crimson makeup. It made her look pretty crazy. And while I'm sure the rest of the teaching staff at my old alma mater didn't care for it, all the boys didn't mind because Red Lid's was a fox. It was the same thing with Mrs. Zuplez who could have been her double or her younger daughter, only without the crazy makeup. I told her to take a seat and we got right down to business.

"On the phone you mentioned that your husband disappeared."

"Yes, that's right," she sobbed. She took out a hand-kerchief and started balling.

"When was the last time you'd seen him, Mrs. Zuplez?"

"It's been three weeks now." She blew her nose and snorted.

"Had you heard from him in that time?" I was asking routine questions while I fumbled through the papers on my desk searching for a pad and a pen. I found the pen but continued looking for the pad.

"No, I haven't heard from him."

"You brought the photograph that I asked for, right?"

"Yes, here it is. I'm sorry it's a little sticky for some reason."

"That's O.K. I need this for your husband's file." I put the photograph into a manila folder that I'd prepared in advance. I wrote the name Zuplez on the label and that reminded me of something. "You know, I don't think you ever told me your husband's first name, Mrs. Zuplez."

"It's Edward."

"Edward." I made a note of that too on the file label. "Has he ever done anything like this before, your husband? Gone away and not called you?" I started looking for the pad again as she spoke.

"Absolutely not. It's entirely out of character for him to do something like this, to go somewhere and not give me a call. He's always been so responsible that way." She was choked up. "Why, he'd never let me worry needlessly." Zuplez blew her nose into the handkerchief in her hand and dried her eyes with it. I noticed blood on the handkerchief and saw that some of it had inadvertently spread to her eyelids. The sight of this sickened me and for the moment I forgot all about finding the pad. I reached for a box of tissues that I kept on my desk and was about to hand it over to her when I realized it was empty. I tossed it aside into a pile of case histories in the corner of my office. "More garbage. Go on, Mrs. Zuplez . . . Didn't you tell me over the phone that he flew to New York?"

"Yes. He went there on business. He never checked into his hotel."

"How do you know that?"

"Because I called the hotel!"

I finally found the pad and made a quick note to

myself, 'Husband flew to New York. Zuplez hasn't heard from him in weeks. Never checked into hotel.'

"Did he have any enemies?" I asked, asking more routine questions as a matter of routine.

"No. He didn't have any enemies. He didn't even have any friends."

"So there would be no reason for him to go into hiding?"

"He was an unemployed writer. He'd been in hiding for years but not from anyone or anything . . . unless you count the whole world."

She continued to dry her eyes, spreading the snot and blood all over her face as she did so. It repulsed me but I couldn't find a tactful way to let her know what it was she was doing. "Do you want to use the toilet to freshen up a bit, Mrs. Zuplez?"

"No, that's alright. I feel better now." She gained composure for a half a second but lost it in a maelstrom of sudden tears, which made the snot and blood run with her mascara all down her clownish countenance.

"Um, where was I?" Such rhetorical questions always brought me back to reality. "You said your husband went to New York on business. What was that all about?"

"He went there to meet with a publisher."

"So, he was invited out there?"

"Yes, that is correct. I miss my husband so very much." The pain of her circumstances painted a wounded expression on her face. "I think of him night and day . . . just like the Cole Porter song. Oh, I do hope you can help me find my husband . . . Mr. Syrup."

I smiled sweetly. "It's *Serop*, actually."

"Mr. Serop, I'm sorry. I'm sorry I called you Mr. Syrup." She folded the mucus moistened, blood stained handkerchief neatly in her lap and kept it there, as she stared across the desk at me.

I cleared my throat. "It's alright. You said he never checked into his hotel, is that right?"

"Right." She reached for a suck candy from the little tray I kept at the corner of my desk.

"Go ahead," I said, "help yourself. Now what was the name of this hotel?"

"Thank you . . . It had a French name. *Le Hotelier Baroque.*"

"An unusual name," I replied. "Are you sure such a hotel exists?"

She un-wrapped the candy and examined it in her hands. "Oh yes, it exists. I saw it listed in a travel guide and everything. My husband showed it to me."

I watched her turning the candy around in her hands, as if examining it. "Did your husband make reservations at this hotel?"

"Oh, yes. He called." She put the candy back into the wrapper and rolled it up again. I waited to see if she was going to put it back in the little tray from which she had originally retrieved it and that was exactly what she did.

"And what made your husband pick that particular hotel, Mrs. Zuplez?"

"The publisher recommended it."

"The publisher recommended it." I reiterated.

"Yes," she confirmed again.

"You said your husband never checked into this Hotel Baroque. Is it possible that he checked into another hotel for some reason?"

"I don't think so. If he had, he'd have called me."

"Well, what do you know about this publisher?" I asked.

"Only the name. Do you want to know it? It's a very strange name."

"Yes, of course. What is it?"

She said the name with great trepidation, "The Big Game, Inc."

"That's the name of the publishing company?"

"Yes, the publishing company."

I made a note. "O.K that's helpful, but what is the name of the man your husband corresponded with, the man your husband was supposed to meet in New York?"

She shook her head. "I don't think my husband ever told me his name and I didn't think to ask. He just gave me his flight schedule on TWA and the name of the hotel."

"O.K. let me ask you this, how did your husband ever get in touch with this publishing company in the first place? What was it called?" I looked down at my pad, "The Big Game, Inc."

"My husband got the name out of a writer's market guide and sent some samples. He used to do it all the time, send samples of his writing out to publishers, sometimes to literary agents." Zuplez peeled an adhesive bandage from a wound on her right hand and then lifted it up to touch the raw skin underneath.

"And so this particular publisher wrote him back?"

"Yes, that's right."

"Presumably, the publisher had encouraging words and expressed an interest in meeting him."

"Yes, right again. He invited my husband to give him a call, to set something up."

I could see the wound beneath the adhesive bandage on her hand was dried with crusted blood.

"Is your hand alright, Mrs. Zuplez?"

"Huh? Oh yes." She left the wound on her hand alone and began refolding the snotty, bloody handkerchief in her lap, which made me regret ever saying anything about the hand in the first place.

"Tell me, was it really necessary that they meet, your husband and this publisher?"

"What do you mean?"

I put the pad and pen down for a moment and re-adjusted myself in my seat. "What I mean is I don't really see why they had to meet at all. If this fellow wanted to publish your husband, he could very well have done so without their getting together as pre-requisite. If they were each in the same city that would be one thing, but to have to fly across the country to discuss a book deal when it could have been done over the telephone . . . This is how it seems to me, anyway. Do you mind if I smoke, Mrs. Zuplez?" I shook a cigarette out of the pack on my desk and placed it in my mouth, expecting her O.K.

"No I don't mind."

She thought about what I said while I lit up.

"I suppose you're right. I never really gave it much thought. May I have one of your cigarettes?"

"Huh? Oh yeah. Of course."

I passed her one over the desk and offered a light.

"Thank you, Mr. Serop. The thing is all of this was not only new to me. It was also new to my husband. He'd been writing for years, contacting agents and publishers all the time. This was the first time that one of them got back to him with something other than a rejection. My husband was very excited by that and I suppose, not knowing the ropes, he never gave it any thought the publisher wanted to meet with him. I didn't either."

I took a long hard pull on the cig while she talked, admiring the heaving chest that spout all these words out in a sexy soughing way that left me breathless. Her pouting lips pursed at several points that left me daydreaming about what else they could do besides talking. When she paused, I asked her: "Exactly what kind of a writer was your husband, Mrs. Zuplez?"

She didn't understand the question. "What kind of writer?"

"Yeah. What did he like to write about? Was he a fiction writer?"

"Yes." She took a drag of the cigarette and exhaled, spewing the smoke in my face.

I coughed slightly and probably grimaced.

"I'm sorry," she said, realizing her faux pas.

"It's alright," I told her.

"Tell me, Mr. Serop, do you really think the publisher is to blame for my husband's disappearance?"

I took a drag and held it for second thinking about that one. "Well, we don't know anything yet. I'll have to fly out to New York to find out for sure."

Her face lit up with excitement, "So you'll take the case, Mr. Serop?"

She looked ridiculous with her red lids fluttering and the mascara and mucus streaks running from her eyes down to the corners of her mouth. I caught a fit of laughter rising up from my abdomen, but was able to effectively stifle it in the back of my throat before it ever reached my lips. My whole face was rigid with artificially imposed composure. "Sure. I'll take the case, Mrs. Zuplez." I wanted to reassure her and at least affect a professional demeanor. After all, this was no laughing matter. "I'll fly out there and see what I can dig up." Realizing my poor choice of words, I cut myself off. But Mrs. Zuplez didn't seem to notice. She was too busy thanking me. I reminded her that my incentive to help out was not entirely altruistic. "Of course, in order to take the case I'm going to need that flat fee we discussed on the phone and I'm going to need it up front, for expenses."

"Of course, of course," she exclaimed. She opened her purse and pulled out a business envelope with a dollar sign drawn on the face.

'That's not too obvious,' I thought, accepting the envelope. It was unsealed and I peeked inside to have a look at the bills. I didn't count it but it seemed to be all there, so I folded it up and put it in the inside pocket of my sports coat. "This will be fine for now, Mrs. Zuplez." I told her. "But like I said on the phone, this is just the flat fee. Once you leave here, I'll also be charging you that hourly fee we discussed."

She sniffled and wiped a tear from her eye, expressing her gratitude again in a manner that I would describe as excessive. "Oh! Thank you. Thank you, Mr. Serop! Thank you so much!"

"No problem." I finished the cigarette and put it out in the ashtray just before she did the same.

"I'll book the airlines, the hotel and all that today. I'll probably fly out there tomorrow. You can reimburse me for those things, the airlines and the hotel, later. There's no need to go into that now."

"Great," she replied. "Just let me know what I owe you and we'll settle it when you say."

I decided that I liked this lady, particularly her attitude about money. If there's one thing I can't stand it's a deadbeat. They leave me disinclined to do a good job, to get the whole story. I started thinking about Mr. Zuplez and his story, how it might relate to the stories he'd written. I have heard it said that the truth sometimes reflects fiction, or vice versa. I followed up that angle with a few questions that I thought pertinent. "Tell me, Mrs. Zuplez, what was your husband's latest book about? Do you recall the premise at all? You never know, it could be relevant to the case."

"Yes, I remember. It was a collection of short stories. He read me bits and 'pieces,' as he used to say. Most of them were mysterious in nature."

"So, he was like a mystery/suspense writer?"

She considered the thought. "Yes, I guess you could say that."

I was about to ask her something else when she added, "My husband wrote all sorts of things, most were what he called, 'experimental.' His latest writings, the stories that the publisher expressed an interest in . . . they were short stories about the supernatural.

"Were you about to say something, Mr. Serop?"

I'd lost my train of thought, but quickly thought of a filler question, "How did you hear about my services, Mrs. Zuplez. I'm just curious."

"Oh you were in the book."

"Thanks, I like to keep track of such things." I made a note and just as soon recovered my thread of thought. "Oh, I know what I wanted to ask you . . . Before you said that your husband had telephoned the publisher."

"Yes, that's right. After he got the letter back praising his work. My husband was very flattered and I was so very happy for him."

"Uh-huh. I'm sure you were. Do you happen to have the publisher's number with you or perhaps you have it somewhere at home?"

"No, I'm afraid not. You see, Mr. Serop, my husband took all of that information with him when he left. I didn't even think to ask him for it. What would I need it for?"

I nodded. "That's O.K. We have the name of the publishing company. I can always get the number from an operator. Don't worry about it."

Zuplez looked at her watch. "Goodness. Will you look at the time?" she exclaimed. I watched as she folded up her soiled handkerchief and for the love of God finally put it away in her handbag. "I almost forgot about another appointment that I have today," she added. "I'm going for a facial."

Good luck, I thought.

"Will you be needing anything else from me, Mr. Serop?" She stood up from the chair and smoothed her skirt.

"No, I don't think so," I answered. She handed me her card and I took it, somewhat surprised by her sudden impulse to leave. "O.K. I'll be in touch." I put the card in my sports coat inner pocket and came around the desk to shake her hand and show her to the door. Before I did I hesitated, remembering to give her one of my cards. I kept them in a little keepsake on my desk and handed her one. "I almost forgot, Mrs. Zuplez. Here's one of mine."

"Thank you, Mr. Serop. You've been so kind to me."

She offered me her hand and I held it for a moment. "Don't worry. I'm going to do everything I can to find your husband." I was surprised at myself for making such a promise and regretted it instantly.

"I have complete confidence in you, Mr. Serop," she said pulling her hand away suddenly.

I opened the door for her. "Please give me a call, Mrs. Zuplez, if you can think of anything else related to your husband's disappearance, anything you might have forgotten to tell me. Even if you don't think it's that important. You never know what might be helpful to the case."

"O.K. I will." She smiled. "Thank you so much for your kindness."

"There is just one other thing," I added.

"Yes?" She moved closer to me, closer than I would have ever expected her to. "Did you forget to ask me something?" Her breath was hushed and it smelled sweet. I would have probably grabbed her in my arms at that moment had it not been for the big booger that I saw hanging off the corner of her right nostril.

"I forgot to ask you, do you happen to have an extra copy of your husband's manuscript, the one that the publisher was interested in?"

Zuplez paused for a moment and reflected on the matter. "An extra copy of the manuscript? You mean like a carbon copy?"

"Yes, a carbon copy."

"H'm, let me think about that," she replied.

Her leg brushed against mine, as I waited for her to finish thinking. The only sound in the room was the sound of our breathing and she was so close I had to do everything I could to keep my eyes above her heaving bosom. I told her impatiently, "If you can't find a carbon copy, a rough draft will do just as nicely."

She pulled away suddenly. "I don't think I've seen any carbon copies around the apartment, but I'll check again."

"Please do. I'll give you a call before I leave for New York."

When I said, 'New York,' she smiled one last time before she turned and walked away, down the hall, toward the elevators where someone else was already waiting. He was probably someone from one of the law offices that I share the floor with. I didn't recognize his face. By the time Zuplez got to the elevator, the doors opened and she stepped inside. The gentleman followed. I watched them leave and then closed my office door to pack and call the airlines. Since Zuplez had mentioned her husband traveling with TWA, I decided to be consistent and booked a reservation with them. I'd leave San Francisco the next morning, giving me enough time to tie up a few loose ends around here before I departed. Borrowing again from the itinerary of Mr. Zuplez, I made a reservation at *Le Hotelier Baroque.* At first, I felt silly even asking for the number. The long distance operator, herself, wasn't nonplussed which immediately restored my confidence in the veracity of my client who had stated quiet plainly that there was such a place. When I was connected with the hotel's front desk, I was even more pleased. I am what some would call conspiracy-minded. It is the line of business I'm in that creates such tendencies for paranoia. I guess you could call me mistrustful. As a detective, I prefer to say that I'm cautious. I've learned the hard way not to assume all my clients are good eggs. Assuming too much can be hazardous to your health. I've been set up too many times for taking the word of someone I don't know at face value. But my suspicions, at least in this one case, proved to be unfounded. Indeed, *Le Hotelier Baroque* did exist. According to the fellow who took my reservation, it was located on East 27th Street. While I had him on the phone, I asked if there was a record of reservation for Mr. Edward Zuplez. I told him the reservation would have been made a few weeks earlier. He put me on hold for a couple of minutes to check the record book. When he got back to me, he said that a reservation had never been made under that name. That was of course in conflict with what Mrs. Zuplez had told me. I asked the clerk if the hotel would still have a record if the reservation had later been neglected or cancelled. He said it would. I was at a loss for an explanation. Why would Mrs. Zuplez lie to me about her husband making a reservation at this hotel? Perhaps she had assumed he had made a reservation when in fact he had done otherwise. I reminded myself that this discrepany could easily be explained as a record keeping error on the part of the hotel, but decided to try Mrs. Zuplez at home tonight to make certain. I'd give her a call right after I finished packing.

After I hung up the phone with the hotel, I had planned to contact the mysterious publisher Mrs. Zuplez had mentioned, the Big Game, Inc. I even dialed the long distance operator back with the intent of asking her for the number in New York. But at the very last second I didn't do it for two reasons. For one, I realized it would be safer and wiser to drop in on them unannounced once I got into town. The other reason I didn't call was because of a sound I'd heard, or thought I'd heard, in the building that contains my office. A family doctor might call it an auditory hallucination. It sounded just like a school bell ringing and it was so real to me, that I actually got up and opened my office door to check down the hallway. I stood there for a second, looking down the empty hallway, listening carefully, but heard nothing else. For a moment, I thought I was going crazy. It was right then that I realized I was doing myself a big favor getting away for a little while. I had spent too much time in that stuffy old office and it was going to my head. The trip would do me good. I grabbed my trench coat and hat and locked up the place. 'Good riddance,' I thought. I took the elevator down to the street. Once outside, I was lucky enough to find time was on my side. A trolley I take home everyday was just coming down the block. I hopped on it just as it was passing. The trolley's familiar bell rang out as we soared up and down the city's familiar hills, like a roller coaster ride on tour beneath the pagoda rooftops of Chinatown, through to North Beach where I lived. It was a short ride for me. I got off in front of this grocery store I went to sometimes that sold bottled, canned and packaged goods on their shelves. I had my jaw broken recently and I was reliant on baby food for dinner, since I still found it difficult to chew. I picked up an eclectic assortment of the baby food, making sure that I accounted for all of the major food groups. Maybe I wasn't eating well but I was eating healthy. I thought to buy a couple of beers to go along with the food, but remembered that I had all the ingredients for a martini at home and that was all that I needed to have, anyway. From there, it was a short walk to the apartment that I called home. I opened the door and drudged up the stairs with my groceries, passing the wiseacre landlady who said to me something like, 'Play it again, Serop." As usual, I didn't have any idea what she was talking about. She was very strange and often made a habit of inane remarks around me. Once inside the apartment, packing went smoothly. I planned to be in New York City for no more than a week, at the most. Since I had been there before in the Spring, I knew what to expect from the weather. It was pretty much the same as here. I mixed up some martinis and ate my baby food out of the jars, watching a little television. I had to bang on the silly box a couple of times and then play with the antenna just to keep the picture going. It was a variety show I was watching with girls dancing around this guy in a top hat and tails. The girls were singing a goofy song off the Hit Parade that I'm still trying to forget. They probably would've been singing and dancing all night were it not for the custard pies thrown at them from offstage. It couldn't have been the audience throwing the custard pies, they were laughing and applauding like idiots starved for entertainment. I failed to see the entertainment in any of it, frankly, so I shut the TV off. I was about ready to hit the hay when I remembered to call Zuplez. I dialed her number but no one answered the phone. I would have tried again later but I fell asleep.

The next morning, I awoke in my easy chair with a backache and cramps in my legs. I got up and stretched, made a pot of coffee and had a couple of cups with a couple of cigarettes for breakfast, before I shaved and showered. I was ready to leave about an hour later and called the cab to take me to the airport. I thought to give

Zuplez a try on the phone again, but just as I dialed her number the cab arrived. I heard the driver beeping the horn for me outside, something I positively can't stand. I threw on my trench coat and hat, grabbed the luggage and locked up the apartment. One of the neighbors has a little girl who sometimes plays with her toys on the landing. She's in the habit of calling me Bogey Man for some unapparent reason. When I saw her this morning she asked me if I was going to hunt for the Maltese Falcon. I thought that so cute and clever that I just had to reward the little girl for her comment. I had nothing else, so I offered her a cigarette. She accepted it, probably out of curiosity. I told her that she was not allowed to smoke it, only to look at it. The idea seemed to boggle her tiny mind. The little brat stared at me, saying nothing as I dragged my luggage down the stairs toward the door. She will learn to be afraid of me, I thought, and with any luck will avoid me in the future. When I got outside, I spotted the driver leaning on his cab, waiting for me. He asked if I needed help with the luggage, offering to open the trunk. I told him that it wasn't necessary, that I'd just keep it in the back seat with me. The driver was polite and quiet, only speaking to me when invited. He reminded me of a janitor who worked in my old high school twenty years ago. Was it the janitor or my old guidance counselor? Anyway, he was a good driver. Before I knew it we were on Bayshore headed for the International Airport. On the radio I heard some kiddy rock and roll playing, a song called 'Dog Gone Detective.' Actually, I just made that up. I don't know what it was called.

When I first caught sight of some airplanes, I told the driver to pull into the TWA terminal.

What happened at the airport was pretty much what you would expect. I checked the baggage, got my boarding pass, found my departure gate and when told to do so by announcement, lined up to board the aircraft with the rest of my fellow passengers. I had my ticket checked by this sexy stewardess who smiled at me and told me I looked like someone famous. Later on in the flight, when she served me lunch, I asked her who she thought I reminded her of. She said, "You know, that guy that always plays the detective in all the movies. You look like him." I couldn't believe it. Did she mean, Humphrey Bogart? I thought. That was when the whole scene got totally ridiculous, because the stewardess stopped another stewardess who was serving lunch to the passengers on the other side of the isle and asked her, pointing to me, "Hey, who does this guy remind you of?" Sure enough, the dame said, "Humphrey Bogart." At that point, every passenger who could look over and stare at me did so. Some were straining to do so. One character even handed me a glossy photograph of Humphrey Bogart and asked me to autograph the damn thing. I flatly told him that I wasn't Humphrey Bogart and that if he didn't get it out of my face, I was going to shove it up his snot nose. Some people might be flattered by a comparison to Bogart, but I wasn't particularly. More than anything it bothered me because as the stewardess so aptly noted, Bogart often played a detective on the silver screen. Since I was a detective for real, it couldn't help my situation if someone thought of me as guy who plays a detective. It's too close to the truth. I go through this thing all the time, because my face looks a little like Bogart's and I sound like him. I guess it doesn't help that as a detective I tend to dress like him. The thing is, if I don't wear a trench coat and a fedora I don't feel like a detective and I have to feel like a detective if I want to be a good detective. I just wish Bogart would wear something else, in those movies. He shouldn't have to look like a detective just to play a detective. But as a detective for real, it helps me if I look like a detective and it helps my clients. They want me to look like a detective, after all. They take one look at me and they know their money is well spent. My look inspires their confidence. I've tried to go undercover. It just doesn't work. I don't feel like me, I feel like an actor, like I'm trying to be something else other than a detective, which is what I am.

Anyway, five or so hours later we landed at Idlewild Airport. I couldn't wait to get off that plane. The guy behind me kept whistling the theme to Casablanca the whole flight. I wanted to punch him in the face. The funny thing is, he sort of reminded me of James Cagney. I strained not to look at him, because I was too afraid of him bringing up the whole Bogart thing. But I caught a glimpse of him out of the corner of my eye a few times during the flight and from what I could tell he was a dead ringer for the actor. Maybe it was Cagney. I couldn't be sure but told myself I didn't care. When I went to claim my luggage with the rest of the passengers from the flight I surreptitiously (and Seroptitiously) glanced around the group of us then huddled near the baggage claim area. But I never saw a sign of him again. I did see my little suitcase on the conveyor belt. When it came close enough I grabbed it and made a beeline for the cab line outside. I only waited ten or fifteen minutes before I had a cab and that wasn't too bad, especially for a Saturday. The cabbie offered to put my luggage in the trunk but like with the cabbie back home, I told him I'd just keep it in the back seat with me. I then gave him the address of the hotel on East 27th Street. We made good timing. He dropped me off at *Le Hotelier Baroque* about an hour later.

The lobby looked like a bohemian love pad of some kind, with beatnik kids lounging around in plush seats. Some of them were talking but most were either quietly writing or necking. Bebop music was playing from a radio at the front desk. I took a look around while I waited for the kid at the desk to get off the phone. The whole place was painted flashy colors and there were modern art pieces, giant hands and lips and other less identifiable objects, strategically placed all around the joint. Straight off I said to myself, "Serop, you're in the wrong damned place." I can't say exactly what I expected but I can tell you it wasn't this. Truthfully, I should have expected something like this from a hotel with such a ridiculous name. The Weird Hotel, said it all. When the kid at the front desk was finally off the telephone I asked him about the reservation book he was writing in. I asked how far it went back. He answered me by asking me a totally different question, did I have a reservation.

I told him the name and he flipped through the pages looking it up. When he finally found it, he clarified that I was only staying a week. I told him, "If the book says I'm staying a week, I must be staying a week." He simpered and told me how much the total was for the week and flatly stated that I would need to pay him in advance. I gave him the cash and he gave me the key to a room on the ninth floor. He then asked if I'd need help with my luggage. I told him no and brought up the reservation book again. He rolled his eyes and asked me what I needed to know. I told him, "I'm trying to find out if a particular person was booked at this hotel three weeks ago. He may or may not have checked into the hotel. Would you have a record of that in this book?"

The desk clerk shrugged his shoulders. "I don't know, Pops. Maybe."

There was another kid fussing around beneath the desk, ostensibly looking for something. When the desk clerk called me Pops this other kid started laughing. The desk clerk smiled at that, appreciating his audience.

I told him, "Look. I'm not going to play games. Are you going to help me or not?"

"Maybe, Pops. First tell me why I should, like are you a cop?"

"No, I'm not a cop and don't call me Pops."

"Well then you must be like some kind of private eye, seeing that you're dressed up like one. What are you, on a big time case? Is the Maltese Falcon stolen again?"

The other kid beneath the desk started laughing.

"No, I'm not a detective either," I lied. "I'm here looking for a friend of mine that disappeared a few weeks ago. If you don't want to help me I'll ask the manager of the place to help me or maybe I will bring the police into this. I'm trying to find my friend."

I could tell that everyone in the lobby had heard me because they had stopped whatever they were doing and were all looking my way.

"Oh if you're trying to find your friend, that's a different story," the desk clerk relented. He turned the reservation book around to face me. "Here, be my guest . . . *friend.*"

"Thanks," I told him, bringing the book closer to me. I knew that the punk would show me some respect sooner or later.

Apparently the other kid beneath the desk found whatever it was he was looking for, because he muttered something like, "Got it," before he walked away. As he was leaving the desk and walking around me I could feel him giving me a dirty look. The desk clerk confirmed this suspicion of mine, when I heard him say to the other, "Yeah I like his hat too. The Bogart Special." I couldn't believe that one, as if no one but Humphrey Bogart ever wore a fedora. I tried to ignore the puerile remark, reminding myself that only the reservation book and the dates therein were worthy of my concentration at that moment. I was pleased to see that there were dates at the top of each entry page. Since I knew that Mr. Zuplez had allegedly been registered for the week beginning the ninth and ending the fifteenth, I paid careful attention to those pages. I scrutinized each hand written entry, working my way up and down the columns of names from one page to the next, for the most part ignoring the corresponding telephone numbers. If there was an address next to a given name I took note of the town. That's how I finally came across the entry of Edward Zuplez. The name was very hard to read because it had been scribbled over and crossed out, but his was the only entry in the book for those dates with a home address given as San Francisco. That was how I found him in the book. If I hadn't seen San Francisco, I might have glossed right over the entry, ignoring the blotch of black ink as nothing more than an error that had been expunged. This was the reason the desk clerk had told me over the phone the day before that he had no record for Edward Zuplez. He never saw the entry, but in fact it had been there all the time. So that answered that question. Now I wanted to know why it was crossed out. Was the reservation cancelled, and if so by whom? I asked the desk clerk about it.

He looked at the entry and shrugged his shoulders. "How should I know why it's crossed out, man," he replied. He was popping bubble gum. "You'd have to ask the clerk who was here on that day about it."

"Well, who was the desk clerk on that day," I asked him, "on the second of March?" I took out a cigarette and lit it.

The clerk picked up an ashtray from the other end of the desk and put it down in front of me, on the book. "Don't get ashes on the floor, Mister," he warned me. "I'll have to clean it up later when you're upstairs reading through your Eye Spy magazines."

I moved the ashtray off the book and then grabbed the clerk by the collar. "I asked you a question, wise guy. I want to know who took the reservations for the second of March." I pointed at the reservation book entry with my free hand while I held him with the other. "Either you took this entry or it was someone else. If it was someone else, let me know who it was. Are you reading me loud and clear, buddy boy?" He heard me alright, as did the rest of the beatniks in that joint. They all cleared out of the lobby like rats off a burning ship, some ran outside but the majority went up to their rooms. I could hear them scampering up the stairs behind me in a panic. I guess they could smell trouble. In a heartbeat the whole lobby was empty with two exceptions, the desk clerk and his little helper (the wiseacre kid who'd been fidgeting behind the desk earlier). The latter saddled up next to me and asked for a cigarette. I let the clerk go and turned to him. "Do you know anything about this book?" I asked. He asked me for the cigarette again, so I gave him one, even offered him a light.

The kid inhaled deeply and then exhaled. "Thanks," he said.

I waited for him to say something about the book but since he didn't I asked him again.

"Oh the book," he suddenly remembered. "Yeah. Smitey and me, we take turns at the desk, taking the reservations and such."

By Smitey, I knew he was referring to the clerk I'd had by the collar. He had looked over at him when he'd mentioned the name. "What's your name?" I asked him.

"It's Smitty," said the kid.

He leaned over the desk to look at the book, when he did his waist bone brushed against my crotch. I wasn't sure if he did it on purpose, but I got out of his way. I started thinking the two of these characters were homosexuals.

"Oh yeah," Smitty said, studying the book. "That's my handwriting, alright. You want to know about this reservation that's scribbled out, is that it?"

I nodded, taking a drag off of my cigarette.

"Let me get a puff," the desk clerk asked Smitty, gesturing for the kid's cigarette.

Smitty gave it to him, keeping his eyes on the book. Finally he turned to me, "You know I'm trying to remember the reservation in question but it was just so many weeks ago now. I mean, here at the desk we take god knows how may reservations in a given night and all those reservations get kinda blurred night after night, day after day. I really don't remember too much about this particular one. I really wish I had something to jar my memory, then I'd tell you everything you need to know."

I handed him a twenty-dollar bill. Smitty took it and stuffed it in his tight jeans, then he started babbling, "Yeah, that was a weird one. The man's old lady called to make the reservation for him. I recall the incident because when I was talking to her on the phone, taking down the information: name, address, phone number, reservation dates, etc. I overheard a male voice laughing in the background. I mean this joker was really cracking up, man. For a moment there, I thought the whole thing was a prank phone call, because the lady on the phone was laughing herself right into the receiver; I guess in response to some of the things the jerk in the background was saying to her. I don't know. My only other thought was that the two of them were kinda sauced, you know—drunk."

I took a last drag off of my cigarette and put it out in the ashtray. "The guy in the background, you think that was the husband? The man she was making the reservation for?"

Smitty shrugged his shoulders. "I don't know, man." He shifted his wait onto his other foot and waited for me to ask him something else.

I asked him what he thought they were laughing about.

Smitty shook his head like he didn't know and at that point the clerk next to him remembered something. He reached across the desk and took Smitty by the shoulder. "Hey, didn't you tell me that the guy in the background said something about a book. 'I'll have to put that in the book,' or something.

"That's right," Smitty acknowledged. "Thanks, Smitey. I forgot all about that."

Smitey nodded and smiled at me. "Do *I* get a twenty?" he asked me.

Smitty punched his co-worker in the arm and grabbed the remains of the cigarette from him.

Smitey grunted and gave Smitty a dirty look. "That hurt, you bitch!"

Smitty took a last drag of the cigarette and put it out in the ashtray. "Go sweep the floors or something," he ordered.

On that note, Smitey left us alone.

Smitty picked up where he'd left off, his story-telling abilities rejuvenated again, "Like my friend said, the guy that was laughing on the other end of the phone kept mentioning a book to the woman giving me all the information. I got the impression that this book was the source of their mutual hysteria, because whenever the guy brought up the book the two of them would immediately start laughing again."

"What did the man say about the book?" I questioned.

Smitty tried to recollect, "Um, I don't remember exactly. It was something like, 'If I put it in the book, that means it will come true.' I don't know something weird like that. 'I'm going to make it all come true and then the book will be an oracle.' I remember he used some weird word like that, 'oracle.' And the woman said back to him—she was carrying on two conversations, one with him and one with me—it was very rude—she said, 'the truth will come out in the end.' It was something like that. The both of them were so weird."

I asked Smitty if the reservation was cancelled and if so, who cancelled it.

"Well, the thing is no one cancelled it. The guy just never showed up. A week later the woman called again and asked if her husband had arrived. I told her he didn't."

"Did she seem upset?" I asked.

Smitty shook his head. "Not at all. She was laughing with that same guy again in the background. I really thought the whole thing was a total joke and that was why I crossed the reservation out, scribbled it out. I never gave it a second thought again until just now when you showed up asking about it." There was a pause. The kid shrugged his shoulders and gave me a blank stare, as if to tell me there was nothing else to say on the subject.

I had nothing else to say either, as I was completely baffled by his story. Why would Mrs. Zuplez call the hotel to make sure her husband arrived then show no concern upon learning that he had not arrived? Wouldn't that sufficiently arouse her alarm at that moment as it did the day before in my office? Wouldn't she have panicked and insisted that there was a mistake or at least asked if there was a forwarding address for her husband? According to Smitty, that was not the case. To the contrary, Mrs. Zuplez exhibited a good deal of mirth and merriment, laughing it up with whoever the other mysterious person was with her on the other end of the phone. What was this person's identity? According to Smitty, the jocular fellow was in the background for the first and the second call. If that was the case, he could not have been Mr. Zuplez. Why would Mrs. Zuplez call the hotel to confirm the arrival of her husband if in fact, Mr. Zuplez was right there with her? I couldn't make heads or tails of it, so like Smitty I just shrugged my shoulders. "O.K. You told me everything I need to know." Reaching for the suitcase at my feet, I added, " I'm going up to my room now. I'm a little tired. Thanks for your help."

"Sure thing. Hey, you need help with that luggage?"

"No, I got it. I hauled it all the way from San Francisco, I think I can make it up the stairs."

"That's nine flights for you, Mister. You could make it easy on yourself and take the elevator over there—"

I turned around to see him pointing at the other end of the lobby.

"Oh," I heard myself exclaim. "I didn't see it. I saw all the kids take to the stairs before, so I just assumed you didn't have a lift."

Smitty laughed. "Most of those *kids* are on the first three floors."

I walked over to the elevator and pressed the button. "Do I have a phone in my room?" I asked.

Just then Smitey walked by with a mop and answered the question vicariously. "Yeah, there's a phone. You can dial out. But messages come through the front desk. You get your messages down here."

The elevator doors opened and I stepped in. I turned around and pressed the button numbered nine. The last thing I saw before the doors closed was Smitey making a stupid face at me, he had his lips pushed out and his eyes rolled back into his head. 'What a jerk,' I thought.

When the elevator doors opened again, I saw a dark, dingy corridor. It was quite a contrast to the bright, colorful lobby downstairs. A melancholy wave swept over me, but it was quickly removed with the help of a happy sound bellowing out from one of the many doors that now faced me on both sides. It was an acoustic guitar strummed by someone with a knack for creating positive moods. I took the room key out of my pocket and saw number ninety-six written on it. That was the number of my room. I found the room soon enough, after all there were only ten rooms on the floor. I unlocked the door, hoping the room would be a little more inviting than the corridor and to my relief it was. I dropped the suitcase on the floor, locked the door and took a look around. It was simple, but accommodating. There was no sign of a television or even a radio, but there was a telephone on a little night table, a private bathroom and some curtains on the window. Most importantly, there was a bed. I took my hat and coat off, loosened my tie and flopped down on the mattress to test it out. To my surprise, it was very comfortable. I thought, 'I'm going to sleep well in this place. The mattress is more comfortable than my own back home.' Soon after that I drifted into sweet slumbers. I don't know how long I slept, because I hadn't looked at my watch since arriving at the hotel. It is entirely possible I hadn't looked at it since arriving in New York. I didn't remember looking at it, at any rate. When I awoke, I heard my stomach growling and knew it was time to feed that animal. Though before I went in search of food I wanted to get in touch with the publisher that allegedly made Mr. Zuplez an offer to come to New York City. I needed their address. I looked over my notes and found their name again, The Big Game, Inc. That's when I picked up the phone and heard Smitey answer downstairs.

"Yellow."

"Smitey?"

"Yeah. Is this Mr. Bogart?"

"Serop, Smitey. The name's Serop."

"What can I do for you, Mr. Syrup?"

"I need an outside line, wise guy."

"Oh sure. Hold on for that."

A second later I heard a dial tone. I dialed the operator and asked her for the number of the Big Game, Inc. I was hoping there was such a business entity. The truth was, whether the publishing company existed or not, I'd still have to find out what happened to Mr. Zuplez. Of course, if the publisher did exist it would make my job that much easier. At least, I would have a place to start the investigation. To my relief, The Big Game was listed in the New York directory. The operator gave me the number and tried to connect me. I did not expect a publishing company to be open for business on a late Saturday afternoon. But to my surprise, someone did answer. I composed myself and spoke:

"Hello? I'm trying to reach The Big Game, Inc."

"This is The Big Game," I heard someone say.

"Oh, it is? I didn't expect you to be open for business today," I explained. "Is this an answering service?"

"No, this is The Big Game," the party clarified. "How can we help you?"

"Well, I have some business to discuss with you."

"Is this about a book?"

"Yes, it is. I want to know your address."

"We're on West 57th Street, on the corner of Broadway."

"What floor?" I asked.

The person on the other end of the line laughed at me, which I thought a peculiar reaction to my perfectly legitimate question. I was about to admonish the voice when it informed me that the business was located at street level. That I thought equally peculiar. Why would a publishing company be located on the street? Street level was usually for restaurants, shops and stores in New York. All of the major businesses demanded large real estate space, the kind of space that just wasn't available on the street. My thought was, 'The Big Game must be a mighty small operation.'

"Will there be anything else?" the voice asked me, waxing impatient.

I didn't know quite how to respond. Of course, I had a million questions more, but if I was going to ask about Mr. Zuplez I knew it would serve me better to do it with someone face to face. The phone was no place to discuss business, after all. Keeping it simple, I asked him how late they were open tonight and what their hours were during the week. I expected to hear that they would be closed by this evening, but to my surprise the voice told me that they were open until eight p.m. Weeknights they were open until seven p.m. 'How convenient,' I thought. 'I'll pay them a visit this evening, after I have a little dinner.' I thanked the voice but received little courtesy myself. The party simply hung up the phone without a goodbye. I had the impression that the voice was rather anxious to get rid of me, leading me to believe that they were very busy down at the Big Game, Inc. But busy doing what? I opened my suitcase and checked my thirty-eight pistol. She was loaded and I strapped her on.

My stomach was growling louder than ever so I put my hat and coat on with intent of finding some food to feed that beast. Once outside in the corridor, I heard the same acoustic guitar playing as I locked up the room and waited for the elevator. When the elevator door opened this time it was crowded with freaky kids headed for the lobby and crazy Saturday night madness in the big city. We all unloaded in the lobby and the beatniks spread out. A bunch of them were hanging around in the plush chairs that filled the lobby. They were listening to jazz and carrying on in suspicious ways. I tried my best to ignore them but had little success. How can you ignore punks that constantly clap their hands and snap their fingers? How can you ignore punks that shout obsceni- ties and then drop kick into bad poetry? How can you ignore punks that feel up under age girls in public places? These are the same punks that will wave a knife under your nose to make a point on some dark and star- less night, when you least expect it. How can you ignore them? The thing is you can't ignore them. That's why I moved to North Beach, because when you can't *beat* them, you join them.

I walked out the front door and turned right, heading toward Madison. Smitey was hanging out by the entrance smoking a cigarette. He called to me as I walked passed him, "Hey schweetheart, where you going? Give my re- gards to Ingrid Bergman and Lauren Becall . . . Oh and say Hi to Katherine Hepburn for me." I was going to turn around and let him have it, but I told myself that it wasn't worth bothering about. Stupid kids like that are a dime a dozen. I concentrated on what really mattered, finding some cheap food and a bottle of something for the room. I kept walking west until I got to Sixth Avenue, then I turned right and started walking uptown. Somewhere in the thirties near Herald Square I found a grocery store that sold baby food. I bought my usual combination of vegetables and meat for a well balanced diet. I made sure to get a spoon from the vendor, as well. I decided to take Broadway back downtown, spotting a liquor store on the way. There, I bought a bottle of scotch. I couldn't remember if the room had a drinking glass, but if it hadn't I could always use one of the emptied baby food jars. I'd just have to wash it out first.

When I got back to the Hotel Baroque with the groceries and my scotch, I passed Smitey again by the entrance. He was still there, like he'd never left. As I reached for the door, he asked me if I'd been up to Times Square. I told him not yet. "That's too bad," he said, "You could find your *African Queen* there on a lucky night." That gives you an idea of this character's caliber. It was pretty low. I knew what I was dealing with here. The last thing I wanted was to give this kid encouragement to pass out future comments from his cornucopia of cornball. If I let him know he'd got my goat he'd try again, for sure, and I'd be playing right into his hands. The kid was so obviously starved for a reaction and for that reason I didn't give him one, not even a grunt or a grimace. I wore my poker face and pretended he was a figment of my imagination.

I passed through the lobby on my way to the elevator when Smitty stopped me and told me I had a message.

"From who?" I asked. He ran over to fetch it from the front desk and bring it over to me but I met him half way. It was from Mrs. Zuplez. The message was cryptic and I read it and re-read it, trying to read into it. It read, 'The Big Game is that you are a character in someone's detective story.' I suddenly realized that the beatnik kids were dancing around me. They were swaying languidly to bebop music blasting from the radio at the front desk. They brought me back to the circumstances of my reality. I asked Smitty, "Don't you think that music is a little loud?" Smitty ran over to the front desk again, while I walked to the elevator, still trying to make heads or tails of the message. By the time I pushed the elevator button to go up, I heard the music lowered. A second later I looked over my shoulder to see Smitty running back over to me. On his way, he fielded complaints from the beatniks who were upset that the radio volume was now being played at a reasonable level.

Smitty got to me just as the elevator doors opened. He said, referring to the message in my hands, "Do you see what I mean about her being weird?"

I stepped inside the elevator and pressed nine, but held the doors so that they wouldn't close. "Was she laughing again?" I asked Smitty, timorously. I was afraid of the answer that I'd get.

"Oh she was laughing alright," he confirmed. "And guess what else? I heard the same guy in the background with her. They were cackling like a couple of jokesters."

"Alright, thanks." I let the elevator doors close around me. As I came up to the ninth floor, I held onto my groceries and scotch like they were my only friends in the world. I felt lonely all of a sudden and stupid, as I was possessed by the paranoid idea that I had been the butt of someone else's joke. Could it be true that Mrs. Zuplez was playing a game? Did she really leave that message for me? Was Smitty truthful about his conversations with her over the phone? I did not entirely exclude the possibility he invented the message from Zuplez and the phone conversations that he recollected having with her. Could it have been an invention of his sick sense of humor? It seemed to me that either he was playing a game with me or Mrs. Zuplez was playing a game with me. It was either one or the other. That indigestible thought depressed me and made me feel like a complete loser. After the doors opened, I stepped out of the elevator onto the ninth floor and heard once again the familiar acoustic guitar being strummed. The difference this time was that the music sounded less cheerful and more melancholic in feeling. I also had the distinct impression that this sad music was being played only for me. I tried to snap out of my depression, searching for my room keys. In the difficult process of fumbling through my pockets while holding the groceries, I accidentally dropped the bag and everything broke right in front of my door. I couldn't believe my stupidity. I was hoping at the very least that the bottle of scotch had not broken, but it was just as busted up as the baby food jars. There was nothing to salvage. The trip to the grocery store and the liquor store had been a complete waste, not to mention the money spent. I did manage to find the room keys, however. I opened the door and went inside and called downstairs to tell them about the mess in front of my door. Smitty said it wasn't a problem and that he'd send Smitey up with the mop. I hung up the phone, took off my hat and coat, praying that Smitey would leave me alone. The last thing I needed was to hear that moron knocking at my door. I didn't want any disturbances, especially if I was going to give Mrs. Zuplez a call. I took her card out of my wallet and compared the phone number printed on it to the phone number written on Smitty's message. They were the same. This could mean Mrs. Zuplez had called, but then again I had not told her that I would be staying at the Baroque Hotel. Of course, she might have assumed that I would be staying at the same hotel that she'd reserved for her husband. But what about the other possibility? What if my friend Smitty had invented the message that she'd called? He could have easily copied her phone number from the reservation book. That seemed to make more sense as I thought about it, given the nature of the message and the inclination I had not to trust him. Of course, the only way to know for sure was to make the call. As I picked up the receiver, I heard what I presumed to be Smitey out in the hall cleaning up the broken glass in front of my door and a second later I heard his pal Smitty's voice sieving from the phone into my ear:

"Is this room ninety-six? Hello? Mr. Serop?"

"Yeah. Hi Smitty, it's me."

"You need an outside line, right?"

"Yeah, that's right."

"You're going to call that crazy lady out in Frisco?"

"Huh? Oh yeah. Is that Smitey I hear out in the hall?"

"Yeah. I sent him up with the mop. I told him not to bother you."

"Good. Thanks."

"Hold on for the outside line, Mr. Serop."

"Thanks a lot."

I dialed the operator and told her I needed long distance. She transferred me after asking me to please hold. After a couple of rings, the long distance operator came on. I read her the phone number off the card Mrs. Zuplez gave to me and in no time at all that number was ringing. I was hoping Mrs. Zuplez would be home. To my relief, she was. I heard her pick up:

"Hello?"

"Mrs. Zuplez?"

"Yes?"

"It's Serop, Mrs. Zuplez."

"Oh, I didn't recognize your voice at first. I apologize."

"No problem. Listen, I'm in New York."

"Yes. I was hoping you would be."

"I'm staying at the Hotel Baroque."

"Yes. I figured as much. That's why I called you there."

"Oh, so you did call?" I asked her.

"Yes. Didn't you get my message?"

"Yeah. I got it. That's why I'm calling. It's rather a strange message, Mrs. Zuplez."

"What do you mean? I only left my number with a request that you'd call."

"You didn't leave a message that read . . . " I picked up the message that Smitty had given me and read her the cryptic line written at the bottom of the memo, "You didn't leave me a message that read, and I quote, *'The Big Game is that you are a character in someone's detective story.'*"

Mrs. Zuplez laughed. "Goodness me. No, I never left you a message of that sort. How strange would that be?"

"Exactly."

Mrs. Zuplez started to laugh again. "I think someone must be playing a joke on you, Mr. Serop."

"I think so too," I agreed. I had a vision in my head of strangling Smitty downstairs, when a weird thing happened that made me forget all about it. I heard Mrs. Zuplez whispering. It sounded to me as if she was carrying on a furtive conversation with someone else. I questioned why she was whispering and when I did Mrs. Zuplez started laughing again. I asked her if there was anyone else with her but I don't believe she heard me. I was talking over her laughter, which had risen to a crescendo. This laughter continued unabated for a couple of minutes or more. Ultimately, I heard it in stereo. That is to say, I am positive that I heard the laughter of two distinct people. One was in the foreground and the other was in the background. I was quite confident that Mrs. Zuplez was in the company of some other person at that moment though she would not acknowledge it. Eventually the laughter stopped altogether. Mrs. Zuplez cleared her throat and gave me the indication that she had regained her composure. Quietly, I waited for her to give me an explanation or at the very least an apology for her behavior. I still had no idea what it was all about.

After a couple of seconds, she demurely apologized.

Again, I asked her if there was someone else in the room with her. She denied that there was and then abruptly told me that she had to get off of the phone, that she had an appointment to keep.

"An appointment to keep?" I echoed her. "Mrs. Zuplez, I am calling you long distance about your husband. He's missing remember? You haven't even asked me if I'd discovered anything yet."

She protested, "Well, I just assumed that if you had found out anything about him you would have told me by now. Certainly, you wouldn't keep me guessing about my husband's welfare. I am paying you handsomely to find out what happened to him, if you recall. I was also cutting you some slack, Mr. Serop. After all, you only just arrived in New York. I would hardly expect that you discovered anything about my husband yet. I mean, am I wrong?"

Suddenly, I felt foolish. "No, you're not wrong."

She started sobbing. "I mean, I only just called there to make sure that you arrived safely. My dear husband never even made it that far."

If there was one thing I couldn't stand it was a woman crying and it choked me up. "Listen, don't start balling. I didn't mean to hurt your feelings. Come on, I didn't mean anything by it. Look, I'm sorry. Mrs. Zuplez, I'm sorry. Don't cry, Mrs. Zuplez. Don't cry." At a certain point, I realized that she was not crying in the sense that most of us understand crying. Mrs. Zuplez was snickering into the phone at me, at my empathy for her easily manipulated emotions. She changed her emotional disposition as quickly and as effortlessly as a chameleon changing its colors. If she'd been crying at all, the tears were incidental as the culmination of her intense joy. She was laughing hard again in no time, no doubt for successfully putting one over on me. I tried to get her attention, to give her a piece of my mind when again I heard the second voice in the background telling her to hang up the phone. The last sound I heard before the line went dead was the uproarious laughter of two people. There was no mistake in my mind about what I had heard.

I hung up the phone and put my hat and coat on to head over to the Big Game, Inc. I had a lot of questions and the Big Game seemed to me the best place to start asking them. I opened the door and saw Smitey crouching to the floor. He was carefully picking up the busted shards of glass from the bottle and jars I'd dropped earlier. Smitey looked up at me contemptuously as I stepped out of the room and into the corridor with him. I ignored his nasty gaze and shut my door. I then started walking toward the elevator, half expecting him to say something to me. He did too, after my foot accidentally knocked over the mop that he had leaning against the wall so that it fell on the water bucket beside it and spilled the contents all over the corridor in both directions.

"Boy, for a big time movie star detective, you sure are one stupid, klutzy, mother f___ er."

I pushed the elevator button and then walked back over to him and picked him up by the collar, tearing his shirt in the process. The kid stood up on his feet and tried in vain to get me to release my grip. He was remonstrating until I shook him and told him to shut up. I was so angry at that moment that I truly think I could have killed him. Instead I decided to give the kid a warning. I looked him straight in the eye and said, "If you ever talk to me like that again, sonny boy, I am going to hit you so hard that your nose is going to be pushed back into your brain. You'll be so unrecognizably dead that the morgue will need your whole family to identify your ugly, contorted, distorted face. Do you understand me, jackass?" I must have seemed pretty angry, like I meant business, because for the first time my friend Smitey showed me a little respect. "Yes, sir," he replied, nodding his head repeatedly. I let go of his collar when I heard the elevator doors open. As I left him and walked back toward the elevator, I passed the overturned bucket and I kicked it. "Remember what I said," I warned. I took one last look at the little bastard as I stepped into the elevator. The kid was still shaking his head up and down like a private first class just given an order from a superior officer. I tried to compose myself, as there were four beatniks in the elevator with me acting up. I could just see myself slugging one of them on account of the way that they were behaving in this confined space with me. In short, they were squeezing at each other's pectorals and then laughing about it. I think one of them said something about a, 'purple nurple,' but I can't be sure. When I finally felt one of their elbows brush up against my arm I was about to let them all have it and I can honestly say that it was lucky for them that the elevator doors opened at that point. Otherwise, I might have pistol-whipped them all. If there's one thing I can't stand its tactile contact with a beatnik.

I passed the front desk heading for the door. I heard Smitty's voice asking me, "Did you give it to her good, Mr. Serop?"

I realized he was asking me about Mrs. Zuplez and I answered him, "Yeah. I gave it to her good." It was bologna. But what else was I going to say? That she gave it to me good? That she was playing me for a jerk? I don't think so. I might have thought it, but I certainly wasn't going to say it. I stepped out the front door and made a left, walking up to Park Avenue. On Park, I hailed a cab and told the driver I wanted to be dropped off at West 57th Street, on the corner of Broadway. The Big Game, Inc. was going to get a visitor. In the cab, I couldn't help speculating why Mrs. Zuplez would leave me such a strange message, about me being a character in someone's detective story. By this time, despite her bogus denial, I had no doubt in my mind it was she that had left the message just as Smitty had said. Not that he was beyond reproach, but that she was so amused by the content of the message as I related it to her. I started asking myself, why would a woman pay a private dick to fly to New York to find her missing husband and a day later leave him cryptic messages implying he had been duped? The only explanation I could see was that

I had been duped, but I kept coming back to this question: Why? Why would a woman pay so much money for a practical joke? It didn't add up...unless she was completely crazy. And who was the man on the other end of the phone with her? Could that have been Mr. Zuplez? Were they both in on this? Did they both want to make fools of me? If so, why? I knew neither of them. I had never met Mrs. Zuplez nor heard of her or her husband until yesterday. What on earth was this all about? I told myself, there was a lot more to this than met the eye and that the only way to get to the bottom of it all was to simply continue the investigation just as if nothing had changed. In other words, I was going to act under the presumption everything I had been told by Mrs. Zuplez was true. I knew that if I followed my instincts on this I might eventually be in a better position to draw some logical conclusions, or at least I hoped so.

I was glad to see the traffic moving. We'd been stopped at a light and I had grown impatient. I was anxious to get to the publisher before he closed. I looked at my watch. It was 7:30. That meant I had a half an hour to get there and find something out. Otherwise, I would have to go back on Monday morning and that sounded like an eternity to me. I was trying to recall if the publisher had hours on Sunday. I did not remember the person on the phone saying they had hours on Sunday. I wouldn't have expected a business like theirs to be open on Sunday but then again I wouldn't have expected a business like theirs to have such late hours on a Saturday. I tried to be hopeful and told myself I'd get to the Big Game in time and settle all of this tonight. I couldn't stand another day, much less two, of not knowing what Mrs. Zuplez meant when she said I was a detective in someone's story and that that was the big game. It was too mysterious to pass off as just nonsense. If, as I suspected, Mrs. Zuplez had not brought me to New York to find her husband, exactly why then did she want me out here? I had to know why. The cab driver had been quiet up until this point but he interrupted my thoughts as we passed the Ed Sullivan Theater. He asked me if I ever watched Ed's show. I took a look at the letters CBS in big lights and told him no. I noticed the signature eyeball that the TV network used as a kind of symbol and I wished then privately that I had such an eye. With any luck I'd see a little more clearly the next time somebody tried to pull the wool over on me.

The cabbie let me out at the corner of Broadway and 57th Street, as I'd asked him to. Sure enough, I saw a big sign with yellow letters that read The Big Game, Inc. The sign was over what appeared to be the entrance of a bookstore. From the street, before I even walked into the place, I could see tables with piles of books, standing displays of books and wall-to-wall shelves filled with books. I said to myself if this place is a publishing company, it could sure double for a bookstore. But my suspicion wasn't aroused, so much as my curiosity piqued. After all, it wasn't an unusual idea that a company in the business of publishing books would have a lot of books lying around. It was just that I'd never heard of a publishing company that sold its own books on the street. Only an underground press would need to control every facet of its operation. It made me wonder about the kind of books that the Big Game published. As soon as I walked into the place I saw my suspicions confirmed. Books were being sold. I saw a cash register with a cashier behind it. There was a line of people in front of this register and each person on that line was holding at least one book. As they came up to the register they presented their books to the cashier and the cashier rang them up. She then told the customer what they owed and the customer then promptly paid their bill. The cashier accepted the cash and in some instances gave the customer change. She would then place the customer's receipt into a bag with the book or books that they purchased. The customer would then accept the bag of books from the cashier, thank her and leave the premises. This process was repeated again with the next customer. I had to hand it to the people that ran this joint. They were making money hand over fist. Why did these books have such a demand? I wondered

I walked a couple of feet over to a display table of books. There was a sign over the table that read, Best Sellers. I picked one of them up and started reading. It was a self-help book. The author offered the reader 'psychic tips' on how to predict the future. One of the tips suggested drinking goat milk from a human skull. I thought to myself, 'I'll stick to drinking scotch out of a dirty glass and worrying about the present.' I guessed I must have looked out of place, because a sales clerk came over to me and asked if he could be of some assistance. I put the self-help book down and took the picture of Mr. Zuplez out of my wallet, the one that his wife gave me the day before in my office. "Yeah, you can help me," I said. "Have you ever seen this guy?"

The clerk looked at the photo and then at me. "No, I have never seen him," he replied. "Why do you ask?"

"Because he's a friend of mine. I am trying to find out what happened to him. He disappeared a few weeks ago. I was told by a mutual acquaintance that he had some business dealings with the Big Game just before he disappeared. Is there someone I could talk to about that?"

"You could talk to the store manager," the salesman told me. He pointed across the room at a man that was seated behind a desk with a big sign over it that read, Information.

The big guy behind the Information desk must have seen the salesman pointing him out, because our eyes locked before I even got to him. Before I could open my mouth, he asked me how he could be of assistance.

I handed him the picture of Mr. Zuplez. "Ever seen this guy?" I asked.

The man glanced at the photo and shook his head. "Nope."

"Are you sure?" I asked.

The man handed me back the photo. "I've never seen him. What's this all about?"

"You manage the Big Game?" I asked.

"That's right," he said. "I manage the store, this store."

"You publish books?" I asked.

"Publish books?" he repeated. "No, we don't publish books. We *sell* books." He stated petulantly.

"The Big Game doesn't publish books?" I asked.

The man leaned over the desk and scowled at me. "The Big Game is a bookstore, mister. It's a chain of bookstores around the city. This is one of the stores and I manage it. Now, what is this all about?"

I put the photograph back in my wallet and told him what it was all about, that a friend of mine had disappeared and I was trying to find him, the last piece of information I had on this friend was that he had flown from San Francisco to New York to meet an alleged representative of the Big Game, Inc. This person claiming to represent the Big Game had expressed an interest in publishing a book that my friend had written. He'd expressed his interest in writing and over the phone, enticing my friend to fly across the country to meet with him. All of this had taken place three weeks ago and my friend had not been heard from since.

The scowl on the store manager's face faded and was gradually replaced with a smile. "Are you nuts?" he asked me.

I was startled by this response. I had not expected it. "What do you mean, am I nuts?" I asked him back.

The store manager laughed to himself and then explained, "The little vignette you just gave me is the plot outline to a short story written by Steven Orion."

The name Steven Orion rang a bell, but I didn't know why. "Who is Steven Orion?" I queried, trying to digest all of this.

"He's a writer and he wrote a short story with the exact same premise you gave me. It's entitled, *The Case of the Lost Writer.* It's part of book of short stories he wrote called, *Roots and Seeds* . . . Just in case you're interested."

I couldn't believe my ears. "Are you sure that the plot premise of this book matches the story that I just told you?"

"You really are a character, mister. You think this is funny?" He asked me evenly.

"Look," I told him, "I'm not pulling your leg, but someone might be pulling mine. Are you sure that the plot premise of this book matches the story that I just told you?"

"I'm positive," the manager declared. The writer had to get permission to use the name of our store in his book. It was a big deal in the book business, a kind of endorsement."

"Well, where can I find this book?" I questioned, hungry for any kind of clues or leads.

"You can find it in fiction, over there—" The manager pointed toward the back wall. You'll find it listed alphabetically under the author's last name, so look under the O's for Orion. Again, the book's called *Roots and Seeds.*" Another customer was standing behind me and the manager turned his attention to this individual, "Can I help you?" I took this as my signal to go and look for the book.

Back against the wall I saw a big sign that read, Fiction. 'This must be the place,' I thought. There were shelves and shelves of books. As the manager said, they were all alphabetized by author's last names. I looked for the O's and found a few books authored by Steven Orion. I was hoping to find the one entitled *Roots and Seeds*. Otherwise, I was going to have to run out and look around for another bookstore that was still open. And it was getting late. There was simply no way I could put this off another day or two. I had to find the book tonight or I was going to go insane. To my great relief, I found one copy of *Roots and Seeds* still left on the shelf. The binding looked a little tattered, like it had been damaged in shipping. But this did not matter. I walked toward the cash register, passing the Information desk on my way. The store manager looked down at me as I passed him. "You found the book, O.K.?" He asked me. I nodded. I think they were anxious to get rid of me. I was the last customer in the place and as I looked at my watch I saw that it was 7:55 p.m. That meant they were closing in five minutes. The cashier already had her jacket on. I handed her the book. She took it and rang me up. After she told me the price, I gave her the money and she bagged the book. She put the receipt in the bag before handing it to me with my change. I expected all of this, as I had memorized her little routine. There was a linebacker guarding the entrance/exit to the store. He had the door locked to prevent new customers from coming in and he had to unlock it to let me out. "Goodnight," he wished me. I wished him the very same. Outside, I saw a pizzeria and thought to give some solid food a chance. My jaw still ached a bit but I had little hope of finding a grocery store where I could purchase baby food at this late hour. Instead, I settled for two slices of pizza and a bottle of Coke. Chewing the pizza was a little difficult at first, but I got used to it. Afterwards, I walked out on the street corner to search for a cab to take me back to the hotel. As I looked around me, I saw that the Big Game was closed. Down the block I spotted a big neon sign that read, BAR. I forwent the cab and capriciously headed in that direction. Inside the bar I found an empty booth with a light and settled into it. The barmaid came over and asked me if I wanted to order food. "No," I said, "Just a scotch on the rocks."

I took the book out and flipped through the pages. Like the manager of the Big Game said, it was comprised of short stories. Sure enough, one was entitled, *The Case of the Lost Writer*. I was about to read the story when the barmaid brought my scotch on the rocks over. It had a stirrer in it and I gave it the once around before relegating it to the little napkin that the barmaid had placed beside the drink. I took a healthy sip of the scotch. I thought it would be good medicine for what I was about to read. I was right. The first thing I saw on the page was my name, Serop. I couldn't believe my eyes. I realize better than anyone how unusual my last name is and I'm not accustomed to seeing it in print. As I read the first paragraph, written in first person, I realized that this Serop character was a private dick. Like me, he was from the Bay Area. The coincidences became even more bizarre by the sixth sentence when this detective mentioned the name of his female client. It was Zuplez. Further down,

I read that this woman resembled a High School English teacher from the detective's past. Uncannily, that woman's name was Ms. Red Lids. I could feel my heart beating faster as I progressed in the reading. The similarities in the story and my own experiences in this case became more acute when I read that the detective had been hired to search for his client's husband in New York. This plot development was not much of a surprise to me as I had been enlightened to it by the store manager of the Big Game. But it certainly was a surprise and yet another bizarre coincidence to learn that while in New York the detective stayed at a hotel named, *Le Hotelier Baroque*. It was located on East 27th Street. Furthermore, characters named Smitey and Smitty worked in the lobby of this hotel. I drank the rest of the scotch in my glass and scanned the rest of the story. My avid reading was disrupted only by the barmaid's voice when she came over and asked if I needed another scotch. I didn't remember telling her I did, but I must have, because she brought it right over. I stirred the scotch and then placed the stirrer on the napkin beside the drink. For some reason, this insignificant action gave me a profound sense of déjà vu. I thought to myself, 'Oh, it's nothing. I did the exact same thing before with the other drink. But then when I picked up the book again I read that the detective put his stirrer down beside his drink. Just like me, he was sitting in a booth in a bar scanning through a book that he'd bought at the Big Game, at the advice of that bookstore's manager. It gave me pause for thought. The strange short story ended with these words:

"Magine that!" I heard myself say, incapable of saying much else at that moment and in a way those were fitting last words for a private detective that was never anything more than a fictional character in a short story written by a man with a familiar name, Steven Orion. As I paused and reflected about that name I realized why it was familiar to me. Steven Orion was the name of a friend and fellow student in my 12th Grade English class. Like me, like all of us in that class, he was a creative writer. Perhaps there was a good chance he had written this very story. I considered the possibilities. If indeed he had written this story and his words were my constitution, he was the one responsible for bringing me to New York, was thereby responsible for my being in this bar, drinking and pondering the likelihood of my own existence, reading a book that I realized I was part of. I took a long drink of my scotch and finished it so that the ice in the glass touched my lip. Was this my first or second scotch? I didn't know for sure and I didn't care, but somehow knew it would be my last. My thoughts turned to the Baroque Hotel, how there was no need for me to ever go back there. I thought about San Francisco and how I would never again see my hometown or even my apartment in North Beach. There was no need for me to go anywhere or be anywhere other than right here in this no-name bar. It was the perfect place not only to finish a drink of scotch but to also finish a story.

Secret
Sentient

Imagine being a soft puppet the size of a human being. Now imagine being a soft puppet the size of a human being with the hidden intelligence of a human being. The world looks at you and all that they see is a soft puppet, but secretly you are much more than that. You have a sentience that no one knows about and it is to your advantage that no one else knows about this secret sentience. People will say and do things in front of you that they would ordinarily never dare to say or do in front of someone else. You are inanimate object and thereby foolishly perceived as a non-threat by others around you. As a consequence you are safely undetected as witness to the perverted crimes that bloom from their lascivious desires. Isn't that kind of neat? At first, I did not appreciate my unique situation as much as I do now. I used to hate it when others would look at me, point and pass lowbrow jokes back and forth, as if I was the joke and not they. Most of all, I hated their infernal smirks. I had to assuage my anger and my need for reciprocity by reminding myself that one day I would have the opportunity to wipe those smirks away forever and a day. Luckily, I somehow sensed that day wasn't long in coming and damn if I wasn't correct. I might have gone insane, otherwise. I will certainly tell you about that wonderful day, but first I will need to tell you a little more about myself as background so that you will appreciate what that day fully meant and how it was that I recognized it as the greatest day of my entire existence.

I am an Auto-Icon. Many of you will be unfamiliar with that term and so I will now courteously explain. In brief, it is what is colloquially known as a corpse but with one small difference: an Auto-Icon is stuffed. I am a cadaver, albeit preserved as one might a favored family pet kept in the parlor. And fittingly enough it is a parlor that I do make my home, although it is not mine technically. This parlor that I call my home is in a house that I do not own, therefore it is not mine. I cannot have my own house to live in if I am dead. At least that is what the state decreed and what my estate (that is, my surviving relatives) greedily acknowledged at the time of my death. Those mooching blackguards moved in before I had the chance to get cold, forget about being properly stuffed. But that was all a long time ago. Now this house that I once called mine belongs to distant descendents. You know I don't even know their names and I honestly don't care to. Generation after generation they all start to look the same to me. I don't exactly know how long I have been deceased. But I would venture to guess something like seventy five to a hundred years, who knows maybe more than that. The world has changed greatly, or so I hear. I hear the family members talk amongst themselves about these changes and I've seen weird gadgets that they've brought into the house that are evidence of change. The video box, for instance. Occasionally I have seen signs of change depicted on this video box. I am not personally privy to the full extent of what is going on outside, however, because all I ever do is sit in the parlor of this house like an ugly old museum piece. I will share with you that I do not remember what it is like to have a bath. I have not had one since I passed from the world of 'the living.' If my nose worked I am quite sure I would be appalled at the extent to which I reek, not that I am desiccating. That was foreseen and prevented in the process of preserving the body, obviously. What I meant by reek is, I bet I smell like a collection of old shoes or some other pile of crap that has been sitting around for generations. I can safely guess this, because the people who own this house spray me with a can of chemicals every now and again. But getting back to the matter of Auto-Icons, they are the invention of a brilliant Philosopher named Jeremy Bentham. It was he in the 19th Century that proposed the idea that corpses could be made useful as props and decorations in family homes as opposed to relegating them to the Earth and consuming maggots. Personally I will admit Bentham was a little eccentric for proposing such an outrageous idea but like many eccentrics he might have bordered on genius. After all, I am most useful. Useful is my middle name. Come to think of it, I haven't told you my first name or my last name so it will be helpful for you to just think of me as Useful. I can usefully prop things up, serve as a punching bag for children and as a confidential pal to adults. What I mean by that is, I am a good listener and usually discreet. Meaning, I do know how to mind my own business when I want to. For instance, a young couple leaned all over me the other night while they were making love on the couch and I minded my business. I simply pretended like it wasn't happening. My meditation was only broken when the girl started moaning. The girl I know was the baby sitter because I've definitely seen her before, but the boy (he was more like a young man) was a complete stranger to me. I'd never seen him before then, of that I'm sure. The slut used to bring a different boy over, this wiseacre kid with a basketball jacket. He used to talk to me as if I weren't there to hear him. Like I said earlier, that's the kind of thing that gets on my nerves. I don't like to be made fun of. Who does? The truth is, I'm the but of everyone's jokes sitting on this couch. I don't care for it at all. No one takes me seriously sitting on a big fluffy thing. Do you know what I did like? I used to sit on an elegant chair. It was an antique, made of cherry wood and it was carved beautifully. Those were the days when things were all handmade. I sat on that chair for so many years. Then one day, the family sold it on me. I know they sold it because I heard them arguing about whether or not they should get rid of it. The Father said he knew of a place that would buy such furniture for a good price. The Mother didn't want to sell it because it was a 'family treasure' and had 'sentimental value,' but in the end the

Father got his rotten stinking way. I especially hate the couch because everyone takes it as an invitation to sit next to me merely because there is room. I don't want anyone to sit next to me, especially the little brat of a kid that they have around here. He has this penchant for spilling things, and more often than not it's on me. The other night the little bastard spilled vanilla ice cream on my favorite paisley vest. It's actually my only paisley vest and now it has a big vanilla ice cream stain. I bought that vest back in 1865 and if anything were to happen to it, the odds are I would not be able to purchase another one quite like it anywhere. And even if I could find a vest like it, no one in this household would ever take me out to be fitted for one. I'm glad I mentioned the kid. He's also the reason that slut of a babysitter comes over here on Friday nights with her beaus. This will lead us to the day that changed my life. The significant event correspond- ing to that day occurred in the evening, so I suppose it might be even more appropriate for me to refer here to the night that changed my life. It is forever with me, as a treasured memory.

If I could have smelled that night, I imagine the babysitter would have smelled heavenly as the basket- ball star leaned her against me. How good it must feel to have her flesh against mine instead of his, I remember thinking as I envisioned her lustful face. I could not ac- tually see her face. I could only envision it, on account of the fact that I could not move my neck to turn my head. As you must have realized by now, Auto-Icons do not move. At least in theory they should not be capable of movement because they are comprised of dead matter, stuffed with feathers and then painted. Where is the possibility of movement occurring in such an entity? And yet I did move, somehow. I surprised not only myself, the kids nearly jumped out of their skins and they cleared the couch as if it had been set ablaze. That is, once they perceived my movement (and I do mean to include tactile contact in their perceptions), the babysitter in particular. It was satisfaction at last for me, when I finally heard her shriek because of something I had done to her. I've heard her shriek before, but never anything quite like this. There was fear in her cry instead of the usual lust. Both have a nice sound, but somehow only the former is truly satisfying for me.

The basketball star told the babysitter to be quiet. She was practically hysterical and he was afraid that she would wake the kid upstairs. I think that he might have been shaking her. I could not see for sure. He very confidently told her that I was a dead body and thereby incapable of movement. He explained this to her in his teenage parlance, quite ingenuously. As I've already intimated, I hated the guy with a passion. Not just because he had something that I wanted and couldn't have (a crime if ever there was one) but more importantly because he managed to make a fool of me and worst of all, he did it in front of her. In the effort to convince the girl that I was dead he slapped me . . . and then he laughed (the laughter was worse than the slap). To further convince her that I was incapable of movement, he then derided me, "Come on, Grandpa. Let's see you move, you big jerk." He then picked me up for a second and dropped me down again on the couch, requesting that I 'get up and dance.' Never had I been so humiliated.

I had resolved to take my revenge and to strike while my will was hot. The basketball star refuted the babysitter's claim a second time and slapped me a second time. I summoned all of my hidden energies into my eyes and a second later I blinked at the bastard. He stumbled back as if he had just seen a ghost. I wanted to laugh like Richard Widmark, but I could only think like Fyodor Dostoevsky. The babysitter was overcome with terror. She ran for the door and fled into the dark night, completely forgetting about the kid upstairs (what responsibility) and her boyfriend (what romance). The basketball star stood there cocky. He didn't want to believe that I had scared the living Jesus out of him. But I did and I knew it and I'm sure he knew it and that was what he hated most, sensing his own vulnerabilities. He slapped me a third time and that was when I miraculously successfully imparted the message to him that he should push his head into the glass screen of the video box.

It only took about a second before he acted on my will. Clearly, it was homicide. It was as if his whole body had been my toy and I had telekinetically killed him. Of course, everyone but the babysitter thought the hooligan had killed himself. I guess the babysitter will never be sure. The police assured her that it wasn't me, that I was a dead body incapable of movement. But I know who killed that boy; having witnessed the whole thing reflected in the mirror that hangs so prominently in the parlor.

I saw the boy put his head into a screen of thick glass and though I did not see the force behind the action, I saw the eyes of the killer reflected in my own. Others will make the unforgivable mistake of drawing conclusions that exclude the impossible with regard to that beautiful night, but I will know better and in so doing will think better of it all. And best of all, the babysitter still comes back to me every Friday night. Each week it is a different boy that she brings to the couch. It is as if she secretly hopes that I will murder again to confirm her own sanity and is hoping that sooner or later she will bring home a boy that I like as much as I did the son-of-a-bitch basketball star. And in between those Friday nights, I simply wait, watching the hands of the old grandfather clock move clockwise and then counter-clockwise and then clockwise again. I love to kill time almost as much as I love to kill basketball stars. And who better to kill time than one that lives outside of time and can survive it? There is only one witness to this crime. He stares out at me from the mirror that hangs in the parlor and is mute. He will keep his lips sealed as I will keep mine sealed. We have a vested interest in mutual silence.

The Cadaver and the Scholar

Mr. Low was not himself today. The gray, misty morn left him empty and wishing for something more beyond what he saw. The stray people wandering in search of fodder for their hopes and the sight of the bare trees spiraling up to the sky saddened him. The branches were like great brown hands reaching for something that wasn't there. It was a cold reminder to him of just how blind the world was to itself and he said so. When Mr. Low spoke to himself he made sure he did it in a hesitant whisper, as if it were a sin to speak and his words were forbidden for the rest of the world. No one would understand him, anyway. The poor, wanting devil was lost in the autumn of his days and the winter of his dreams as might be a lonesome traveler trying to recall the road less traveled. "But I know where I am going," Mr. Low told himself, "and as long as there is an end in sight, there is hope of deliverance."

He was wondering if he would make the express bus this morning or if he'd miss it like the day before. Like most people, Mr. Low owned a watch, but unlike most people he did not like to wear it. It was a reminder to him that his life was not his own. 'When you live on your own watch, you don't need to wear one.' This was what Mr. Low deemed his personal philosophy. Mr. Low also did not like to carry a wallet. He kept what little money he had in the pocket of his jeans. If he could have made his way around without the money, he'd have left that home every day too, just like he did all forms of identification. Names meant little, as did social security numbers and photographs to prove to anyone who or what he was. Was it even possible to have a constancy of being from one second to the next? Mr. Low wondered. He shook his head and whispered, 'No. If I am continually changing from one second to the next, I cannot be the same being I was a second before. For that reason I say I am not myself today and I never was. But who am I then?' Mr. Low wasn't sure how to answer that question. He only knew that he felt like nothing in this life and that he saw life itself as meaning nothing and being nothing . . . But under no circumstances did Mr. Low wish to be called a Nihilist. He would reply, 'How can I be an advocate of nothing when I am nothing myself. I am incapable of advocating anything because I am nothing.' According to Mr. Low, the word, the meaning, the concept of Nihilism only existed in the minds of men; therefore it was based on chimerical substantiation. Mr. Low was philosophizing on this bleak, gloomy morning because he would ordinarily be heading to a philosophy class at this particular time and on this particular weekday. But as it happened, he impulsively changed his mind about attending the class this morning. The reason for his decision was unclear. He just didn't feel like going. If he was headed in the direction of school, it was only because he didn't know what else to do with himself.

After Mr. Low bridged the overpass crossing Henry Hudson Parkway he paused at the corner of 235th Street and waited patiently for his bus like he usually did on school days. He lived in Riverdale with his parents and so was dependent on public transit to attend classes at New York University. The commute took him about an hour. It was May and soon classes would be over for the semester, then he could look forward to a fun and restful summer if he was so inclined. 'But a person has to live life day by day or else he runs the danger of getting too ahead of the game,' Mr. Low reprimanded himself. He could see the West Side express bus coming around the bend as he looked over his shoulder. He saw a local blue bus behind it. They were stopped at the light. Most mornings Mr. Low had a routine. He took the West Side bus to 57th street and caught the R train there to 8th Street. Occasionally he caught the local bus if the express did not show up. But that meant he would have to take that bus to the 231st street subway station to connect with the 1 train and later make a second connection at 42nd Street for the R train. It was a whole production and definitely not an easy way to start the day.

When the express bus pulled up Mr. Low let the other people at the stop board before him. It was a matter of courtesy but it also made life easier. Struggle of any kind exhausted Mr. Low. Besides since this was only the third stop on the bus route, he knew he was guaranteed a seat. He liked to take a seat not only to be more comfortable but also to read his philosophy books. Even though he was not going to class today, Mr. Low still wished to leaf through a few pages of the Schopenhauer book that his professor had provided for the class. There was a lot in it that Mr. Low found himself identifying with. It was sort of a prescription for life. What Mr. Low liked best was the writer's dark nature. Just the other day he had learned something in class that he liked. 'What was it again?' he asked himself. 'It was something about the optimist making a mockery of the struggle synonymous with existence.' Mr. Low's cracked a grin that nearly split his head in half and he sustained it with a self-satisfied air.

Making himself comfortable, Mr. Low mused over the irony that he had used the last three dollars on his metro card and would therefore not have money left for a return trip. That was fine, he told himself. He would cross that bridge later, if it came up. What was there to return to, anyway, more of the same day after day? It was always the same story with the same boring people lecturing him, telling him what to do with his life. The grin upon Mr. Low's face disappeared and was replaced with a menacing scowl. How he hated his life and hated the world that had given him life, because too much of it was spent suffering. He often daydreamed of destroying this world and if ever there was a day to realize such complete destruction, today was the perfect day for Mr. Low. He entertained visions of mushroom clouds endlessly rising into the stratosphere until he realized he could achieve the same ends more easily and more efficaciously by cutting the thread of his own consciousness. He looked down at the Schopenhauer book in his lap, considering the philosophy assignment that Mr. Notall had given to the class. He leafed through a couple of pages, but then closed the book almost as quickly as he'd opened it. He was too depressed to give the assignment a second thought. What was the point of it? Even if he could be enlightened to the misery of the world, what was that worth to him? Exactly what was the knowledge of one's misery worth? Was it even worth the paper it was printed on?

A young couple sat in the back seat behind him. As the bus pulled away, Mr. Low could hear the soft kisses of their lips and their giggling in between. It was like they shared a clandestine secret that only they in the whole world knew and their outward expressions of joy reflected that esoteric mirth. Mr. Low was never very popular with the ladies, himself. He reasoned that his dark and anomalous nature made such sharing with anyone impossible. He was too wrapped up in himself to seek unity with anyone else. Mr. Low squirmed in his seat and sighed. 'What is the point in this macho posturing?' he questioned. It seemed to him then that he was in denial. Mr. Low knew that he needed to be loved and needed to love, just like every human being in this miserable world. 'But how can I love another person when I can't even love myself?' he wondered. Mr. Low hated himself. He hated himself like he hated the world.

In fact, he hated himself *even more* than he hated the world. Could he blame the world for failing to accomplish the things that his will deemed most important in life, for denying him the deserved recognition of being the world's most unique artist? Blame had to go somewhere, after all.

As the bus continued its journey toward the city, Mr. Low remembered the creative writing class that he would also be missing later that afternoon. He had written a wonderful short story for that class as was his assignment to do, but he reconsidered ever submitting it for approval or rejection and the comments that would inevitably follow. True, the assignment itself was the impetus for the story's creation. It would not have ever been written otherwise. But now that it had been written Mr. Low did not deem it necessary to let anyone else read it. He was most proud of this short story and he had enjoyed writing it and that was more than enough reward. Mr. Low would not give someone the opportunity to use this short story to pass judgement on it and on him as its creator.

The title of Mr. Low's short story was *The Cadaver and the Scholar*. The hero is a nineteen year-old student named Mr. Owl. Like Mr. Low, he lives in Riverdale with his parents and regularly commutes to NYU in Greenwich Village to attend classes. As the story begins, Mr. Owl prepares to catch a bus to the one train that will take him into the city. The reader might presume he is on his way to class, but not as much is said. From the outset, Mr. Owl is an unpredictable character with a dark outlook on life. There is only the obscure mention of his dissatisfaction with the fairer sex and with himself as an artist offered as an explanation for this disposition. To add to his complicated character, the reader learns Mr. Owl has a keen interest in Nihilistic philosophy. In particular, he has avowed an admiration and respect for the 19th Century German writer and thinker, Arthur Schopenhauer, for his persistent portrayal of the world as an essentially bad place. As each piece of the puzzle is connected it is made plain to the reader that once Mr. Owl reaches his destination, the 8th Street subway stop, he will not proceed from there to his scheduled morning class at NYU. He will instead wait on the platform for the next oncoming N or R train and throw himself in front of it. Mr. Owl believes that by following through with his self-destructive plan, he will have a greater impact on his philosophy class than that class ever could have had upon him. In a bizarre twist of fate, Mr. Owl's philosophy professor, Mr. Tallon, is riding on the subway train that ultimately kills him. The irony here lies in the fact that the professor is preparing a Schopenhauer lesson that might have saved Mr. Owl's life, had it ever been presented to him. The basic tenet of this lesson is that a person takes their own life because of an inability to change the world in accordance with their own will. Stubborn to the end, they destroy their life rather than abandon their dreams for it.

Mr. Low was proud of his morbid story. He giggled with an air of snobbery, bowled over by his own perceived genius. He considered himself to be a greater individual than his fellow students and many of his professors because of the greater imaginative power he had proportionate to his being. Imagination was the key to grasping what really mattered in this life. According to Mr. Low, without an imagination to sustain oneself, a person was worthless. For what would be left for such a person, but a very dull and plant-like consciousness? Imagination was the essence comprising deities, the gods that ruled the world. A man intuitive enough to know this magical ether within himself would know how it feels to be god and master of the world around him. He would see the world for what it really is, an illusion of his own creation.

As the bus passed Yankee stadium, Mr. Low affirmed this reasoning with the nod of his head. It was hardly noticed by his fellow passengers. As slaves of perception, they were far too busy reading their paperbacks, newspapers and magazines, searching to find meaning between the spaces separating things or listening to music through headphones, nodding to hypnotic rhythms of time that played in their minds. In contrast, Mr. Low's thoughts were removed from space and time, abstracting from a well hidden within his own brain. He was glad that he decided to not read his philosophy book this morning. He reasoned it would be better to create his own concepts rather than satisfying himself with the concepts of others. If he wanted to be a god he would then need to form his own ideas and couldn't be reliant on books for information. The reader does not afford himself the opportunity to think for himself, if he is perennially digesting the thought processes of others, Mr. Low reminded himself. He thought that Schopenhauer would agree with him there. Mr. Low thought about what Schopenhauer might say if he was seated beside him right there and then. Art might say, "Don't read the book, even if it is mine. Look out the window and think about what you see! A realist would tell you what you see is nothing but matter. It would exist whether or not you were beholding it. An idealist would tell you what you see is actually coming from inside of you—it is a representation. In other words, Yankee stadium is contingent upon your beholding it in order for it to be. But I can resolve the conflict by pointing out that you cannot have one (physics), without the other (metaphysics). Together they create the world."

Mr. Low then imagined turning to his loquacious fellow passenger and grabbing him by the throat. "Don't tell me what to think! I can think for myself! Let me think for myself!" Then it suddenly occurred to Mr. Low, what if the inner voice that carried Schopenhauer through his life and helped him to compose all of his brilliant ideas was the very same voice that carried him through life and spoke to him in a meaningful way. That would mean that Schopenhauer's concepts were his concepts and vice versa. It would mean that everyone and no one could lay claim to concepts, that all concepts, all thoughts belonged to the world; that the inner voice was a common thread uniting the world, enlightening the world to a reality which each and every one of us was a participant in and that meant that no single participant was any more important than another and that the reality which we helped to constitute was greater than the sum of its parts which could be conveniently altered at any point. Mr. Low now recalled Schopenhauer's idea of the Will as a universal, singular force present within all living beings, governing them and the world around them. If this were the case, it would mean that people like himself and Mr. Notall, for example, were only the instruments of the Will; that was the Will of the World and the World as Will.

In that flash, Mr. Low saw his life as being meaningless in the vast scheme of things. He imagined his own demise like the Mr. Owl of his story and realized it would make no difference to the world at large. Certainly, the philosophy class would continue without his presence. Mr. Notall would give a lesson that he would never hear, perhaps on suicide, and life in the world would continue in an unbroken flow. But what if he was not the one to disappear from the world? What if it was Professor Notall? Mr. Low entertained a vision of himself teaching the philosophy class in lieu of Notall. After all, who in the class would be more capable? Wasn't he the prodigy of the class and by Notall's own admission? Granted, such a scenario was crazy to imagine but not inconceivable. It might become a reality under the right circumstances. But what circumstances? Mr. Low searched himself for the answer. Then it occurred to him, what if the professor's wife killed him over a long-standing dispute. After all, Mr. Notall had missed the Wednesday class because of an alleged domestic problem (rumors were often whispered in class that Mr. Notall's frequent absences were on account of domestic issues). Mr. Low envisioned Mr. Notall fighting with his wife over something as trifling as expenses, he screams at her for buying a mink coat with one of the credit cards. In a homicidal fit of rage, Mrs. Notall grabs a frying pan off the wall and hits him over the head with it. No. Better yet, she poisons his orange juice and as the old bastard falls to the kitchen floor writhing in pain, she grabs a piping hot frying pan, fresh off the stove, and smashes him in the face with it. She screams, "I deserve a mink coat for putting up with a stingy old man like you, you boring old philosophy professor. I will spend every last dime you've got when you're dead and rotting in your grave!"

Mr. Low was having fun. He reached into his schoolbook bag and brought out a pen and paper with the intent of putting together a hypothetical lesson for the class. Lastly, he reached for the volume of Schopenhauer and turned to the pages that he had been assigned to read on Monday. As he leafed through the book he gave pause at the pages that comprised the German philosopher's words about suicide, *"Our suffering springs from an incongruity between our desires and the course of the world."* Mr. Low wore a wide grin but held it only for a moment, recognizing that the subject deserved a more serious disposition. He cleared his throat and assumed a stern countenance. "Now class," he heard himself say, "the important thing to remember here is that the Will is constantly at war with itself. The manifestations of this conflict are many. It could be a person's ego at odds with another . . . or at odds with the world. In that case, only you can make the difference by disengaging yourself from conflict, by finding peace with yourself. If you can find peace with yourself, you can find it with others and with the world. The only way to find peace is to leave willing and wanting behind you. Only the ascetic who doesn't struggle and doesn't fall prey to the continual wheel of wanting and attaining, boredom and wanting again or what's worse, wanting and then not getting—for here lies the source of conflict—only he will ever have peace with himself and will ever have harmony in his life. Remember then that abnegation is the only true key to happiness." Mr. Low had been jotting down some notes when he looked up and realized that his stop near 57th Street was nearing. He jotted down a final note, 'Money and property will never bring anyone happiness. Money and property will only beget the need to collect more money and property. It is a vicious circle that you will not escape from, because the circle is designed to appeal to the bottomless pit of man's greed. Only the fool stakes his worth in dollars."

Mr. Low's thoughts were violently interrupted as his head flew forward and hit the seat in front of him. He was dazed for a moment, but lucid enough to realize that his pen had disappeared and his pad with it. The bus had hit something hard and come to an abrupt halt. The sudden screeching of the breaks that Mr. Low remembered hearing and still heard like an echo in his mind was his only record of the accident that he could ever later reference. It was the trace of a moment in time when a bus driver made a magnanimous but fruitless effort to avoid an obstacle that fate had mercilessly placed in his path. Sadly, this obstacle was a human being but more relevantly and in a twist of fate and plot this obstacle was Mr. Notall, philosophy professor at New York University who was on his way to catch the nearby N or R train near Carnegie Hall. He lived in the neighborhood and was on his way to work when the bus crossed his path. The poor fellow had been a slightly depressed that morning, because his wife had told him over breakfast that she wanted a divorce. She told him that her lawyers would take him for every penny he was worth. No one would ever know that Mr. Notall saw the bus at the last second and overcome by emotion decided to allow it to make its destined impact into him. No one would ever know the extent to which he contemplated the possibility of ending his own life at that moment. No one would ever know, that is, except for Mr. Low.

The Hand
of Fate

Borg and Crayon were sitting in front of the television. They were undecided about how to spend the evening. Because it was a Friday night neither wanted to spend the entire evening watching television. But since the selected program was entertaining, at least in a superficial sense, the two elected to remain seated until its conclusion. Borg and Crayon were only half-paying attention to what they viewed anyway. Their focus was elsewhere; each was struggling to come up with an original idea that would impress upon the other that he was in the presence of true genius. At the beginning of the fifth cartoon, Borg conceived what he considered to be *the* definitive inventive alternative to the boob tube.

"I've got it!" he declared with his finger pointed to God. "Let's go to Cal Calhoun's grave!"

His friend laughed, "That's 300 miles away, Borg."

"So?"

"*So?* How long do you think it'll take us to drive there?"

"I don't know. What does it matter?"

"Try a good four hours."

"What's the difference? I'll drive."

Crayon looked at his watch. "It's 7:15, man. By the time we get up there it'll be 11:30 p.m."

"So, it's something to do. It could be fun."

"Stop talking crazy, O.K."

"Have you ever been to the grave, Crayon? You've never actually seen it."

"Well, what's there to see in the middle of the night?"

"THE GRAVE!"

Crayon rocked on his chair and thought about it. "How about we go to the bar instead . . . and try to meet some girls. That's what normal guys our age do . . . on a Friday night."

"Normal guys our age are married with kids. They aren't *astronomers* that don't even know what the outside of an *observatory* looks like. We're lucky we got the night off, man."

"I don't know. The whole idea sounds pretty half-baked. I mean, all that driving!"

"Ah, c'mon. Where's your sense of adventure? We'll stop off and I'll buy you some dinner too, as an incentive."

"And you don't mind all the driving?" Crayon qualified. "Because I'm not driving."

"I'll drive. C'mon, get your jacket."

"Well, you can't use my car."

Borg's expression fell. "What?" he gasped. "You know my truck is in the shop. We have to use your car! There's no other way."

"O.K. fine" Crayon reluctantly stood and put his jacket on. "Just don't drive it into a sump or anything."

"I didn't drive the truck into a sump! I was chasing some lights in the sky and the truck slid off an embankment. It's not like I intentionally wanted to crash the truck, Crayon!"

Crayon was counting the money in his wallet. "I'm broke, so it's not like I can chip in for gas or anything."

"Betty left a couple of credit cards before she left. I found them in the drawer the other day. I don't think she even knows. We'll use one of those to pay for everything. I'll buy you a fabulous dinner, if you want, anywhere you like. Give me your keys."

Crayon reached deep into the pocket of his jeans and came out with a big key chain. "Here," he said, handing them over. "It's the big silver one . . . We'll be driving all night you know. It'll take another four hours to drive back. How much time can we even spend at the grave?"

"It'll be great!" Borg replied putting on his own coat.

"And then you want to stop off for dinner? I don't know . . . Well, if we're going to go, let's go. We're wasting valuable time. I guess it'll be fun. I mean, it's true I've never seen the grave."

"Right! Right!"

By the time they got out to the driveway, Crayon was already having second thoughts. "I heard it was going to rain tonight. Why should we drive for hours and hours in the rain? What kind of an evening is that? Besides, we could see the grave anytime. It doesn't have to be tonight. We could even go tomorrow."

"Let me open the door for you, Crayon…"

Borg felt the need to reassure his cautious friend, "Don't worry. It will be great and besides, it beats sitting around talking about what we could have done all night. You won't regret it, I promise. Tomorrow you'll thank me."

"I hear what you're saying. But I'm not as impetuous as you, Borg. I like to plan things out. Driving to that cemetery is a real journey. It will take us forever."

"Who cares how long it'll take? We're finally going to do something that we've wanted to do for a long time. Frankly, I can't believe I've had to talk you into this. You're a bigger Calhoun fan than I am. I thought you'd be thrilled at the idea."

"I am thrilled at the idea. It's just that . . . Hey! You're driving the wrong way, Borg."

"I took a short cut through the hospital parking lot. This way we can get right onto the highway instead of driving down all those residential roads first. Trust me. I know what I'm doing."

"Jesus, Borg. This is the hospital's emergency entrance! You're exiting out of the hospital's emergency entrance. I can't believe this!"

"Don't worry about it. There! You see? Now we're on the highway and no harm done."

Crayon waxed disgusted, "You take too many risks, man."

Borg scowled at his friend. "Where's your sense of adventure? Isn't there an impetuous bone in your body?"

"Impetuous bones are in graves."

"Speaking of which," Borg replied, "I'd like to take this

transitional opportunity to segue back to our pre-eminent subject, Mr. Calhoun."

"Right. Mr. Calhoun."

" . . . whom we are now on the way to visit, thanks to me."

"Right. Thanks to you."

There was a long pause.

Borg tried to read his friend. It was unlike Crayon to be sparse of words. Experience had taught Borg that Crayon was only laconic in instances where his temper had flared. Borg had seen evidence of this temper on such occasions when he tried to solicit from his friend a more loquacious disposition. He knew better than to bother him. Nevertheless, he asked, "Are you upset for some reason, Crayon?"

"Me?" Crayon shook his head. "Nah. I was just thinking about something." His face lit up. "Hey, did you ever read Cal's short story, *The Hand of Fate*?"

Borg shrugged his shoulders. "I read whatever you gave me. To be honest, the title doesn't ring a bell." He adjusted the radio. "What's the premise?"

"It's about these two guys that decide to rob a famous author's grave."

"No, I never read that one." Borg laughed. "Why do they want to rob the grave?"

" . . . for the body, of course."

"What? Are they sick?"

"They want to ransom the body, Borg."

"Oh. I guess there's a lot of money in that sort of thing, huh?"

"Well, presumably in this case. As I said, in the story the body belonged to a famous author."

"I can't imagine robbing a grave. That sounds pretty disgusting. I mean, even if there's a lot of money involved. Where do you hide the body in the meantime while you're ransoming it?"

"Well, in the story they never got that far . . . See, it's like this: they planned to ransom the body to the author's descendants. They were filthy rich. The plan was to sneak into the cemetery at night and dig the body up, so they brought two shovels and I think a pick to break open the casket."

"What stopped them then? The writer came out of the grave and killed them or something?"

"Not quite, Borg. I don't read dumb stories like that. That's kiddy stuff. This is more like *Twilight Zone*, man."

"Well, what happened?"

"The two villains in the story (or heroes, depending on your point of view) do manage to dig up the coffin. They dig up the coffin and carry it into the back of their station wagon . . . "

"Crayon, man, I'm seeing a lot of similarities here, two guys with a station wagon? We're two guys and this is a station wagon . . . "

"Relax. Remember when I said I was thinking about something? That's what I was thinking about. Believe me, it's a complete coincidence. You were the one that wanted to go to see Cal's grave. Remember? It wasn't my idea. It was your idea, Borg. Yours! And we would have taken your truck instead of my station wagon, had you not driven it into a sump."

Borg lost his composure. "I told you to shut up about the truck! Every time you bring it up, you bring me down. Do you know what it's going to cost me to repair that truck? Don't mention it again, please."

"O.K. O.K. Do you want me to tell you what happens to these two guys or not? Maybe you want to read the story yourself sometime?"

"Geez! I can't believe this guy! He sets me up and then leaves me hanging."

Crayon cleared his throat and started fidgeting with the radio. "Should I continue . . . "

"JUST TELL ME WHAT HAPPENS!"

"The two guys dig up the coffin and carry it into the back of their station wagon. Their plan is to bring the body back to this abandoned house in the woods not far from where they're living. But they never get that far."

"The police get them, right?"

Crayon rolled his eyes. "No. They can't get out of the cemetery with the body. They're trapped, because they can't find the exit. They're driving around and around in circles. Hours go by and they start running out of gas. Their situation is getting desperate. Finally they hit on the idea of narrowing down the location of the exit by keeping close to the perimeter of the gate."

Borg nodded. "And do they ever find the exit?"

"Oh, they find the exit alright, but by the time they do . . . it's locked."

"What do you mean? How did they get into the cemetery in the first place if the gate was closed?"

Crayon laughed deprecatingly. "Borg! The gate was open when they drove into the cemetery but at some point while they were driving around in the cemetery, the gates were closed. Cemeteries do have visiting hours."

"So what, they just waited there till the morning like sitting ducks? I'd scale the frigging fence and get the hell out of there. That's what I'd do."

"Borg, they can't do that. Even if they did that, they would still be leaving the vehicle behind."

"So? I'd rather leave the car behind then go to jail, man."

"Yeah but the car's registered. They'd be tracked down sooner or later."

"I'd still split that scene as fast as I could. Then I'd go to Mexico."

"Mexico?" Crayon repeated. "Oh yeah that's what I'd do, I'd go to Mexico."

"Don't be sarcastic. It's better than waiting around to be discovered the next morning with the dead body of a famous author in the back seat of your car."

"Well, I don't know. For all I know maybe they do go to Mexico. We never find out what they do. The story ends there with them looking dumbfounded at the locked gates not knowing what to do."

"I know what I'd do. I'd put the body back in its grave," Borg commented. " . . . then I'd scale the fence . . . and go to Mexico."

"Brilliant plan," Crayon replied. "But they'd figure out what you'd done."

"Who would?"

"The authorities. The next morning they'd be wondering what the hell you were doing in that cemetery overnight. And they'd take a thorough look around, especially if they found shovels in your car."

Borg had a pained expression. "Yeah, well, I'd never be caught in that situation, because I'd never be caught dead robbing a grave. So that's that, then."

"Oh I give up. Let's just drop it."

Borg had a worried look. "Well now you have me not even wanting to go to Cal's grave. What are you trying to do, bug me out with this story? What if we get locked in the cemetery like those two idiots?"

"*The Hand of Fate* is never that obvious, Borg."

"Hey, it's starting to rain." Borg turned the windshield wipers on. "Maybe you were right, maybe this was a bad idea. You know, it's never too late to turn around. We could go back and go to the bar. Pick up some chicks?"

"Oh you're afraid of a little rain now?"

"I'm not afraid of a little rain!" Borg was indignant. "You're the one that said it was going to rain and that you didn't feel like driving around in the rain."

"When did I say that?" Crayon asked. "I don't remember saying that at all."

"You said it just before we left!"

"Oh I get it, Borg. You don't want to go now. Need I remind you that this whole thing was your idea, going to the cemetery."

"Listen, I might have been the one that thought of it tonight. But you're the one that first put this idea in my head months ago! You're the big Cal Calhoun fan. You're the one that's read everything the man ever wrote. You're the one!"

"Borg, if you don't want to go to the cemetery tonight just say so."

"No, no. I want to go. I quite like the idea of seeing the grave. I was just being considerate of you. You said earlier that you didn't want to be driving around in the rain."

"Well, the rain doesn't bother me. And I like the idea of seeing the grave, especially tonight."

"Why especially tonight?"

"Because I'm anxious to see what *the Hand of Fate* has in store for us."

"Why, what do you think is going to happen when we get there? I mean, maybe nothing at all will happen. Maybe we'll find Cal's grave, yawn and go home. Meanwhile, we could be getting laid."

"All of sudden you want to get laid. You're afraid we're going to get locked in that cemetery, aren't you?

Borg was silent.

"Borg, don't you see? Because you're so fearful of being locked in the cemetery, there isn't the slightest chance of that happening. It's just like what I keep telling you about the UFO's. You're never going to see a flying saucer, man. You know why? Because you're always looking for one!"

"I did see a flying saucer, Crayon. That day I drove the truck into the sump."

"That was probably s shooting star."

"No man, it wasn't. That was a UFO. I saw three of them, in fact. They were flying in formation. I wouldn't make that stuff up. Don't you think I know what a shooting star looks like? I'm an astronomer, for crying out loud!"

"You're not getting my point, man. So just forget the whole thing."

"I do get your point."

"No, you don't."

"Yes, I do! Let me tell you something . . . If I think there's a possibility of rain on any given day, I always bring the umbrella. Because I know that if I bring the umbrella I am greatly reducing the chances of it raining that day. It has nothing to do with me being prepared in case it does rain, mind you. By bringing the umbrella I am reducing the chances of it raining at all. But if by chance I say instead, 'you know what, to heck with the umbrella,' then man . . . you can just bet I am going to get caught in a torrential downpour. If I simply forget the umbrella, a number of things could happen. If I realize that I forgot the umbrella and I begin to expect that I will get caught in the rain then I have an even chance of not getting caught in the rain. But I have to sincerely fear the rain. If I have other things on my mind and I'm not thinking about the rain or an umbrella I am probably going to get rained on at some point that day . . . and probably at the moment that I least expect it."

"EXACTLY!" Crayon shouted. "That's my point. When you least expect it! The expectation is key. It is the key factor always."

"Crayon, this is not just about expectation. There is also the issue of tempting fate. I'm beginning to think we might be tempting fate tonight with this whole cemetery thing. I'm very superstitious about it."

Crayon rebuked his friend, "No. You can't live that way, man. You have to take chances and you have to tempt fate because that's why you're alive and that's the only way you're ever going to know you're alive."

"You think so, huh?"

"Absolutely!"

Borg wore a considerate expression. "Well, alright. I mean, we've come this far. We might as well see this through to the end."

"We have to!"

"Well, no, we don't have to," Borg objected.

"Yes, we do. *The Hand of Fate* has decided it or else we wouldn't have come this far. We have to see this through to the end, because it is our ontological imperative."

Borg laughed. "Now, you're getting dramatic on me."

"No, I'm getting real on you."

"Well, let me ask you this, how do you know it's not our ontological imperative to go back home. Who knows what fate has in store for us back home."

"That's ridiculous, Borg. There's nothing for us at home. We were bored there. That's why we left, to find our fate, to chance fate. It can't be any other way."

"Well, let me ask you this, do you think Cal Calhoun could have written his story any other way?"

"Yes, he could have . . . But he didn't."

"But he could have."

Crayon considered the supposition. "Yes, I think I read somewhere he had another premise for that story, a slight variation."

"A slight variation in the premise?" Borg queried.

"Yes, but again it doesn't matter because he didn't write it."

"Maybe it does matter, Crayon. Maybe that slight variation in premise matters to us. Maybe that story is our story."

"Do you hear yourself, Borg? Do you know how crazy you sound?"

"Tell me about Cal's other idea."

"I won't."

"Just tell me one thing. Do the two characters in that 'alternative' story still go to the cemetery with the intention of robbing the writer's grave?"

Crayon sighed. "I can't tell you, Borg. I was going to tell you before, but now I can't. At first I thought if I told you the outcome of that alternative story you would reasonably think us absolved of a similar fate but now I'm not as confident of your reasonability. So let's just drop it, alright?"

"What happens?"

"Oh you're impossible, Borg. They see two other guys robbing the grave and they frighten them off. That's the only difference in the story."

"Then what?"

"I forget. I don't know."

"What's this? You have to at least tell me if they get out of the cemetery?"

"No, I won't tell you. Perhaps the best thing to do here is to just drop the subject and simply resign our selves to *the Hand of Fate.* We don't have an alternative."

Borg was indignant. "You know, you keep talking about this *Hand of Fate* like you know what it is, like you understand it or something, like you're familiar with how it works."

"I do know what it is," Crayon replied. "I do understand it. I am familiar with it."

Borg grew frustrated. "Oh yeah? Well if you're so familiar with it, why don't you tell me what it is, define it."

Crayon widened an already infernal smirk. *"The Hand of Fate* is the unknown and I am its envoy. You, my friend, are merely my chauffeur."

Borg didn't hear Crayon. He was staring out on the open road searching for some sign of the exit that led to the old sawmill that he knew as a teenager. The heavy rain made it very difficult to see and the windshield wipers were not working properly. Finally he recognized the damaged telephone pole that his father crashed the family station wagon into twenty years ago. It was where he had been killed. Borg knew that the next right would lead them to the old sawmill. When the opportunity presented itself, he exited the highway and drove the car in the direction that his memory dictated.

"Hey, where are we going?" Crayon asked. "Why did you drive off the highway?"

"I want to show you something, Crayon."

"But I thought you were driving me to the cemetery?"

"All in good time. We have to do something first."

"What? What's going on?"

Borg widened an already infernal smirk but said nothing else. He didn't want to spoil the surprise for Crayon. Also, he wanted to stay true to the nightmare that he had suffered through for the last seven nights. The nightmare had always played out the exact same way without variation. He would entice his friend for a drive using some spurious pretense and then bring him to the intended destination of the old sawmill. So far everything had been as he had foreseen, even the rain. Now the only thing left to do was lure his friend into the sawmill itself. Good thing he still had the key. Borg wondered how it was going to feel cutting Crayon in half.

Meditations on Acting . . .

Mack looked down at the bar and stared at his pint of ale. He reminded himself that he was at O'Reilly's Pub. He had to remind himself because he wasn't really at O'Reilly's Pub. He was really at the Reality Theater, pretending he was at O'Reilly's Pub. Likewise, he knew it wasn't a pint of ale in front of him on the bar. It was something that looked like ale, but it wasn't ale. It was a prop just like everything else: the bar, the bottles of booze behind the bar, etc. Even the stool that he sat on was a prop, because it was only there for him to sit on in this scene. The actor that played the bartender was cleaning the glasses behind the bar. Two stools down from Mack, just as it was written in the script, was a fellow actor friend, Marty. Mack was staring at his drink, waiting for Marty to deliver his opening line. In the play they were in together, Mack's character was named Fled and Marty's was Moigle. Fled and Moigle were actors just like Mack and Marty were in real life. They were also friends like Mack and Marty and liked to have a drink like Mack and Marty after work, discussing their craft and what it meant to be not just a good actor, but a great actor.

Moigle finally turned to Fled and said, "You know we always come here after the show and talk about what we said and did on the stage, as if we thought there was something to gain from talking about it."

"I know what you mean. We never leave here with any more than what we started with," said Fled.

"There's nothing to be gained," Moigle told his friend. "It's always the same lines and the same delivery. It's like we're constantly re-living the same experience on stage over and over again. I know what you're going to say and you know what I'm going to say, because of the script. It's the worst kind of déjà vu I can think of."

"Mm." Fled took a sip of his ale, put the glass back down on the bar and swallowed. "It's like the past never dies or something."

"The past is never dead for us," said Moigle, "only dormant until the hearth of the imagination is rekindled."

"Very poetic."

"But we are subject to the past and to memory," Moigle continued, "never free in the moment. As the eyes of our audience observe our every move and hang upon our every word, they don't see that we are slaves to the opiate of mimeses."

Fled took a sip from his glass. "Only if we are great actors do they forget that we are actors."

"There should be no scripts," Moigle replied. "We should just improvise."

"Improvise?" Fled gasped.

Moigle readjusted himself on the stool so that he faced his friend. "Yes, that's right. Improvise. We should only say what we want to say, stand where we want to stand."

Fled shook his head. "I prefer to work from memory. It's safer."

"Think so?" Moigle laughed. "Memories are like shadows, no more substantial than the dreams that spark beneath your curly brows at night. You cannot rely on them to be anything more. You have to learn to rely on yourself and live for the moment, impulsively."

Fled took another drink and swallowed. "Wow. You're like a raging storm tonight!"

Moigle explained, "There are storms raging within ourselves, Fled. Only when we recognize hallucinations for what they are, will we know the reality of the web of the world."

Fled considered that. "The web of the world? I don't think I follow."

"That's alright," Moigle reassured him. "Truth comes in flashes that are too fleeting to fully comprehend. We can only get a sense of what is true. To fully grasp it conceptually would require an omniscience; a concentration powerful enough to balance a sphere on a pin's point."

"I see you're a philosopher and a poet," Fled granted, turning on his stool to better face his friend. "What is your point, exactly? Do you have a point?"

Noting Fled's impatience, Moigle confided, *"The point is we can only know best what is false."*

"What do you mean?" Fled asked, wincing. "Are you false?"

"With each passing second, I am changing," Moigle elaborated. "Since I am changing all the time I am never who I think I am. With this reasoning, it is easy to understand why I must invent a past. There is nothing else for me to do. There is a past but it is not mine, unless I pretend that it is. This is why I find it so amusing to see ignorant, slavish people searching the past with fine-toothed combs to explain the enigma of their present circumstances. I am only who I am at this moment and never was the same person at any other moment," Moigle declared. "Just as I will never be the same person I am now at some later moment."

Fled finished his ale and turned to his friend, and said, "I am only who I am at this moment and never was the same person at any other moment. Just as I will never be the same person I am now at some later moment." He paused to order another pint from the bartender and then asked Moigle. "Have I got it right, old chum?"

Moigle nodded. "As an actor, this train of thought has taught me that I can become anyone at any time and place. That's quite a gift. Not only do I have the ability to assume a new personality, I do so in the heartbeat of a flying sparrow. I invent a personal history for that new personality just as quickly. In the time it takes a newborn baby to draw a breath, I can be someone else that quickly."

As the bartender placed Fled's drink down he expressed his thanks and then smiled at Moigle. "You can be someone else and I can be someone else. I could be you!"

"EXACTLY!" Moigle screamed. He realized the exceeding tone of his voice when the bartender gave him a scathing glance. He quieted himself with a long drink from the cold beverage that was in front of him. He finished the drink and just as soon asked for another, "Bartender . . . one more, please." Moigle returned his attention to his friend and implored, "I ask you, Fled, with such talents, why should we waste our time with scripts? I have it in me to be anyone that I desire, to live as many lives as I desire, as quickly as I desire them. Just like that!" Moigle snapped his fingers. "These individual experiences are collectively experienced as an eternity of being. That is to say, they are a continuum. For instance, if I have been eleven different persons in a single day, it is as if I have lived a thousand years in a single day. I have seen the flashes of what could have spanned a millennium of living. I have enjoyed first hand, all of the feelings and emotions of these eleven lives, without the nasty trappings of their individual limitations."

Fled swallowed a sip of ale and commented, "I've always felt the parts that I play are like little pieces and stems from a never-ending storyteller who will never appreciate what it means to endure a final scene himself. When one story reaches its conclusion, the storyteller takes comfort in knowing there will always be another story for him to tell."

"That's right!" said Moigle. He took a sip from the drink that the bartender put down before him and shared another thought with his fellow thespian. "An actor is the means by which the writer expresses his ideas to an audience. The actor is a tool . . . the conduit used by the writer to channel his experiences and desires to the audience.

Fled nodded. "You're right. The actor is more necessary than the director himself," Fled added.

"He is more necessary than the director!" Moigle declared. "The actor reveals the drama of life through his actions and words. And they become his words and his actions when he becomes the conduit that I spoke of. The writer doesn't own the words and the actions anymore, but his character does! And even if the actions and words of an actor are the small part of a bigger story, that actor is nevertheless a necessity in that bigger story. He is a link in the chain, bringing ideas to life . . . and when called for, the deliverer of the hammer blow!"

"Death," Fled finished with a flourish.

Moigle nodded as he took a sip of his drink, considering the comment. He swallowed and as soon as he did added, "You know, I have worked with the greatest directors, the greatest writers and the greatest producers and I am proud to say that despite all of their demands not one of them has succeeded in their attempts to destroy me."

"What do you mean?" Fled asked, curiously. He wore a whimsical expression on his face in anticipation of the answer.

Moigle explained, "The directors always told me what they wanted and I always gave them what they wanted each time, even if it was . . . my death. But the parts that I play never die within myself, even after they perish on the stage. I keep all of my parts, especially those that died on the stage. I keep them all living for another day, when they might be useful to me again. The deaths of my assigned characters were my greatest acts, because I feigned their destruction upon the stage. I could never have killed even one of them inside of myself. It would have killed me to have to kill one of them for real."

"You're being overly dramatic."

"I'm being serious, Fled. The greatest part about being an actor is that he lives with death every moment, within himself. But he takes comfort in knowing he will rise from it like a phoenix from the ashes. Even if he is never quite the same again afterwards, he can take solace in knowing he was never meant to be anything for very long."

"Sometimes death comes poetically," Fled offered. "In the form of a pause when for a second the actor forgets who he really is."

Moigle scratched his head, considering what Fled had said. "Can an actor forget who he is?"

"It's happened to me," Fled confessed. "I sometimes lose sight of who I really am. That is a kind of death."

Moigle hesitantly admitted, "When I've forgotten my lines it is the greatest death I've ever known. Though it has happened infrequently."

"What do you mean it is the greatest death you've ever known?" Fled asked, his interest piqued.

"Forgetting my lines is the greatest death I've ever known, because in those painful moments, I had nothing to say. It was like I was dead, standing there frozen on the stage with the fear of my own silencing. I had ceased to exist because I didn't know what to say or do.

It was a flash of what death might be like for me. But you know, maybe those fleeting flashes were only a means of realizing my own immortality. What I mean is, in the end I always found something to say."

"Mm," Fled paused, shaking his head approvingly.

Moigle continued, "I am made of that immortality as you are, Fled. We spend our days wallowing leisurely, breathing in and out of an endless cornucopia that is time. Once more, we deserve this eternity. We deserve it for realizing it is there to take and for realizing it is there for us to take."

"Truthfully," said Fled, "Can you even conceive of such an immortality?"

"I would guess not," Moigle consented. He grew pensive.

"Don't look so upset," Fled told him. "Don't take this too seriously."

"You're just like the rest of them, Fled." Moigle quipped. "You lack the perennial depth of true imagination. By contrast, my imagination is as infinite as the universe itself."

"Oh, c'mon . . . " Fled protested.

Moigle went on, "But I don't care if you can't appreciate what I'm trying to tell you, Fled. In fact, I hope you can't relate to what I am saying."

"You hope I can't relate to what you are saying?" Fled questioned, growing petulant.

"Of course, I don't care,' Moigle insisted. "Your denial of my immortality, conscious or otherwise, is an indication to me of something that I have long suspected."

"Oh and what is that pray tell?" Fled asked.

"You can always make your envy known to me, Feld, by your denial. You demonstrate the limitations of your imagination then, the limitations of your intellectual being."

After a long slug of his ale, Fled put his pint down on the bar and wiped the foamy residue from his mouth. *"The limitations of my intellectual being?"* he mockingly repeated. "Now you're not only pretentious, you're insulting . . . and talking like a madman."

Moigle confessed, "I know you think I'm a madman. Perhaps, you're thinking that I am only acting like a madman because we are in a play."

Mack didn't recognize Marty's line and for a second he fell out of character as Fled. He laughed and improvised a line. "Oh are we in a play, Moigle? I thought we were in a pub having a drink?" Mack could hear the audience laughing. It was a nervous laughter that made him nervous.

Marty continued to break from the script. "Perhaps you really think I am the character of Moigle. Perhaps you think I am only that character. You think I am the character of Moigle in a scene from a play that takes place in a pub, is that it? Am I supposed to be a madman in this scene? Ask yourself that."

Mack shrugged his shoulders as Fled. "I don't know where you're going with this. I thought we were in a pub." He took a look around. "It sure looks a like a pub to me." He stared at Marty, annoyed with his friend's impulse to further improvise the lines.

Marty shrugged his shoulders. "What's the matter? You don't like this, Mack?"

"It's Fled," Mack corrected. "My name is Fled, remember?"

"Perhaps you're right, Fled," Marty obliged. "Perhaps this is a pub and not a pub set on a stage. Perhaps the world is not a stage."

Mack grew sullen. "I prefer not to address the subject directly," he replied. "I prefer to parry around it with a few shallow remarks," he joked.

"Like for instance?" Marty invited.

Mack decided to play along, hoping to salvage the performance. "Well, like for instance," he began, "A great actor lives on the stage. There is no differentiation between his role and himself. He becomes that role."

"Right," Marty agreed. "The actor plays with his mind, tells himself that he is where he isn't and isn't where he is."

Mack recognized Marty's line from the script. He smiled hopefully. With any luck they could now return faithfully to their intended lines. He recalled his own character's words and spoke them, "The actor tells himself he is who he isn't and isn't who he is."

"Right! Right! That's the ticket!" Marty obliged him, reading Moigle's lines faithfully. "That's the ticket, Fled! And that way of thinking, telling yourself you are where you aren't, you aren't where you are, you are who you know you're not, you aren't who you know you are, is an invitation to a kind of madness. The actor confuses himself in the effort to confuse his audience that he is someone else other than who he really is, that he is somewhere else other than where he really is."

Fled nodded and took another sip of his ale. "I see what you mean, Moigle. I see what you mean."

"And so as an actor, I say to you, if I sound at all like a madman . . . I am doing my job very well." Moigle nodded, self-righteously. "And maybe I'm more sane than the rest of you by recognizing my own insanity," he added for good measure.

Fled raised his eyebrows. "So I am to dispose of myself completely in the process of acting so that I don't know what is real anymore?" he qualified.

Moigle smiled and leaned closer to his friend. "Look around this pub and see it for what it is, it is no different than a set on a stage. It might as well be a pub set on a stage because that is the same thing. And you are nothing but a character on that stage."

Mack rolled his eyes, realizing that his friend had departed from the script again.

Marty asked him. "Are you having difficulty grasping the message that I am trying to impart to you, Mack?"

"It's Fled," Mack protested. "My name is Fled."

"Oh right," Marty replied, condescendingly. "Since I don't know who you are it is that easy for me. Since you don't know who I am it is that easy for you." He turned to face the audience and addressed them. "Stay with us, folks, as we progress with these words of wisdom and accept all that is said between us as a given. It may or may not be what the writer intended, but you will appreciate it nevertheless as a product of the Reality Theater."

Marty gestured with his arm out to the edge of the stage. "If history is being re-written it is being re-written for all of you."

"So you decide what's in and what's out of the script?" Mack asked, humoring his friend. "Are you the script writer now?"

"If only because you are reading me," Marty explained. "Are you reading me?"

"Loud, but not so clear," Mack replied. He could hear the audience growing restless and it bothered him. He took another sip from his glass. He could only imagine what the director was thinking now.

Marty continued to badger him. "These words we're sharing, Fled, our whole conversation, is the script of this play," Marty defined. "It is our whole world. I say to anyone who hears us that their voices are our voices and our voices are their voices. We're all here tonight as Fled and Moigle."

"So now, it's not only you and I in O'Reilly's . . . and the bartender," Mack said, remembering to mention the other actor who was there. "It's also everybody in the audience. Everybody's in this pub with us, is that it?"

"YES!" Marty laughed. "The whole audience. They are living this life of ours, this scene that is a microcosm in our lives. They are here with us. We are only here for them, living the microcosm for them."

"Of course," said Mack, humoring his renegade friend.

Marty turned to face the audience. "It might be more facilitating for all of you to just think of me as your conscience in this or that given situation," he offered. "As we go along, I'll be acting out the thoughts of others but the audience must allow me that opportunity. That is what an actor does, that is what they pay him to do, to portray the words and acts of others, to bring them to life for still others. The actor imagines himself as another, namely the writer who maybe imagines himself as someone else—an invented character. So you see, folks, it is not so confusing to be someone else for a little while. Remember, it is only a chance of fate that you are not someone else other than yourself, anyway."

Mack was laughing with the actor who played the bartender. "He's lost it."

Marty heard them but persisted, "And the audience members can share in this world of make believe from the safe distance of their theater seats. They're in the pub with us but they aren't really. But all of you can have just as much fun as any of us on the stage, even if you are enjoying it vicariously."

Mack yelled over at Marty. "The audience may wish they had the courage to sit through the rest of this," he contended. "I see that half of them are walking out."

"RIGHT!" exclaimed Marty, growing excited.

Mack addressed the bartender and asked him if he had any real ale behind the bar. A few of the remaining audience members heard this remark and laughed.

Meanwhile, Moigle left the bar and walked to the far end of the pub. He addressed an imaginary audience in an imaginary play, "I must apologize for my behavior here tonight, folks. This must seem so strange to all of you. But if all of this seems rather strange to you, that is a good thing indeed. You should feel strange, when you consider what this play is all about. It is no coincidence these enigmatic sets were designed by Expressionists, with an appreciation for bizarre, theatrical perversions. It is very dangerous to be up here. But most of you are just too weak to live the lives that we live here up on the stage. Fled and I question everything, including ourselves, including you. I can read all your faces from up here. I see you're getting uncomfortable at the prospect of my addressing you directly. You don't like to be acknowledged in such a familiar way or do you? It is why you are in the audience, after all—to know our world intimately. Why else would you buy orchestra seats? You want to sit as close to the stage as possible. You want to feel our pain, to know the fear and the paranoia along with Fled and I. You're too embarrassed to admit these truths and so I admit them for you. At least you should be honest with yourselves if not with me—a perfect stranger! But then again, is anybody really a stranger? I ask you. Isn't one man's nature just the same as the next? What does my name matter, couldn't my name be your name?

"Someday, friends, you'll learn this lesson from me and teach it to someone else. Maybe someday you'll be in the position of power to upend all logic before perfect strangers. But those strangers will have the same appetites that you have and they will want to learn the little theatrical tricks that upend the world as they know it. It's a world we only thought we knew, but that world never really existed. That world is a world of silly, childish games. It is a world existing more in your confused mind than anyplace else. Just like everything that ever was, is, and can ever be . . . a daydream."

"What are you doing over there in the corner, Moigle," Fled called to him, "talking to yourself? Come back here and have another drink, for crying out loud."

Marty pretended not to hear his friend and continued speaking to the pictures hanging on the pub wall, pictures of the greatest Broadway actors ever to grace the stage. "You are all nothing compared to me!" he ranted. "You played the game by the rules, by the rules handed down to you. I invented my own rules! I learned to think for myself and demonstrated to the whole world that the world itself makes no sense. There lies the strength of my artistic prowess. I have proved the reality we know a web of lies, and I have done so by stepping out of it! The world is not to be understood, because it is a world of confusion. And that is how this world shall finally be portrayed." Marty beat his chest. "Even I am a confusion, folks. Do you want to know why? Because this world—this play and its characters—exist in my head. Even you, the audience, exist in my head, as does Mack, Fled or whatever you want to call him—and that no name bartender over there—" Marty gesticulated toward the other two actors absorbed in conversation. "To make matters worse, I'm in all of your heads! Search yourselves and you'll know it's true. This strange world is a vortex, continually replenishing itself with you and me. If you can't understand that, walk away from all of this and don't think of it again. If simpler minds get caught up in this vortex, it is like a farmhouse coming up against the greatest tornado in history. The foundations are obliterated."

"Moigle do you want another drink, or what?" Fled joked with the bartender, "I'm sorry, Joe, but I can't take the kid anywhere . . .He thinks the world is a stage."

Marty didn't respond to his friend's call. He just stood there, at the far end of O'Reilly's Pub by himself, as the scene faded to dark and the curtain fell. He decided there would be no curtain call that night. He would wait there until the last audience member went home, until his fellow actors went home as well and the stagehands cleared the stage, so that the set of O'Reilly's Pub no longer existed. He would wait on the empty stage until he heard perfect silence, if not perfect silence then the lonely, chafing rub of a single cricket's legs telling him the night was finally over. Then he would go home and get a much deserved rest from the world of the theater.

A Costly Gift

Novogno was a fortuneteller. The gift was in the patriarchal line of his family going back many generations. Over the years, Novogno's family blessed many lives with the foreknowledge of impending events, preventing catastrophes and unhappiness. It was a noble and rewarding livelihood to serve their community in such a caring and unselfish way. But this gift of omniscience came at a high price for each man in Novogno's lineage. Before he entered the family business, Novogno's father, Vled-Totl, explained to his son, "As a fortuneteller you will hold great power in this community and carry much responsibility because of it. It is this responsibility that requires you to make personal sacrifices. Some of these sacrifices may be in direct conflict with your conscience."

Novogno's father told his son that at some point during his life he would encounter a man that would ask him to interpret a dream, in order to determine whether or not it was a prophesy. The dream would depict the dreamer in mortal conflict with a fortuneteller and would conclude with the fortuneteller attempting to stab the dreamer with a silver dagger. When Novogno heard the words, "silver dagger," he would know he was being tested by the same circumstances once faced by his father and his father before him, ad infinitum. How he responded to the matter depended heavily on whether or not he felt personally threatened by the individual revealing the dream. If he did feel threatened, he was to take the silver dagger hidden beneath the table where he sat and kill the customer with it. If he did not feel threatened, Novogno was to reassure the man that the dream would not come to fruition. As he understood his father, he simply had to search himself for the appropriate response at the climactic moment. But to Novogno this sounded like too light-hearted an approach to take. Fortunetellers second-guess themselves just as ordinary people do. A misjudgment under such dire circumstances could prove fatal.

To bolster his son's confidence, Novogno's father related the story of his own encounter with a customer revealing such a dream. It was to Novogno's father's credit that he calmly assessed the man with a level head and an even temper. In this equanimity, he was able to see into this man's future and knew then that he was a kind and gentle fellow, incapable of hurting anyone or anything. Novogno's father had seen him helping an old lady across the street, giving a young child a lollypop and another a quarter. How could such a good man be a murderer? So instead of reaching for the dagger, which would have been his visceral response, he laughed off the idea of killing such an innocent man. Novogno's father not only laughed off the idea of killing the customer, he laughed the customer right out the door. The silly man was insulted, of course. How could he have known his sole purpose in life was to help determine a fortune-teller's fate?

Novogno's grandfather, Gdorke, was not as fortunate as his son. He had an encounter with a man that was less amusing to relate and whenever Novogno's father shared the story, a tear would swell up in his eye. The sight of it there always brought a tear to Novogno's own eye. He often asked himself, was it for his grandfather, his father or himself that he wept? It was for no one if not for all three and the rest of his father's line stretching back into incalculable pages of history books. There were more sad stories than happy ones in Novogno's line but his grandfather's story was perhaps the saddest of all. It seemed that fate had made a mockery of this man for the benefit of future generations. His poor, impulsive judgment stood out as the example that should never be repeated. Novogno's father related the story to his son in this way, "On my father's fateful day, he had practically no business. He was happy to have finally heard a knock on his door. He invited the visitor in with a good deal of hope and cheer. But from the moment that he caught sight of this visitor he recognized that the bane of his existence had finally come calling. Like a man, he accepted it. He was even happy the prophesy had finally come true. My father was nearly seventy years old by this time. He had waited his entire life to take the test of his mettle.

When the fateful moment arrived, he was level headed at first. He politely invited the visitor to sit down at the table with him, opposite corner from where he sat. This enabled my father striking advantage with the dagger if he ever needed it. As the man related the anticipated dream, my father's fears eased. He saw clearly that the man was incapable of murder. But as time passed something was revealed to my father. He saw that while this man could never intentionally kill another man himself, he could be an accessory to such a crime. That is to say, my father had a clear vision of the man causing the death of another indirectly. This frightened my father, because he envisioned himself as the dead man. He reacted impulsively, brandishing the silver dagger from beneath the table and plunging it into the man's chest. This did, of course, fulfill the prophesy as foreseen by the victim himself in his dream. My father watched as he fell back with his chair, convulsed and died. With the light in his eyes completely extinguished, my father then closed the man's lids and dragged him by his feet into the adjacent, empty room. He thought to hide the body until nightfall when he could covertly sneak it out of the building.

"My father suffered no pangs of conscience for the bloody deed. He even felt a certain satisfaction in killing a man so much younger and able bodied than he. He relished the thought for a couple of precious minutes until disturbed by an unexpected knock at the door. With a dead body being in the other room, he decided it prudent not to answer the door. Instead, he lingered silently in the hallway listening, waiting and hoping for the visitor to go away. But the visitor did not go away. He banged at the door and screamed out a man's name. My father realized this name belonged to the recently deceased fellow lying on the floor in the next room. All at once, he changed his mind and decided that he should open the door. He told himself that he had to at least make a fainthearted attempt of assuring the visitor no one had been there to see him on that day. Otherwise, the visitor might just pay a visit to the local police station and that would be very bad, indeed. So my father pulled himself together and unlocked the door and turned the knob. But the second that he caught sight of the person on the other side, my father knew that he had made a mistake. It was not that he recognized the face, just the imminent danger this stranger posed him. He immediately tried to close the door again, but the man on the other side forced it open and pushed his way inside. Being much bigger and stronger than my father, the stranger tossed him across the room and then stormed from one room to the next calling out the name of his friend. He found him soon enough. Our place of business is so small. Do you know which room the body was in? It was in the room where you keep your library today, my son. It was in that room that your grandfather died, for he ran in there chasing the intruder. He had the silver dagger in hand, to kill again. But in his rush, he did not notice the dead body directly at his feet. He fell over it and accidentally stabbed himself with the upturned dagger. Your grandfather died the following day in the hospital, after relating the story to me."

Novogno always remembered his father's words and wondered when he too would have to face the challenge of the dreamer and the dagger. In his thirty-sixth year, it finally happened. Novogno heard a knock at his door. He answered the door and invited a stranger in to sit down with him. After the man was seated, Novogno invited him to speak and when he did he spoke of the dream with the "silver dagger." Novogno was surprised, for he'd felt no danger in this man's presence and would never have guessed him to be the vassal of his family's curse. Since he felt no danger, Novogno smiled and relaxed, thinking that perhaps he'd been spared the burden of deciding whether or not to take another man's life, always quite a troubling decision to make. He had hopes of laughing off the silver dagger dream as his father had done years before. But then the visitor said something that frightened and disturbed Novogno. He stated that he was the grandson of a man murdered by a fortuneteller three decades earlier. Hitherto, the men that shared the silver dagger dreams had never been relatives as their fortunetellers were. Novogno asked himself what if anything did this new scenario mean? Should this silver dagger dreamer be treated more cautiously than his predecessors? Novogno's inclination was to let the man live, for he seemed to be harmless. Novogno could not even envision him being an accessory to a crime much less a murderer. Novogno only wavered because this fellow was the grandson of the man murdered by his grandfather. It made sense that the man was visiting Novogno to take his revenge. The fortuneteller's hand reached for the silver dagger beneath the table. The palm of his hand caressed its handle as he considered the options available to him. Might it not be most prudent to swiftly gash the man's throat, to render him verifiably harmless, or was it not more apropos to look upon their meeting as a unique opportunity to make amends? Novogno thought to correct his grandfather's error of judgment in killing a man that should never have been killed.

As Novogno listened to the customer speak about his dream, he decided to let him live. If he could break the curse of his family lineage with a single act of goodliness, it would be worth the chance. When the man asked Novogno what he thought of the silver dagger dream, Novogno laughed good naturedly and reassured him it was not a prophesy. More than likely, it was a mental rehashing of the murder suffered by his grandfather thirty years prior (thirty years, six months, three weeks, nine days and three hours earlier, to be precise). Novogno also admitted to the customer that it was his own grandfather that had committed the murder and he humbly apologized for his grandfather's actions. Furthermore, he told the man if his family ever needed anything at all, to simply ask for it and his family would do what they could to oblige them. No sacrifice was too small to make amends. With these sympathetic words, Novogno sent the customer on his merry way. Not long afterwards, Novogno ate his dinner and went to sleep in the adjacent room where he kept his books and his bed. He fell asleep reading one of his favorite books, the Old Testament. The next morning his brother, Sevlor, found him dead.

As Sevlor (and Novogno's parents) later discovered, their last customer had been the carrier of *Angevence,* a deadly and incurable disease. Depending on the carrier's chemistry, *Angevence* can kill quickly or remain dormant for years. In this instance, the disease had been dormant for thirty years (thirty years, six months, three weeks, nine days and three hours, to be exact). Just before the carrier passed away, he had the privilege of knowing that his infirmity had infected Novogno and also Novogno's brother. Because Novogno and Sevlor had never sired offspring, the carrier was able to single handedly end their family line. Novogno's father buried his two sons just one month apart and then took his own life. He killed himself with the family's silver dagger. Everybody called it a suicide, except for Novogno's mother. She called it a very bad dream.

A Bad
Day for Bob

It's sad to see a friend breakdown and fall to pieces. That's what happened to my buddy, Bob. June and I have known Bob and his wife, Ethel, for thirty years. They're our neighbors in Spring Hill, Florida, but Bob and I first met at Rankel's Department Store in Albany, New York. Not long after we started working together in Women's Wear, I invited Bob and his wife over to our place to play bridge. June and Ethel took to each other quickly, as Bob and I had. It was the beginning of a long friendship. We've had some good times and a lot of laughs over the years. About ten years ago, when Bob and I became eligible for retirement, we mutually decided on Spring Hill, after researching several possible retirement communities. It was just what we wanted, quiet but lively. June and I realized the value of having two close friends by our side at this new phase of our lives, and I think Bob and Ethel did too. Having them living next door to us would be like having a slice of Albany next door—a taste of home. We've had many fun filled afternoons with Bob and Ethel in our backyard; lazing around the poolside, eating barbecued hamburgers and hot dogs. While the girls sunned themselves and gossiped, Bob and I would have a few beers and talk sports. When the sun set, we would take the party into the den to play bridge. It was a great life . . . until the day Bob fell apart.

I remember that morning well. Bob rang the bell repeatedly. I must have answered the door in a huff. I was expecting to see another neighbor who only rings my bell to tell me that our cat is humping his cat. He rings the bell repeatedly to emphasize the exigency of the matter. When I opened the door, I was surprised to see Bob on the porch, crying. My first thought was that something had happened to Ethel, so I asked Bob if she was alright. Bob reassuringly nodded his head but then contradicted himself by sobbing, "Jesus, I don't know." There wasn't anything I could do for him on the porch, so I told him to come into the house. June was still asleep, so I directed Bob away from the hall where the master bedroom is located and led him to the den. I'd just made a pot of coffee so I sat him down and told him I'd get some. When I went into the kitchen I could hear Bob talking to himself. It was strange talk: "If the bogus Ethel is in the backyard and the bogus Bob is in the garage, then where is the real Bob and Ethel?" I'm paraphrasing, but it was something to that effect. I placed the coffee mug down on the table in front of Bob and noticed his hand trembling when he reached for it.

I said to him, "Bob, why don't you tell me what's wrong."

He took a sip of the coffee, holding the mug with both hands. They were still shaking.

"Bob, did you hear me?" I asked. There was no reply. He stared into space, like he was in deep thought; thinking about Ethel, I suspected. "Bob, where's Ethel? Is she alright?"

Bob nodded. "She's in the backyard."

"Oh good," I sighed. I was happy to hear him respond casually, like everything was fine. But then he said something that puzzled me.

"She's in the backyard," he reiterated, "and apparently I'm working on the car in the garage."

"What are you talking about, Bob?"

He smiled and shrugged his shoulders.

It's out of character for Bob to joke in a less than obvious manner, so his behavior threw me off. I repeated my question.

Bob took another sip of coffee and used both hands to rest the mug on the table. He had to make an effort to place it on the coaster and almost spilled it at one point. He cleared his throat. "Listen Larry, I have to tell you something. It's going to sound odd. All I ask is that you hear me out."

"Lay it on me," I said. "I'm all ears."

"You promise not to laugh?"

I reassured him, "Of course I won't laugh. Bob, you and Ethel know if anything is wrong, you can always count on June and me."

He scrutinized me for a moment and then said something peculiar. "I think you're a mannequin."

I broke my promise and laughed. *"A mannequin?"*

Bob was visibly upset by my laughter. He stood up. For a second I thought he was going to leave, but then he sat down again. "I told you not to laugh," he said sharply.

I lit a cigarette. "Bob, tell me what this is all about. What happened this morning?"

"Weird stuff," Bob sighed. "I woke up this morning and thought it was like any other morning, except I couldn't find Ethel anywhere . . . anywhere. I looked all over the house, in every single room. I couldn't find her. Then I checked the backyard . . ."

"So, she was in the backyard."

"Yes and no," Bob answered. His expression soured. "From behind, it looked like Ethel sitting in a lounge chair. I called to her but she didn't answer me. I said, 'Honey, I've been looking all over for you.' I remember being confused because I saw what looked like a margarita in a tall glass with a little umbrella sticking out of the top. The drink was resting on the ground beside one of the chair legs and right beside it was an ashtray filled with cigarette butts, like forty or fifty. Now, you know as well as I do Larry that Ethel doesn't smoke or drink, especially not at seven o'clock in the morning! I was like, 'Ethel, are you alright?' I approached her and grabbed her shoulder. I was shocked to feel how cold and hard it was to touch. As I shook the shoulder slightly, I realized why it was cold and hard to touch. It wasn't a human shoulder. It was a mannequin's shoulder, a mannequin of Ethel! I turned it around to get a better look and to my disbelief the head fell off and rolled onto the lawn."

I shook my head in disbelief. "Oh Bob, that's crazy!"

"Of course it's crazy!" His eyes widened. "Can you imagine if that happened to you? I mean, what if you went looking for June and that happened? What would you think?"

I shrugged my shoulders. "I'd probably think it was a joke."

Bob shook his head. "No, it isn't a joke."

"Of course it's a joke," I insisted. "What else could it be?"

"No, Larry. You don't understand. Ethel is nowhere to be found."

"I'm sure she'll turn up," I told him. "Right now, she's having a laugh at your expense. You'll see. She'll turn up." I forgot my promise and laughed out loud. "What did you think, your wife suddenly turned into a mannequin?" I finished the cigarette and put it out in the ashtray. "Relax, Bob. You're beginning to worry me."

Bob held his head in his hands and I heard him mutter something.

"What was that?" I asked.

"I said that's not the end of the story."

"Well then finish it," I told him. "You have my attention."

"I looked all over the house for her, Larry. I looked in every single room. I couldn't find her any place. Finally, I thought to look in the garage."

"What happened in the garage?" I asked him.

"The hood of the car was opened and it looked like someone was examining the engine. I couldn't see who it was at first."

"Was it Ethel?"

"No. When I went around to see who it was, *or what it was*, I saw . . . " Bob stopped and took a deep breath. "I saw that it was a mannequin of *me*."

"What?" I smiled at Bob. "Are you kidding?"

"OF COURSE NOT!" Bob screamed.

I told him to keep it down, reminding him that June was still asleep down the hall.

"Of course I'm not kidding," Bob whispered. *"I would never joke about something like that."*

Up until this point in the story, I thought Ethel might be pulling her husband's leg. Now with this latest development I thought Bob might be pulling mine. But I was indulgent. I lit another cigarette and told him to continue.

"Well, like I said, the mannequin was positioned beneath the hood of the car, as if examining the engine. It looked just like me, down to every detail—even wearing the same pajamas. Now I know what you're thinking, Larry. You're thinking this could still be part of some elaborate hoax perpetrated by my wife—even though this kind of humor is totally out of character for her."

I shook my head, confused. "Actually, I don't know what to think."

"One mannequin might be a joke," Bob acknowledged, "but two never."

"Listen, Bob. This story of yours is a little hard to believe. I'm beginning to think . . . "

"It gets worse, Larry. It gets much worse. After I saw the second mannequin, I panicked. I ran outside to look for Ethel. I'd already checked every room and closet in the house. I just couldn't imagine where she was. I started to think a madman was responsible for all of this, that a madman had stolen my wife and replaced her with a dummy. Perhaps he had meant to get me too. I know how crazy this sounds but you have no idea how spooky it was seeing an exact replica of me looking under the car's hood."

"I can only imagine," I replied, calmly. "Bob, you're sure you're not imagining all of this."

Bob sighed and grimaced. "No, I'm not imagining it."

"If I went over to your house right now, I'd see the mannequins?" I clarified.

"I think so. Unless someone moved them."

When he said that I sighed. "Go on, Bob."

"You don't have to humor me, Larry. I'm going to the police after I leave here. In fact, maybe we should call them right now."

He made as if to stand and I motioned for him to sit back down. "Let's just go over the details first, you and I, alright?" I waited for him to say something else, but he was quiet, so I asked him, "What happened after you ran outside, Bob?"

"I saw my neighbor watering the lawn. You know that old Canadian couple that moved next door to me. They have the Maple Leaf flapping in the wind everyday?"

"Yeah. That's, um, the McPhersons." I said, remembering the name.

"Yeah, the McPhersons. That's right. The guy's name is Jack. I saw him watering his lawn, so I asked him, "Hey

Jack, have you seen my wife anywhere?" He didn't answer me right away, so I repeated myself. He still didn't answer me, so I shouted to him, "HEY JACK! SEEN MY WIFE? I CAN'T FIND HER ANYWHERE." Again, he didn't answer me. I was going to drop it and come over here, but I don't like being ignored. I grabbed a stone and threw it at him."

"You did what?" I asked, incredulous. "Bob, why did you do that? You shouldn't have done that. *Have you lost your mind?"*

Bob shook his head. "It's alright. Nothing happened. The stone struck him in the shoulder and I saw the hose that he was holding fall. You know what, he wasn't watering the lawn. He'd been holding a hose, but the water couldn't have been on. Nothing was coming out of the spout. I went right up close to the fence and saw for myself. The hose was at his feet and it was obvious that nothing was coming out. I waited for him to say something about the stone. He just stood there quietly, staring straight ahead."

"He didn't move at all?" I clarified.

"Larry, I swear he was in the exact same position that he'd been in when I first spotted him, with his arm extended, only now without the hose."

I considered just how bizarre and rude such behavior might seem. It didn't sound at all like the Jack McPherson I'd met at the Senior Citizens Country Club a few months earlier. He and his wife were friendly with June and I. We'd played shuffleboard together and had a very pleasant exchange.

"Can you believe that?" Bob asked me.

"No," I answered. "I can't."

"Well," Bob continued, "I didn't pay it any further mind. I was too interested in finding my wife."

"So then what, you came over here?" I asked.

"I headed in that direction," he explained, "but something happened along the way. I saw something."

"What did you see?"

"I saw a little dog saluting one of your shrubs with his hind leg."

I grimaced. "That's Mrs. Wilson's dog. It piddles all over the place."

"It wasn't really piddling, Larry, only positioned in such a way so as to convey that impression. When I got close enough I saw that it was not a dog at all. It was a dog mannequin."

I stood up and extinguished my cigarette in the ashtray. "OK. That about does it, Bob."

"Wait. I'm not finished." He stood up too. "There's more, Larry."

"No, there's not." Just then the doorbell rang. "Excuse me. With any luck, that'll be your wife."

I saw my suspicions confirmed as I opened the front door. Ethel was on the other side of the screen door with a worried look in her eyes. "Hi Larry. Is Bob here, by any chance? I can't find him."

"Hi Ethel. He's here. Would you like to come in?" I opened the door for her and she started to explain something to me as she came in but quieted herself once she caught sight of Bob.

He greeted her, leaning against the wall in a cavalier fashion. "Hi Ethel. Welcome to the party."

"What happened to you?" she demanded. "I've been looking all over for you!"

Bob laughed. "You've been looking for me? *I've been looking for you.*"

Ethel turned to me and said, "I didn't know where he was. He just disappeared."

Bob interrupted her, "I was in the garage, looking at the car engine. You didn't see me?"

Ethel ignored him. "He's been acting so strange. You know he threw a rock at one of our neighbors?"

"Yeah. He told me."

"Mr. McPherson. You know him?"

"Yup."

"The man said he was going to call the police the next time it happens. I told him, there isn't going to be a next time. I apologized to him. Larry, I was so embarrassed."

All of the commotion in the hallway had awakened June. She opened the door and came out of the bedroom, squinting her eyes. "What's going on? Ethel, is that you?"

"Hi June. I'm sorry to bother you so early in the morning. I came to get Bob."

"Bob?" June was puzzled. "Is he here too?" She adjusted her bathrobe.

"Hi June." Bob waved to her from the den.

"What's this all about?" she asked, turning to me.

I shrugged my shoulders. "You feel like some coffee?"

"What's this all about?" she asked me again.

I told her, "Bob thinks everybody's a mannequin. It's a long story."

"He what?"

At this point I noticed Bob and Ethel arguing. I stepped in to defuse the situation. "Hey, how about some breakfast? You kids must be starving."

"I have to use the bathroom," Bob said, storming off.

"Go ahead. Help yourself, Bob."

The second he was gone, Ethel threw her hands up in exasperation. "That's it, Larry. I've had it with him," she said.

I tried to reassure her, "Don't worry about it, Ethel. He'll be alright."

June whispered something to her, before I could say another word.

"What, are you two having a private conference?" I asked.

Ethel whispered something back to June and June relayed the message to me. "Larry, Ethel would appreciate it if you would simply end all of this aggravation."

I turned to Ethel. "Well, what would you have me do?"

June answered vicariously, "She wants you to take Bob apart."

"Take him *apart?*" I repeated. "You mean, beat him up?" I laughed.

"You know what we mean," June replied impatiently.

"But why?" I asked. "Bob's a good guy!"

"He's become too much of a problem," Ethel answered on her own.

June shook her head. "I can't believe he mentioned the mannequin thing," she grumbled.

"Ah, that's nothing," I said, defending Bob. "I'm sure he won't do it again. I'll talk to him."

Ethel gave me a hard look. "All the same, Larry, I'd appreciate it if you would take him apart."

"And do what with him?" I asked, indignant. I really thought they were overreacting.

June finished the thought, "Take him apart and put him back in his little box."

"What box?"

"Larry you know what we're talking about, the box that you shipped him in from Albany."

Trying to avoid an argument with the wife, I agreed. "Alright, I'll do it. Where's the box?"

"It's in the guest room," June told me. "And don't make the mistake of putting him in *my* box."

"Or mine . . . " Ethel added.

They both looked at me demandingly. I felt bad about putting Bob away in a box but knew it was the prudent thing to do under the circumstances. No doubt, I would miss that crazy guy. I consoled myself with the thought that I might be able to take him out of the box again, at some point down the road. In that case, compliance with the girls' wishes wasn't a huge sacrifice. It only meant Bob was going away for a little while; until he sorted out his problems and was able to join Ethel, June and me again as the positive, friendly, fun loving guy we once knew. In the meantime, I'd have to reconfigure my relationship with the ladies. I had the responsibility of making two women happy now, instead of just one. After all, Ethel knew no one in Spring Hill, aside from June and me. For the time being, it would have to be a threesome.

I heard the bathroom door open down the hall and I heard Bob's voice mixing with the sound of the flush. Ethel and June both gave me a little push and I stormed down the hall after him. I surprised Bob in my rush and quickly overwhelmed him with my body weight. I threw him to the ground and ripped his arms and legs off. In hindsight, I should have gone for the head first, because he was laying a very heavy guilt trip on me the whole time. He was yelling out, 'I thought we were friends, Larry. I thought we were friends.' That sickened and saddened me but it didn't stop me from doing what I had to do. Needless to say, he did finally shut the hell up after I pulled his head off. June and Ethel roared with laughter as they saw me bumbling down the hall with all of Bob's pieces, stumbling toward the guest room. I dropped Bob's torso at one point.

"You did the right thing, Larry," I heard June say. It didn't make me feel any better.

Anyway, one good thing did come out of this tragedy. After I boxed Bob up, June and Ethel gave me a nice reward for all my troubles. They teasingly invited me to take their clothes off and I greedily did so. Oh, we had such a lovely day together. At first we only tanned and talked, with our arms around each other in the pool. But later we took it into the bedroom. That night, we fell asleep in each other's arms. To my surprise, I learned that Ethel snored (the same problem I'd had with June all these years). Now, I had that problem in stereo. I had no choice but to remove their heads until the morning. Otherwise, the three of us got along great together. The truth be told, it even occurred to me to leave Bob in his box permanently. Knowing myself, that is more likely to happen than not. Meanwhile, Ethel has been spending a lot of time with June and I and I'm here to tell the world that while two is company, three is not necessarily a crowd.

City of the Mind

Vondel adjusted the tripod of the movie camera then looked into the lens.

"Is everything in view?" his assistant asked him.

"We'll have to pan," Vondel replied, "but from here, we can get all the close ups." The director continued to look through the lens, admiring the narrow oak table in view and the gothic high back chairs surrounding it. The tapestries above, depicting religious scenes, were a perfect compliment. The entire set was medieval in appearance.

"There's plenty of shadow," his assistant commented, "as you requested."

"Yes, plenty of shadow," the director admitted. He pulled himself away from the lens in order to better appreciate the expertise of the lighting crew. "This is even gloomier than I had anticipated; darker, more mysterious."

"Is it too much?" his assistant asked.

"No, not at all," Vondel answered. "This will do nicely." The director paused, trying to collect his thoughts. He'd suddenly forgotten the name of the picture.

"Is everything alright, sir?" The assistant took a sip of coffee, awaiting the answer.

Vondel turned and looked over at him. "Sky, I have to ask you something."

"What is it, J.P.?"

"Why are we shooting this scene?" Vondel inquired. "You know, I don't remember giving the order to shoot this scene."

"What are you talking about, sir?" The bewildered assistant stared at the director questioningly. "Of course, you gave the order. That's why we're all here, because you told us to be here."

Just then the director heard a loud thud over his left shoulder. When he looked around, Vondel noticed actors dressed as clergymen entering the set from a large wooden door. They strolled past the two men on their way over to the long wooden table.

"Nice costumes," Sky remarked.

Vondel counted thirteen actors, all sporting long crimson robes with white trim. The director tried to recall the premise of the scene that they were about to shoot. But no matter how hard he tried to recall a script or a premise that would have required such a scene, the director remained clueless. Vondel was at a total loss to even explain his reasons for being there.

Not knowing what else to do, he confessed this quandary to his assistant. "Listen, Sky, I have to be completely honest with you . . . I don't recall having seen a script for this scene. I don't know what these actors are supposed to do. I don't know how to direct them." He sighed deeply.

Sky was about to reply when Vondel added, "I don't even remember driving to work this morning. It's like I just suddenly realized I was here with you. But how can that be?"

"You don't remember how you got here?" Sky raised an eyebrow. "That is strange."

"Not only that," Vondel confessed. "I don't recognize anyone on this set; that is, except for you. I'm talking about the actors, the make-up people . . . THE CAMERA CREW! Isn't that bizarre?"

At first, Sky didn't know how to reply. After a long pause, he let out a loud laugh. "Oh man, you had me going there for a minute, boss. I'd never seen you like that. You scared me, you really did. Took me a minute to figure it out. But I gotcha now." He laughed again. "Just wait here a minute. I have to check up on a couple of things for the next scene." Sky started to walk away.

"What couple of things?" Vondel asked him, indignant.

"Just a couple of things. I'll be right back, J.P." On that note, Sky turned his back on Vondel and headed for the only available door, the same one used by the actors to enter the 'dining room.'

Vondel watched as Sky disappeared. He stood there for more than a minute, scratching his head. He couldn't comprehend his assistant's callous demeanor. It was out of character for him to be so totally disregarding. Vondel was about to run after him and give him a dressing down, when he felt someone tap his shoulder and heard a voice from behind:

"J.P., I have to talk with you for a moment."

Vondel turned around and saw the face of Bunky Myers. He couldn't believe his eyes. He tried to say something but nothing came out.

"Cat got your tongue, J.P.? Long time no see, Huh?"

"*Bunky*, is that you?"

"Of course it's me. A little older, but still the same old Bunky."

Vondel put his arms around his old high school buddy and hugged him. "Geez, it must be twenty years! What are you doing here?" he asked, smiling.

"O.K. You can let go of me now," Bunky told him, breaking the embrace.

"What are you doing here?" Vondel asked him again.

Bunky laughed. "Don't you know? I'm producing this picture."

Just then one of the actors interrupted their conversation. He spoke to Vondel, "Sir, the 'Cardinal' sits in the middle of the table, right—not at the head of the table? We're going with the revised seating?"

It was obvious Vondel was perplexed by the question and didn't know what to tell the man. "The revised seating?" he hesitantly asked.

The actor stared at him in expectation, Bunky did as well.

The director looked over at the long wooden table and saw that the middle chair was unoccupied. "Sit in the middle," he instructed.

As soon as the actor walked away, Vondel grabbed Bunky's arm. "What do you mean you're the producer?

That makes no sense!"

"Why?" Bunky asked, disconcerted.

"Because you're not a producer!" Vondel argued.

"Who told you that?" Bunky asked. He suddenly grew serious. "Listen, you're supposed to start shooting. Everyone's waiting on your call." He pointed at the 'clergy' assembled around the long dining table, dressed in their red and white robes.

Vondel surveyed the scene and remembered that he was supposed to film everyone seated at the table before moving to the close up of the 'Cardinal' in the middle. He also recalled that the 'Cardinal' was to give a sermon to the 'clergy' present, but that something dramatic was supposed to interrupt his speech. The director could not recall the specifics. He wanted to ask Sky, but he was nowhere to be found. His train of thought was suddenly distracted by an amplified command:

"ALL QUIET ON THE SET!"

Vondel recognized the voice as his assistant's, but his location was still a mystery. 'Why's Sky giving the orders?' Vondel wondered. 'I'm the one who's supposed to say, 'All quiet on the set.'

The director's ego was quickly assuaged when he saw that everyone's eyes were focused on him, especially Cameramen One and Three. They were blatantly staring at Vondel waiting for their instructions to begin filming. The actors were also waiting for their cue. Like a professional, Vondel looked through the lens of Camera Two one last time before relinquishing it to its assigned operator who was then chomping at the bit.

"All ready," Vondel told the cameraman. He stepped back and away into the shadows looking for his own assigned position, a chair with his name on it. He found it soon enough and sat down. Having no idea where the order would lead, Vondel picked up his bullhorn and gave the go ahead to, "ROLL!"

Immediately, the 'Cardinal' began to speak. It was obvious that the actor had been well rehearsed. He articulated every line with feeling and distinction. Even the Latin words and phrases, which Vondel did not understand, were delivered in such a way that they complimented the entire sermon with profundity and a sense of urgency. Despite this proficiency, the director's ear still found something displeasing. There was an uneven element in the actor's delivery. Though the actor's lips were moving fluently and his voice was a boom on the sound stage, certain words were not registered fully in the pickup. The director reasoned that more than likely this occasional inaudibility was probably attributable to inconsistencies in the microphone hidden on the actor. The director had a fleeting thought to break the scene so that he could investigate the matter further. But a contravening voice deep inside Vondel told him not to interfere and to listen to what he could understand of the sermon. It was at this critical point that the director heard the 'Cardinal' refer to the consciousness of God and how that consciousness pervaded the consciousness of Man so that they were one and indistinguishable from each other. Specifically, Vondel heard the words *singularity* and *plurality* used by the speaker. While devoting his attention to the sermon of the 'Cardinal' Vondel's concentration was suddenly and irrevocably broken by an event that left him riddled with horror.

In the middle of his speech, the 'Cardinal' began to choke. His face turned as white as a sheet. Desperately, he grabbed his throat and gasped for air. The rest of the 'clergy' arose from their chairs and slowly backed away from the table in fear. Their languid body movements cast insidious shadows across the face of the dying man. Like everyone else on and off the set, Vondel simply watched as the 'Cardinal' fell back in his chair against the wall, writhing in pain. No one present did anything to help the man in his death throes. Vondel was nonplussed by the event. In every respect, the agony of the 'Cardinal' seemed to be real. But then the director took note of the calm manner and focus that pervaded behind the scene from all levels of production. This was so even at the most climactic event of the 'Cardinal' coughing up chunks of organic matter and convulsing on the floor. The reality check came when one of the actors yelled, "Oh my God, he's really dying!"

Once that was said, it was as if someone had flipped a switch causing everyone to panic; not only the actors, but everyone involved in the production. All abandoned their assigned stations in the rampant pandemonium that ensued, scrambling to the only available exit. Vondel was no exception. Like everyone else, he ran for the crowded door. If his life was in danger, he did not want to wait around to find out why. He was caught up in the pushing, shoving and screaming, like everyone else. Could the mass hysteria be attributable to the dying man, he wondered? Overwhelmed by a morbid curiosity, he glanced back one last time at the 'Cardinal' lying on the floor. The man's head was partially eclipsed by a red, satanic cape. The director strained to see the head of the actor more clearly, but was prevented by unseen hands that pushed him from behind.

Vondel was suddenly thrown off the set and into the daylight of a strange urban landscape. The director knew he should have seen the recognizable back lot of *Wunder Haus Studios*. Since this was not the case, his confusion and fear intensified. The director had no idea where he was or what was going on. His adrenaline continued to flow as the crowd scrambled behind him, panicking to exit the studio door; some were stumbling and falling to the ground. Fearing he might be trampled, Vondel struggled to pull away from the crowd. Once freed, he leaned hard against the building wall, seeking support for his tired frame. He caught his breath, steadied his fluttering heart and waited and hoped for a return to normalcy. It did not take long for the storm to pass; for Vondel to find himself quietly alone again, with only two dead bodies at his feet for company. He gathered himself, trying to make sense of the last several minutes and rationalized that a pandemonium of this scale could not possibly be part of a Hollywood production . . . or could it?

Standing with his back to the wall, listening to the sundry sounds that earmark urban life, Vondel wondered for the second time if he could be dreaming. The first time occurred as he was being pushed out the doorway. Vondel recalled hoping his first step out the door would be his first step in supplanting the crazy world that had been the cause of so much confusion and grief for him that morning. As he stepped over the bodies of the trampled, Vondel optimistically entertained the thought that perhaps they were not what they appeared to be. He gazed into the doorway, partially blocked by the dead bodies. All was quiet and dark in that entrance. Vondel thought to step inside again but reconsidered the idea immediately. For what could it prove to go in there again? Wouldn't it be more prudent to assume that the crew had fled for sufficient reason? What conundrum could he answer on his own in there?

Vondel heard a commotion not far from the alleyway where he stood. When he looked down the avenue he saw what appeared to be a riotous assemblage. His impulse was to walk toward the commotion but the second he crossed the street he was nearly run over by a white van blasting circus calliope music. The vehicle had large amplifying horns extending from the roof, which explained the source of the loud music. Vondel also noticed a motif of laughing clowns painted all around the sides and back of the van. The van sped past him with such ferocity that he might have lost his life had he not had the quick reflexes to step back onto the curb. That van was followed by another. It flew past Vondel at a speed that violated all respect for public safety. Again, it was painted with clown faces and had circus calliope music playing from amplifiers. The volume was nearly deafening. Fortunately, the van disappeared as quickly as it had appeared. Before he had the chance to give it further thought Vondel's attention was diverted to a piercing scream overhead. When he looked skyward Vondel saw a man leaping from the roof of a nearby building. Fearing himself the landing target of the suicide, he maneuvered out of the way in the nick of time. The sound of the body hitting the pavement was horrible. Paranoid and shaken by another near miss, Vondel decided it best to change his location. He scurried to a different doorway and then in between two nearby buildings. He was fortuitous in his timing, as he narrowly avoided the path of a third clown van as it sped around the corner. It came to a screeching halt and the back doors flew open. Vondel saw two Bozos jump out of the van, carrying flamethrowers. Without provocation, the clowns directed their weapons at an old man walking his cocker spaniel. Vondel hid his eyes but heard the burst of fire that followed as well as the abbreviated agonized cries of the old man and his dog. When Vondel looked up again he saw the charred remains of the victims smoldering on the ground and the clowns returning to their van. The circus calliope music increased in volume and the bravado of murderous laughter wafted on the passing wind.

The director was beset with a fear of moving. He cowered until he heard the tires of the van skid off. The circus calliope music rapidly faded. Vondel bore further witness to the trail of carnage left by the clowns; a sight that sickened him physically. Soon the familiar cacophony of the rioters returned. This was an additional excuse for him to stay put. But as Vondel cowered in the alley, a comforting and invigorating thought occurred to him and filled him with an intrepid confidence: if this was, in fact, a dream that meant everything perceived hitherto was imaginary. Likewise, all future perceptions would be just as benign—

in essence, phantasmagoria. Vondel was elated, realizing he could not be harmed, no matter the danger posed him. Gradually he raised his hunched figure from the ground until it stood straight and tall.

With his new found strength, the director felt something cold and heavy in his right hand. He glanced down and saw that it was an old western style six-shooter. 'Where did this come from?' he asked himself. Vondel felt awkward holding the gun, but accepted it as a necessary evil. Knowing he could not hide forever, he emerged from the safe haven of the alley with the intent of facing the rioters. They were picketing and waving fists; more belligerent elements were breaking shop windows and throwing bottles. Vondel was surprised to notice a police presence lacking in the area. When he heard circus calliope music again, that lack of law enforcement became a frightening prospect. Vondel held the gun tightly and made up his mind to shoot it at the clowns if they drove by again. With bold strides he approached the marauding crowd, in the direction of the music, but something made him stop. He spotted a police officer, completely oblivious to the rioters and their looting. Vondel forgot about the clowns and was focused on confronting the police officer about his neglect of duty. The civil unrest had now grown so alarming that Vondel found it incomprehensible an officer of the law could ignore the problem with a clear conscience. As he walked within a few yards of the police officer, Vondel noticed something unusual about his uniform. It was bright blue with gold brocade trim, collar tabs and tassels. It resembled a military costume of the 19th century.

The officer nodded at Vondel's approach. "Hello there," he said.

Vondel was about to reply in kind when something startled him. A full can of beer flew past the officer's head, narrowly missing its mark. Strangely, the officer hadn't noticed. He stared expectantly at Vondel. "Can I help you with something?" he asked.

Despite the rioting and the fear that it inspired, Vondel was obliged to turn his firearm over to the officer. He raised the gun, so as to show him the weapon. He pointed it skyward, careful to keep his finger off the trigger as a matter of precaution.

The police officer shrugged his shoulders. He didn't seem the least bit phased at the prospect of Vondel brandishing a firearm in public. "I assume it's registered," he calmly replied with his hands still clasped behind his back.

"Huh?" Vondel continued to hold the weapon up. "No. I just found it in the alley behind you."

"It's like something out of the old WEST," The officer laughed. He raised his voice just slightly at the emphatic mention of the word 'west,' as if that word meant something to him.

Rather than guess what the police officer was getting at, Vondel simply handed him the gun.

The officer was surprised by this action but accepted the firearm reluctantly. "You don't want it?" he incredulously asked Vondel.

"No. You take it. It's not mine. Like I said, I found it in the alleyway, over there—" Vondel pointed behind the officer.

He politely turned to look where Vondel was directing his attention. "Oh, where the blue dogs are," the officer acknowledged.

Vondel saw that the alley was now partially obscured by a group of people wearing fluffy blue dog outfits with big anthropomorphic limbs and giant snouts. A few of them seemed to look over at Vondel and the police officer when Vondel pointed their way. Because their big, black eyes appeared to be pasted onto their costume heads, Vondel thought they could not really see. His assumption proved wrong. One of the dogs leapt away from the rest of the group and hurried across the street, to the corner where Vondel and the police officer were standing. When he came within a few yards, the man removed the big blue dog head of his costume to reveal himself. It was none other than Jonathan Barnes, the Studio Chief of *Wunder Haus Pictures.*

"Barnes?" Vondel heard himself say, "What the—"

"You two know each other?" the police officer asked.

"Of course we know each other," Barnes replied, "Go take your coffee break."

"Sure thing, Chief," the officer replied. He turned around to leave but a beer can hit him in the head and stopped him. He fell to the ground unconscious and then rolled over onto Vondel's feet.

Vondel couldn't believe his eyes. He quickly looked around, fearing other flying projectiles, but Barnes reassured him it wouldn't happen again.

"Don't worry. They were only supposed to throw two of those."

"Who are *they*?" Vondel questioned, nervously.

"Oh, a few studio hands I have around—kids, mostly."

Vondel voiced his concern. "I hope they aren't too anxious to impress you above and beyond the call of duty."

Barnes laughed. "Don't worry, J.P. I helped them drink the other four beers."

"Thank goodness," Vondel replied. He moved his feet out from under the unconscious police officer's body. "I hope he's not dead."

"No, he's fine. *He better be.* We need him in an upcoming scene." Barnes noticed the gun Vondel had given to the police officer, now lying on the ground. The Studio Chief picked it up and studied it for a second, before handing it to Vondel. "Here, take it. You could use it more than he could, especially in his condition."

Vondel heeded the advice and took back the gun. He was about to tuck it into his pants but was surprised to find a hip holster fastened to his waist. He shrugged his shoulders and stuck the gun into the holster. It was a perfect fit. Vondel was pleased, but at a loss to explain the sudden appearance of the gun belt.

"Now you're just like John Wayne," Barnes laughed.

Vondel laughed too, but only to be polite. He was concerned about nearly everything. The chaos that had accompanied the rioters had briefly died down while the men were talking, but now he saw a fresh wave of picketers marching towards them on the avenue. Even more worrisome to Vondel was the familiar sound of circus calliope music heard in the distance.

"Listen J.P.," Barnes said, taking hold of Vondel. "Cardinal Spengler dying suddenly caught us all by surprise. We need to replace him, pronto. The picture demands it. "

Vondel was only half listening, distracted by his fear of the circus calliope music. It had grown much louder. He realized the clown van was right around the corner from where they were standing. Panic stricken, Vondel brought his concern to the attention of Barnes.

"Oh, don't worry about that." The Studio Chief replied, trying to comfort his director. "They can't hurt you so long as you're doing the right thing by the picture."

Rather than comfort Vondel, Barnes words put him ill at ease. They sounded like a veiled threat. "What do you mean, as long as I'm *doing the right thing by the picture.* How on earth could I do wrong by the picture?"

Barnes smiled. "We'll need your help with the new Cardinal. Sky will talk to you about it later."

"SKY?" Vondel asked. He wasn't sure he heard the Chief correctly.

"Yes, Sky," Barnes confirmed.

"Why should my assistant explain anything to me?" Vondel asked angrily. "Why should he know something that I don't?"

"Don't worry about it, J.P." Barnes told him.

Vondel was indignant. "I am worried about it. What about the new Cardinal?"

Expectedly, the clown van sped around the corner. It partially jumped the curb, as it flew past the two men.

Vondel was shocked to see Barnes wave to the driver of the van. The driver removed a multi-colored wig from his head and threw it out the window at Barnes, blowing a raspberry as he drove away down the block.

"Crazy bastard," Barnes laughed. Seeing Vondel's pained expression, he returned to the subject of conversation, "Don't be paranoid about Sky, J.P. He's been doing most of the research on this picture while you've been working on your other projects. I know how busy you are."

Vondel questioned the veracity of Barnes' argument. He had no recollection of involvement with other studio projects. But then again he had no recollection of anything concerning this picture. He was too embarrassed to admit any of this to the Studio Chief who might consequently think him incompetent.

"You're lucky you have such a smart kid working for you, J.P." Barnes continued. "He's one in a million."

Vondel tried to squelch the growing resentment of his assistant by reminding himself that he was in a dream. 'This isn't reality,' he told himself. At this critical moment, Vondel heard the demonstrators approaching rapidly from behind. The director turned and looked over his shoulder when he heard Barnes say:

"HERE THEY COME!"

Like a giant tidal wave, the masses suddenly overwhelmed the two men.

"JUST STAND YOUR GROUND AND DON'T MOVE," the Chief told Vondel.

The two men watched as the crowd poured around them.

"I'M AFRAID," Vondel confessed. "WE COULD GET TRAMPLED."

"THEY WON'T HARM US," Barnes replied. "I DO HAVE SOME CLOUT AROUND HERE, YOU KNOW."

Vondel noticed that some of the demonstrators were carrying hand made signs. Several promoted the deceased Cardinal, Spengler. Vondel read one that stated, 'Spengler Was Right!' and another that read, 'Spengler = Truth'

"SPENGLER WAS VERY POPULAR WITH THESE KIDS," Vondel observed. He was making conversation but was also hoping to gain some insight from Barnes.

"A PESSIMIST," the Chief blasted. He lowered his voice as the crowd dissipated. "He prophesied an end to our civilization. What the world needs now is an *optimist*. Sky has someone lined up that I know you're going to love!"

Vondel waxed petulant. "Shouldn't I have the final say on who gets to be Cardinal?"

"Well, you'll meet him," Barnes replied. "No one's excluding you from the decision making process. You sound so defensive, J.P. No one's wronged you!"

"But that's precisely the point, Chief—" Just then Vondel felt a pat on his back. He turned and saw the smiling face of a teenaged kid. Vondel returned the smile and greeted the kid, "Hello there. How're you doing?"

"You're J.P. Vondel, the director, aren't you?" the kid asked.

"Why, yes, I am." Vondel acknowledged with pride.

The director felt a playful punch to his left arm. He turned to look and found another smiling kid. "Hello there," Vondel greeted, keeping up his smile. The kid politely nodded but said nothing. He seemed to be in awe of the director.

"We're counting on you. We are all counting on you," the first kid said, giving the director a vote of confidence. "We just know you won't let us down."

Vondel laughed. He was pleased to see that the demonstrators were friendly and not hostile, as he feared they would be.

"Looks like you have some friends," Barnes commented.

"Wow," Vondel chortled, "they really are very nice."

"What did you expect?" Barnes asked.

"A problem, maybe," Vondel answered. "You should have seen these kids earlier."

"They're not going to have a problem with you, J.P. They have to put their faith somewhere." Barnes waved his finger at Vondel. "But don't let them down. They can turn ugly."

The smile evanesced from Vondel's face. "What do you mean, Chief?"

"Everybody's future's at stake here, including yours and mine," Barnes told him.

"You worry me when you say that." Vondel confessed, "But honestly I don't know what you're talking about." He paused and then continued. "It pains me to admit that to you."

"Ah, don't worry about it." Barnes took the big blue dog head out from under his arm and placed it back over his own head. He continued talking with a muffled voice.

"If you do what's right by the picture they'll be nothing to worry about. Just meet the new Cardinal that Sky has lined up—that's all you have to do."

"Why does Sky pick the new Cardinal?" Vondel asked timorously.

"I TOLD YOU WHY," Barnes yelled out from under the dog head. "You know I hate repeating myself. Oh and I almost forgot. Tell the kid I approved the extra clown vans that he asked for."

"THE CLOWN VANS?" Vondel's jaw dropped. "You approved that?"

"Of course, I did." Barnes defended. "Granted, I was a little put off by the number he requested. I thought five or six would have been sufficient. When the kid asked for a hundred and forty seven, I nearly had a heart attack."

"A HUNDRED AND FORTY SEVEN!" Vondel yelled back.

The Studio Chief laughed. "I had the same reaction. But as the kid explained, we really do need that many vans for the picture." Barnes leaned closer to Vondel and lowered his voice, *"The kid cut a deal, you know. We get every third van for free."*

"OH MY GOD!" Vondel exclaimed. He thought of the implications of having that many clown vans roaming the streets.

"Yeah, it was a pretty good deal," Barnes boasted. "You have to hand it to the kid."

Vondel was overwhelmed with a daunting insecurity that he found impossible to hide. "I have to be honest with you, Chief, you should have included me on that decision. As director of this picture, I should know what goes into the budget."

Barnes put his hand on Vondel's shoulder. "J.P. We couldn't find you anywhere when it came time to take care of these things. The world doesn't stop for you, you know."

Vondel censured his boss, "But I'm the director! And if I'm the director, this is my picture."

"It doesn't work that way," Barnes told him.

"Well it should work that way," Vondel insisted. "The thing that I find most difficult to stomach is the fact that Sky went over my head. The budget is my responsibility."

Barnes began doing deep knee bends. "Like I said before, J.P. you weren't around. Things had to get done. Luckily, Sky stepped in and it's good for the both of us that he did. A potential crisis was averted. We could have had a major shortage of clown vans! Now we have more than enough. Be happy about it."

The throng was spreading out and that opened a clearing for Barnes to leave. He stepped over the police officer. "I'll talk to you about it later. Keep up the good work, J.P."

The director watched as Barnes joined the other men standing around in blue dog outfits across the street. He wondered if they were all studio executives like Barnes. "Why would they be dressed like that?" he asked himself. With great interest, he watched the group walk off together, down the abandoned alley.

Vondel was curious to see what the blue dog men were up to but was drawn to the crowd then gathering en masse around him. The director immediately assumed the gathering to be on account of the fallen police officer, but then he saw that everyone was looking skyward. Vondel looked up himself and spotted a man floating down in a parachute. The parachutist waved enthusiastically to the crowd below and specifically to a window washer on the scaffolding of a nearby skyscraper. In response, the window washer tossed a bucket of dirty water at him. Vondel knew that it was dirty water because the bucket landed a few feet from where he was standing, spraying its contents all over his shoes and the hem of his pants. The act did prove beneficial in at least one respect, however. It forced a clearing in the crowd for the parachutist to land. When that surreal event finally occurred, Vondel was at first happy for the man's safety. But he was overtaken with rage when he recognized the dare devil as none other than his assistant, Sky.

"What are you doing in that parachute?" the director asked him. "Is this what I pay you for?"

"I have to talk to you, J.P.," Sky replied. He was trying to remove the straps that secured him to the silk. "It's about the Cardinal. We have to replace him on the picture and we have to do it as soon as possible."

Vondel was cantankerous at this perceived air of authority and he sneered. "What do you mean *we have to replace him*?" he asked.

Sky let out a sigh as he finally freed himself from the straps securing him to the parachute. The crowd enclosed around him and a few women began to touch his long hair admiringly, treating him like a rock star. Sky was overjoyed by their adulation and momentarily forgot about Vondel. "Wow. I could get used to this!" he laughed out loud.

"You came out of the clouds," a boy from the crowd said excitedly, pointed upward.

"Yes, I did," Sky acknowledged. He patted the kid on his head.

A beautiful brunette gave Sky a kiss on his cheek. "You are so brave—and handsome!"

Vondel swelled with jealousy and rage at all of this attention. He desperately wanted to scream at that moment but his better judgment triumphed. He demurely did an about turn and strolled away down the street, away from the crowd, away from his assistant. "I won't be part of *his* fantasy," he said to himself.

"WAIT! WAIT!" Sky yelled after him. "WHERE ARE YOU GOING? I HAVE TO TALK WITH YOU, J.P."

Vondel continued to walk at a leisurely pace. After a few seconds he heard Sky's voice getting closer behind him. "HEY, WAIT A MINUTE! THIS IS IMPORTANT. I HAVE TO TALK WITH YOU ABOUT THE CARDINAL, J.P." The crowd around Sky seemed to be in tow. Vondel heard them as well. When the director realized that a crowd was following him he stopped and did an about face to face Sky.

"Are you trying to undermine my authority?" Vondel asked him.

Sky stared at his mentor in stupefaction. "Of course not! Where is this coming from?"

"Don't look so surprised, Sky," Vondel told him. "I had a little chat with Barnes and I know that you've been calling all the shots lately."

"WHAT DO YOU MEAN?" Sky demanded. "I DIDN'T CALL ANY FILM SHOTS!"

Vondel clarified. "By shots, I don't mean continuous film sequences. You know what I'm talking about."

"I don't. I really don't," Sky objected.

"Barnes told me you had a replacement in mind for the Cardinal."

"Yeah, that's right. So what?"

"He also told me that you hired all of those crazy clown vans—A HUNDERED AND FORTY SEVEN VANS!"

"Yeah," Sky replied, softly. "I did do that on my own. But it's only because you've been busy with other things, J.P. I'm just doing my job. This picture has got a deadline."

Vondel was morose. He laughed disgustedly. "In the first place, Sky, this isn't a picture. It's a dream. A DREAM!"

Not knowing where this was going, Sky humored him. "Yeah . . . "

"And when I say this is a dream, I don't mean figuratively."

"Uh-huh . . . "

Vondel noticed that Sky wasn't paying attention. One of the women in the crowd had cuddled up to him, a beautiful blonde. As well, a child had taken hold of Sky's hand and an old man wrapped his arm around his shoulder. Vondel was incredulous at all of this attention. He did an about face to walk away, just as another person from the crowd was snapping Sky's photo. "Just forget it," he seethed through clenched teeth.

A second after he turned the director heard his assistant's voice calling out after him, "WAIT, J.P. THE COUNCIL OF CLERGY ARE MEETING ON SOUND STAGE 13B. PLEASE TRY AND MAKE IT. THEY DON'T LIKE THE WAY THIS PICTURE'S GOING. THEY SAY IT'S A BIG DEPARTURE FROM THE SCRIPT SUBMITTED BY THE WRITER, JOHNNY DIVINE. DIVINE'S THREATENING TO SUE WUNDER HAUS PICTURES."

Vondel stopped dead in his tracks, spun around and screamed down the block at Sky, "SO LET HIM SUE. WHO CARES IF HE SUES? I'VE NEVER EVEN HEARD OF JOHNNY DIVINE! I MEAN WHO THE HELL IS HE?"

"Don't say that about Johnny," Sky admonished him. "It's blasphemy."

"BLASPHEMY?" Vondel echoed. "DON'T YOU HAVE A NERVE? LISTEN, I DON'T CARE ABOUT ANY OF THIS. I'M WALKING AWAY FROM ALL OF IT."

"You can't do that, *Vondel baby*," Sky warned him.

Vondel was put off by his assistant's egregious address. Everyone at *Wunder Haus Pictures* always respectfully referred to him as J.P. "Don't tell me what I can and cannot do," the director angrily retorted. "And when you address me, address me respectfully."

Sky approached Vondel with the crowd in tow. They were screaming threateningly at the director and expletives lashed from their tongues. Though it was obvious Sky enjoyed their instigation, he quieted the crowd. "WAIT A MINUTE," he ordered with a glib smile. "QUIET, PLEASE!"

Their obedience to Sky's command only furthered Vondel's exasperation. But rather than walk away again, he decided to face his assistant and settle the matter once and for all. Before Sky could speak another word Vondel told him, "You have repeatedly tried to usurp the authority entrusted to me from the executives of this motion picture company in an attempt to undermine me in their eyes. Well, I'll stand for it no more!"

"This is bigger than you and me, *Vondel baby*," Sky said evenly.

"IT'S J.P. TO YOU!" Vondel corrected him.

"This is bigger than you and me, J.P.," Sky replied, correcting himself. "You've got to meet with the clergy because the fate of this picture depends on it—and the fate of *Wunder Haus* depends on the fate of this picture."

"What are you talking about?" Vondel demanded to know.

"They're expecting you to name Toynbee as the new Cardinal," Sky explained.

"I don't care about the Cardinal," Vondel dismissed. "What were you saying about the fate of *Wunder Haus?*" he asked impatiently. "How does it depend on the picture?"

"The fate of the world as we know it depends on this picture, J.P.," Sky answered cryptically.

Vondel could barely control his temper. "WHAT ARE YOU TALKING ABOUT, YOU IDIOT? THE FATE OF THE WORLD! WHAT DRIVEL!"

The old man standing beside Sky objected to Vondel's condescension, "Don't talk to my friend like that! I'll punch you right in the mouth!"

"YEAH, RIGHT IN THE MOUTH!" screamed the little boy holding Sky's hand. The blonde woman hugging Sky's waist gave Vondel a dirty look.

Vondel shook his head, disapprovingly. "Morons," he said to himself.

Sky continued to plead with the director. "You've just got to meet with the Council of Clergy. J.P. You've got to meet Cardinal Spengler's replacement. His fall precipitated the chaos that is now raging all around us . . . " The demonstrators had grown violent once again. Vondel heard windows breaking across the avenue.

"It's only going to get worse," Sky told him.

"I don't care," said Vondel. "I'm not meeting with anyone. Who are you, telling me who I should meet? You don't give the orders around here, I do."

"You've got to meet with the clergy and the new Cardinal, Toynbee," Sky insisted. "If you don't introduce him in the picture, you threaten us all with total apocalypse. Please, for the love of God, just walk through this door." Sky was pointing to a glass door that suddenly appeared before the two men. It was an entrance to an art deco building. Above the entrance was the address 1313 Lucky Lane. A small plaque to the right of the door, Vondel noticed, was in tribute to *Wunder Haus Pictures*. Despite that, the director did not recognize the building.

"Please," Sky continued, "It's on the 13th floor, 13B. They're expecting you. Go in and take the elevator. If you want, I'll accompany you."

"You're not accompanying me anywhere," Vondel informed him. The director sighed disgustedly and then firmly stated, "You are fired, Sky! Do you hear me? *You are fired!*"

The blonde woman cuddling up to Sky gasped and put her hand to her mouth. She was fixed in horror, staring hard at Vondel. The old man beside Sky released a deluge of swear words at Vondel, while the little boy, still holding Sky's hand, shook the clenched fist of his free hand at the director. "You, you, you . . . " was all that he managed to say. By contrast, Sky reacted calmly to the news. He gave Vondel a glib smile and snickered quietly to himself.

Vondel was not detracted by what he perceived as his assistant's feigned disregard. He leaned into him un-abated, "How dare you tell me who to meet with. How dare you hire people without checking with me first. How dare you go over my head with Barnes. You've got a lot of nerve, Sky! A LOT OF NERVE! I've been in this business for nearly twenty years and I've made a name for myself. You? You're nobody. And guess what? You're going to remain a nobody."

"HIT HIM, SKY!" the old man screamed.

Sky ignored the call for retribution. He addressed Vondel as if he had not heard the director's backlash or his scathing refusal to meet with the clergy and the new Cardinal. With the utmost composure he pointed at the entrance to the art deco building and said, "You wouldn't need a camera crew, J.P. Just go up there and let them see that you recognize the new Cardinal. It's a gesture more than anything else." Sky motioned to the throng gathered around him. "I'm asking you to help me to make this a better, safer world for all of us."

On that note the entire crowd applauded with an enthusiasm that Vondel had rarely seen in his lifetime. He scratched his head and looked at the entrance to the art deco building.

Sky noticed this and reminded him, "13B. I'll go with you, if you want."

Vondel couldn't begin to guess the rationale behind Sky's persistence. The only apparent motive was a power play. Therefore, succumbing to any of Sky's suggestions could set a dangerous precedent. The director weighed his choice responses carefully, before ultimately raising the middle finger of his left hand, as an indication of sentiment.

Sky was aghast by Vondel's gesture. "That is base," he rebuked. "You are insulting!"

"And you are unemployed," the director replied with a satisfied smile. He turned to walk away.

"WAIT!" Sky implored. "WHAT ABOUT THE PICTURE?"

"YOU ARE FIRED!" Vondel screamed back at him. The words echoed off the buildings. The concrete and steel created an immense man-made valley for Vondel to disappear into as Sky looked on.

"YOU CAN'T FIRE ME, J.P.," Sky yelled after him. "YOU CAN'T FIRE ME AND YOU CAN'T WALK AWAY FROM YOUR RESPONSIBILITIES TO THIS PICTURE. THE COUNCIL OF CLERGY HAVE EXPECTATIONS OF YOU, DIVINE HAS EXPECTATIONS OF YOU, BARNES HAS EXPECTATIONS OF YOU AND I HAVE EXPECTATIONS OF YOU! THE WHOLE WORLD

HAS EXPECTATIONS OF YOU! YOU CAN'T LET US DOWN!"

Vondel continued to disappear into the urban landscape; oblivious to all calls for responsibility.

Sky knew he would have to say something dramatic to bring the director back into the fold. "J.P., IF YOU DON'T COME BACK HERE AND DO AS I SAY RIGHT NOW, YOU'LL NEVER MAKE IT AROUND THAT NEXT CORNER ALIVE."

Vondel heard that threat. He also heard circus calliope music emanating from around the corner. It was enough to give him pause and in so doing, he could not help but hear the next shocking threat that Sky directed at him:

"YOU THINK YOU CAN WALK AWAY, BECAUSE THIS IS A DREAM? YOU CAN'T BE HARMED IF YOU'RE DREAMING, RIGHT? BUT IN YOUR SHORT SIGHTED ARROGANCE DID YOU EVER ASK YOURSELF, 'WHAT IF SOMEONE ELSE IS DOING THE DREAMING?' WHAT BURDENS COULD I NOT BRING TO BEAR ON YOU IF THIS WERE MY DREAM, J.P. VONDEL? ANYTHING WOULD BE POSSIBLE THEN, IF THIS WERE MY DREAM! *ANYTHING!*"

The circus calliope music was getting louder with each forward step. Vondel knew that soon the clown van would turn the corner and that he could easily meet his end at the wrong end of a flamethrower. He reached for the six-shooter holstered to his side, but to his great disappointment found it was not there. The director reevaluated his options. Maybe it might be worth while, after all, to meet the new Cardinal, as Sky had proposed. The clown van finally turned the corner as Vondel weighed the decision. He saw one of the Bozos lean his head out the passenger side window. The hideous thing wore a broad red smile, cakes of white makeup and an unruly mane of orange hair protruding from the sides of his scalp. A black, elongated weapon was hanging half-way out the window, clumsily supported in the clown's arms and pointed straight at the director. It was only at the last moment that Vondel realized it was not a flame-thrower as anticipated, but rather a bazooka.

Someone screamed, "DEATH TO TYRANTS!" just before the dream ended with a bang.

The Poet's
Voice

I awoke from a dream I could not remember. I had a faint sense of lingering fear, nevertheless. I could not be sure if this dread was a residual of the dream, or a consequence of realizing I had awakened into a nightmare. My entire body was wracked by pain and discomfort, from spending the night on a bed of iron. I was dying of thirst and would have given anything at that moment for a glass of water to relieve my cracked, deprived lips and my parched palate. My tongue felt like a piece of rolled sandpaper in my mouth. To add further misery, my eyes were sealed shut by a thick, gluey crust. It took several minutes of digging with my fingers to remove all trace of this unkind substance from my lids. Despite my agony, I attempted to stand up but was dismayed to realize that task physically impossible, since I am over six feet tall and my cage only five feet high. From my limited, crouched position, I fantasized an escape, but the bars were not going to move. I was furious as I considered my compromised position, but calmed myself by lying flat on the floor. Since the cage was longer in length than in height, this was the most accommodating position for me. My cell was situated in what appeared to be a photographer's studio. I concluded this because three of the surrounding walls were completely covered with large group portraits. I also realized the portraits had all been taken in the room where I was being held. The background of each portrait prominently featured a large mirror, identical to the one hanging on the fourth wall of this room.

One portrait drew my attention immediately, because it featured my wife embracing two children that I didn't recognize, a boy and girl. Upon closer inspection, I noticed the portrait also featured members of my family, including my mother and father and my brother and sister. I was absent, which made sense, since I had no recollection of the portrait ever being taken. It was disconcerting to think that the individual responsible for this portrait might also be responsible for my captivity. 'Who would do this to me and why would they do this to me? Why would they involve my family?' I wondered. As I examined the other two large portraits hanging on the opposite walls, I recognized more familiar faces; one portrait featured various friends that I'd made in my lifetime. The other portrait was comprised of business acquaintances I'd made throughout my career. Additionally, in both portraits I noticed a handful of strangers. Circumnavigating the rest of the room with my eyes, I caught my reflection in the large mirror. My face was partially eclipsed by rows of iron bars.

I laughed, as it was an image I never thought I would ever see. It was so funny to me at that moment that I could not stop laughing. I considered the possibility of my emotional breakdown being observed. Could someone be on the other side of the mirror, watching me? I imagined my kidnappers having a laugh at my expense, listening to me laugh, watching me unhinge. Suddenly, I had nothing to laugh about anymore.

I stretched my legs out fully. It was peculiar being in such a relaxed position, considering my excited state. Nevertheless, I was determined to play it calm and cool; to be resolved in my judgment and resigned to my circumstances. I turned my emotions inward, grimacing and huffing in anguish, but playing it cool outwardly. I told myself that whoever had placed me here would be held to account and that for the meanwhile I'd have to endure the fear and insecurity that my captors had managed to instill within me. I wondered aloud what kind of evil-minded person would be inhuman enough to cage a fellow human being? It was a rhetorical question. I did not believe anyone would answer it, even if they did hear me. I had little doubt, however, that sooner or later, I'd come to know my captors. Surely, they would seek to exploit their foul advantage over me in some swinish way. For why else would they have put me in a cage? I told myself I'd have to hang on for the next development of this tragic and pathetic game, when the demands of my captors would be made known to me. Until then I had to feign patience. But after five minutes of staring at the pattern of my plaid pajamas and listening to my stomach grumble, I grew a little irritable myself. "GO TO HELL!" I screamed. "TO HELL WITH YOU, YOU ROTTEN BASTARDS!" It made me feel better to scream, even if there was no reply. If I'd had a reply, it would have made up for the pathetic exhibition I'd given my captors, groveling in my pajamas in a little cell, railing with wrath against unknown forces with clandestine agendas. I was compelled to continue, "WHAT YOU HOPE TO GAIN FROM THIS I DON'T KNOW, BUT IT WON'T BE MUCH!"

Miraculously, I heard an amplified reply, correcting me, "It's what *you* have to gain from this that matters." The voice came from above the cage. I suspected it emanated from a loudspeaker, perhaps one attached to or built into the ceiling. I could not be sure. The top of the cage obscured the source from my view.

"What did you say?" I asked, hoping the voice would resume. There was a dramatic pause, but it did eventually respond:

"It's not what *I* have to gain, it's what *you* have to gain that matters," the voice reiterated.

"What I have to gain?" I laughed. "I didn't think I had anything to gain from sitting in a cage."

"In this case," the voice said back, "you will have much to gain from sitting in a cage."

"Maybe I'll learn patience and how to exchange banter with a faceless kidnapper," I retorted.

"Very funny," the voice returned, laconically. It was cold and monotone, but still reassuring to hear. As long as I had an exchange with the voice, the possibility existed that I might be able to make an appeal to reason. It was my only hope.

"What did you say your name was?" I asked.

"I didn't give you a name, Jack."

"Jack, that's my name," I laughed, looking around at the portraits again. "You probably know everything there is to know about me, right?"

"That's right," the voice confirmed.

The brevity of response angered me. *"That's right,"* I mimicked. "That's all you have to say? You're short on words but big on ideas, is that it?"

"It's affirmation, Jack. You need affirmation in your life right now," the voice explained.

"Affirmation's O.K, but I'd prefer to get the hell out of this cage, if you don't mind."

"All in good time, Jack."

"All in good time," I repeated. "What's that supposed to mean, when you're good and ready?"

"No, when *you're* good and ready," the voice told me.

"When I'm ready?" I questioned. "I'm ready right now."

The voice fell silent. "Hey, are you still there?" I asked.

"Yes, Jack, I'm still here. You don't have to worry. I'll never leave you."

"Oh great!" I said, facetiously. "I can't tell you how comforting it is to know you'll never leave me. I suppose you want to make sure I don't get bored or lonely. It has nothing to do with making sure I can't escape."

The voice fell silent again.

"You know you're a pretty sick individual, locking me up in a cage," I declared. "Is this your idea of fun? What's with this room?" I inquired.

"It's just a room," the voice answered.

"Why all the photos of family and friends?"

There was no reply.

"Look, why don't you tell me what this is about," I asked, "instead of playing mind games? If it's money you're after, I really don't have much. I'm sure that my family could raise something. We all have bank accounts. But I have to tell you, we're not Rockefellers."

"You're missing the point, Jack."

"What, it isn't about money?"

"It is about money, but money is only part of it."

"Well what's the rest of it? Kicks? Are you doing this for kicks, locking me up in a cage? I want to get out of here, just tell me what you want and I'll make sure you get it."

"I don't want anything that you don't want for yourself, Jack. Please try and understand that."

"I don't want to be locked up in a cage, "I answered. "PLEASE TRY AND UNDERSTAND THAT! I mean, look at it from my side." I moved around, changing positions until I found one that was comfortable, resting on my side with head in hand, supported by my elbow.

"You're in that cage for a reason, Jack."

"Oh, I'm sure. Some sick reason of yours, no doubt." I took another long look around the room and became obsessed with the idea that my kidnapper's face might be featured in one of the portraits. I decided to be direct, thinking I had nothing to lose. "Tell me something.

Is there a picture of your face in this room? You don't have to tell me which one it is. It might be fun to guess. Maybe you want to tell me though. Maybe you're proud of what you've done."

"I can assure you, Jack. I am not in these photographs."

"Really?"

"Really."

"Are you the photographer?"

There was no response, so I asked a different question, "What purpose do the portraits serve?"

"I'm very happy to hear you ask, Jack."

For the first time the voice showed emotion. It seemed pleased by my inquiry and that pleased me. I desperately wanted to seek favor with the voice, thinking cooperation to my advantage. "So you like that question, eh?" I asked, sounding proud of myself.

"It's a pertinent question," the voice affirmed. "What purpose do the portraits serve? It's by asking questions like that and answering them for yourself that you increase the likelihood of your release. Believe me, Jack. I very much want to help you get out of that cage."

"YOU DO?" I heard my voice assume an incredulous air.

"Of course, Jack," the voice responded. "I want nothing more than to help you get out of that cage."

I doubted the sincerity of the voice but wanted to be facilitating. "I simply have to ask the right questions and answer them for myself, is that it?"

"Ask the most pertinent questions and answer them honestly," the voice specified.

I was much relieved to hear this, as I now understood the game that we were playing, which gave me a chance of winning. I suddenly remembered something the voice said earlier. When I brought up the subject of money, the voice admitted its relevance, at least in part. I decided to bring this subject back into the conversation and relate it to the people that I saw in the photographs.

"I have more questions," I offered.

"Good," the voice encouraged. "Think out loud, if you want."

"Well, I was wondering about my connection to all of these people," I explained, gesturing around the room. "In some cases the connection has to do with love and friendship, in other instances, it has to do exclusively with money. But at least to some extent, money is an important factor in all instances. Some of these people I don't recognize, so I can't say for sure—"

"You're on the right track, Jack," the voice told me. "Actually, the unknown faces will someday be known to you as well."

I was baffled by the comment. Before I had a chance to respond, the voice lauded my reasoning. "Very good, Jack. I must say, you're certainly doing well."

"Thank you," I said with gratitude. I was beginning to feel hopeful.

"Please, do go on," the voice urged. "Were you thinking about anyone in particular, when you mentioned money and relationships? What about an example?"

"Well," I thought, "When I break it right down, my wife is to a certain extent dependent on my income. She works and has a decent salary, but we wouldn't live as comfortably as we do unless we both worked. And lately, Jill and I have been talking about kids. I love the idea of having kids, but that would really put the squeeze on me. I would be even more dependent on my employer. As it is, I feel as if I've sold my freedom. Do you know what it's like to compromise your freedom?

"You should know," the voice told me. "You're sitting behind bars."

Of course the voice had a point, but I felt like the butt of a joke. What was the purpose of this *strange* exercise, anyway? To make a metaphor of the cage in my life, to demonstrate how hindered I was in my life? It sickened me to think of such things. I was about to rebuke the voice for its comment, when it allayed my concerns, "Don't be paranoid, Jack. I am not making fun of you. I want this to be a cathartic experience and *strange* only in that sense."

It was as if the voice had read my mind and answered my questions. I did not allow such thoughts to preoccupy me, however. I told myself if I wanted to get out, I would have to continue my indulgence of the voice. For this reason, I gave it what it wanted to hear. "I'm not paranoid at all," I said, reassuringly. "I want this to be a cathartic experience myself."

"Great," the voice replied.

"It feels good getting all this off my chest, actually." I confessed.

"Anything else you want to tell me about your wife, Jack?"

I chuckled. "She's an inexhaustible subject. Did I mention that she wants us to buy a house?"

"No, you didn't."

"Until now, we've been renting a one-bedroom apartment," I explained. "'But if we want to start a family', Jill says, 'we need more space.'"

"I imagine she's right about that."

"Yes, I know. You can't raise a family in a one bedroom apartment."

"A house would be more ideal."

"And a car," I added. "The other night Jill said if we have a kid and move out to the suburbs, we'll need a car, as well."

"You'd need a car in the suburbs, I imagine."

"Say whose side are you on, anyway?" I asked, challengingly.

"Sorry, Jack. I'm just trying to help you sort things out."

Feeling a migraine coming on, I grabbed my head. "I'm sorry too. I didn't mean to snap at you. I just have so much on my mind . . . buying a car, a house, having kids . . . .slaving my life away to pay for all these things."

"You work your whole life away so that you can buy these things because you think they're what you want or what you need and all you really need is a smile at the end of the day," the voice replied.

"AMEN TO THAT!" I yelled. "Boy, have you got that right!"

"Happiness is most important," the voice continued. "Happiness and health. You can't buy either."

"Tell me about it. I can't tell you how often I've said the very same thing. My friends, my family, they just don't get it."

"What don't they get, Jack?"

"They're all on the money trail," I said, throwing my hands up in exasperation. "Their big idea of success is tied in with all those material things, houses, cars, et-cetera—having a smile at the end of the day is not as important. Needless to say, they'd never understand my idea of success."

"What's not to understand?" the voice asked me.

"Are you kidding?" I laughed.

"No, tell me what they don't understand," the voice demanded.

"In their world, the only thing to do is work until you die and accumulate as many things as you can along the way. That's their measure of success. That and rais-ing large families of children who will also grow up, work until they die and accumulate as many things as they can along the way. I would lose their respect, if they knew what I really wanted out of life."

"They'd love you for who you are, no?"

"You don't understand," I complained.

"What don't I understand?" the voice asked.

"My family and friends would disparage me, if I abandoned my career to become . . . oh I don't know, say a poet or something."

"A poet?" the voice questioned.

"Yes, a poet," I replied, sounding defensive.

The voice whispered, *"I knew you'd never give up*

your dreams, Jack. Someday your words will mean so very much . . . to everyone." Because the whisper was amplified through a speaker, it sounded more like an ethereal pronouncement.

"Thank you," I said, feigning gratitude. The sound effects had put me off but I tried to conceal it. Fortunately, the voice quickly resumed its familiar monotone:

"You *always* were a poet, Jack."

I smiled thinking of my youth. "Always," I confirmed. "But my thoughts were most free when I was young. Back then, I lived poetically. Why can't I be a poet today? I should be able to do what I want with my life. After all, Jack Hill only gets one life."

"Jack Hill *does* only get one life," the voice agreed.

"And so why can't I do what I want with my life, what I like, what I do best?" I demanded to know. "Why do I have to waste my life at a nine to five job, thinking about things I don't care about?"

"That's a sacrifice that you make, Jack. You have a sense of responsibility."

"Yes, but at what cost?" I asked thinking aloud. "At what cost do I sell my dreams?" I held the bars of the cage. "How did I ever get into finance in the first place? That's what I'd like to know."

"You graduated college and had to earn a living, right?" the voice suggested.

"Yes, but I didn't realize it would get me here, *in this cage,*" I said, grasping the bars tighter.

"Then you know who was responsible, then?" the voice asked. *"It was you. It was your fault."*

I wanted to humor the voice, but didn't honestly believe I was responsible for my predicament. How could I be responsible? I had no recollection of confining myself to the cage. Furthermore, the voice seemed to be an authority on all matters concerning the cage. Wasn't it more reasonable to conclude that the voice was responsible for my predicament? Why would I agree to absolve it of guilt to blame myself? But realizing again that this was a game that I had to play, I offered the voice a culpable nod. "Of course I am to blame . . . for everything."

"You don't sound convinced," the voice contradicted.

Before I had the chance to offer it further reassurance, the voice persisted, "Do you call finance a living, Jack? You can make a living, but is it making a life?"

"Boy, you are the devil's advocate," I answered.

"Do you call it a life, Jack?"

"I want to be a poet. Anything else is a compromise. If I can't be a poet, what does it matter what I do with my life? But I have to have a means to live, don't I?"

"But at the same time . . . " the voice vicariously added.

"But at the same time, I have to have a reason to live," I finished. "ARE YOU SATISFIED, NOW?" I screamed.

"Are *you* satisfied now, Jack?" the voice calmly asked.

"No. I am not satisfied. I love Jill and everything and I want a nice life with her, with kids, a house, a career, etcetera, and I love my friends and my family, but . . . "

"BUT!" the voice boomed.

I shook my head, staring at the faces on the wall. "Look, I don't want to lose any of them. They mean too much to me."

"You could never lose their love," the voice told me.

"I know," I granted, "but their respect for me would be gone. Anyway, what am I supposed to do, quit my job and chase a childish dream? How can I pay my bills with flowery words? I don't want to be a loser!"

"A winner never worries about losing, Jack. Remember that."

I felt tears swelling in my eyes but I held them back. "A *winner*? How am I a winner?"

The voice elaborated, "You're a winner when you're doing what you do best. You're a winner when you're being true to yourself. Make up your mind today, right here and now, that you are a poet. Put finance behind you and worry about being a good poet."

"What about Jill?"

"She loves you. She'll be true to you. Be true to yourself, Jack, and leave that cage."

I held tightly to the bars. "How do I get out?" I implored. "I have to go to the bathroom."

For the first time the voice laughed. It was reassuring and infectious. It made me laugh.

"I could also use some breakfast," I chortled, *"and some coffee."*

"For a poem, Jack," the voice bartered. "Your words will set you free."

Inspired by the thought of leaving the cage, I quieted the storm of my mind and summoned the words from my heart, *". . . I am a bird, but once I was a man . . . Weathering the wares of his storm . . . Now I region wherever I'm fanned . . . Tethered by the force of a strong gale's* norm . . . *In the spectrum of the sun's giving rays . . . Scaling the love of all I've ever loved . . . Riding on the pulse of new days . . . Renewed, gratefully saved . . . Over the rooftops and spires I inspire . . . Carried by bold dreams that wake me . . . To all that warm a heart's hearth to fire . . . In the bliss of the blessed sky blue sea . . . With an abandon that lords eternal . . . I savor the tranquil peace that time stays . . . As I answer horizon's call . . . Living life, as it plays."*

"Living life, as it plays . . . very nice, Jack," I heard the voice say. "Now, you know freedom!"

Indeed, the cage was gone. It was like I had blinked it away. I stood and looked up at the ceiling, searching for a sign of amplification, but there was none. The origin of the voice was still a mystery. "You are a poet," I heard it say, "a poet that should never be compromised. What does money matter when you own the sky, Jack?"

"You're right," I said, thinking about my poem. "I do own the sky." I took one last look at all of the portraits before walking toward the door.

"It's unlocked," the voice told me.

As I turned the doorknob I had the urge to confess, "I know who you are, now."

"You know who *you* are, now," the voice told me.

How true. How true.

Wrong Number

As a freelance writer for the *Examiner Weekly*, Bud spent much of his time hunched over a home computer whimsically typing the most fantastic of tales. Early on the tabloid recognized the fecund nature of Bud's imagination and gave him license to write about whatever tickled his funny bone. Lately, Bud was on a roll about UFO and Elvis Presley sightings (most occurred within a hundred mile radius of each other). On a large map pinned to the wall of his home office, Bud indicated UFO sightings with red tacks and Elvis sightings with blue tacks. Since several of the Elvis sightings had been reported at roughly the same time in different regions of the country, Bud concluded Elvis had been cloned. He also concluded the Elvis clones were being deposited in various towns and cities across the USA by space aliens. The main purpose for this operation was to gather information on the culture, leading to an eventual takeover of the country.

On one particular morning, Bud was in deep thought over his UFO/Elvis story as he lingered over breakfast.

He stabbed a large piece of French toast with his fork and slid it across the plate, soaking it in a puddle of maple syrup. Bud envisioned aliens with big heads and frail bodies sporting blue suede shoes, as he swallowed the toast with a gulp of orange juice. He sliced another piece and moved it across the plate with his fork. A silly song was on his silly mind, "Blue, blue, blue suede shoes, baby . . . A blue, blue, blue suede shoes . . . " Bud giggled and gulped down the rest of the O.J. in his glass. As he forked the last piece of toast, Bud imagined the aliens pumping the Elvis clones full of amphetamines, to motivate them on their missions. "No, no, no," he said dismissively, "that's too much, even for me." He swallowed the last piece of toast and stood up from the table. "Blue, blue, blue suede shoes . . . Blue, blue, blue suede shoes." Bud poured some coffee as he sang the song and broke into a fit of laughter as he added milk and sugar to his cup. He continued laughing as he carried the coffee down the hall to his office, trying not to spill the cup.

The sun was shining through the window illuminating the room in a way that made Bud feel alive. He cleared his desk and took a seat, sipping his French Roast coffee. The creative thoughts he'd had over breakfast, he now organized into a dramatic flight of fancy. He asked himself what could the government do to protect its citizens from clones of Elvis? It was a difficult question, but it demanded an answer. After a while Bud came up with one, "They could distract the clones with clones of Ann-Margret! Perhaps the government could clone Ann-Margret!" Bud took another sip of his French Roast and envisioned an

Elvis clone with a guitar trying to take over Las Vegas. He imagined the entire city panic stricken and frenzied, screaming hysterically. Suddenly an Ann-Margret clone comes on the scene and dances circles around the Elvis clone. The eyes of the Elvis clone are ineluctably drawn to the hips of the Ann-Margret clone. After a few seconds he becomes cross-eyed and loses his balance, the rhythm of his guitar playing is off and he forgets the words to his song. A minute later, the clone finds that he can barely stand. In a last gasp of, "I'm All Shook Up," Elvis collapses in a whirlwind of scarves and rhinestones.

Thunderous applause reverberates across the Nevada desert as Ann-Margret graciously takes her bow to the appreciative masses. Amid a constant barrage of long-stemmed roses, she humbly smiles. The gleam in her eyes sparkles across the night, consuming the entire scene in a haze of green light. Bud sees the caption, *Viva Las Vegas and Viva the United States of America!* rising high over the skyline of hotels and casinos.

It was at this point that the phone rang. Bud thought to let the machine pick up but remembered that his boss, Stan, the Editor of the *Examiner*, never left him messages. Since the last thing Bud wanted was to hear the phone ring all day, he left his desk and walked to the adjacent bedroom to get the cordless. He answered the phone with dreaded anticipation, "Yes?"

"Hello," replied a woman's voice. "Is Mara there?"

"MARA?" Bud repeated angrily. "Why do you keep calling?" He walked over to the window for a view of the park. "I told you yesterday, there's no Mara here!"

The caller became indignant. "This is the first time I've called, sir."

"BOLOGNA!" Bud protested. "I spoke with you yesterday . . . and the day before that . . . and the day before that!"

"I'm just trying to reach my friend," the caller explained.

"Well, she must have changed her number," Bud replied, peevishly.

The caller was not dissuaded. "I find it hard to believe that Mara would change her number without telling me about it first."

Bud was infuriated by her insinuation. "I'm trying to get some work done, lady! I don't have time for this. There is no one named Mara here. Don't call back!" On that note, he disconnected the line.

"I'm going to have to change the number again," he said, throwing the phone down on the bed. "Now, that's another fifty dollars!"

Bud gazed out the window reflecting on the matter. He focused on a small park area with benches near the planetarium and the museum. An intriguing looking woman with red hair suddenly appeared in the frame. Bud watched as she sat down on one of the benches. What made her so intriguing was her choice of clothing. She was dressed completely in black, from her neckline down to her shoes. The long garment that she wore appeared Victorian or Amish and was in morbid contrast to the beautiful spring day. 'What, is she going to a wake?' Bud guessed.

Just then the phone rang again.

"GOD DAMN IT!" Bud hollered. "I can't think in here." He took another look at the redhead and thought to go downstairs. "I bet I could think better if I were outside," he said, grabbing a pen and pad. "If I change the phone number that means I have to notify everybody in the address book again," he complained to himself, looking for the apartment keys. "I can't imagine going through all that again," Bud said, shaking his head. "Everyone is going to think I'm nuts!"

When Bud found the keys, he locked up the apartment and took the elevator down to the lobby. On his way out the door, he acknowledged the doorman with a wave of his hand. "Hey Gus. Good to see you."

"Oh Mr. Damon," the doorman called, trying to solicit Bud's attention. "I have to thank you for that book you lent me. It really helped me a lot. " He had the book in hand and attempted to return it to the lender.

Bud disinterestedly waved him off. "Keep it. Keep it."

"Thanks, Mr. Damon."

"I'll talk to you later, alright. I'm in a rush now," Bud explained. He had the redhead on his mind and was trying to politely slip away.

"Oh I understand," Gus said, appreciatively shaking his head up and down. "No problem, Mr. D." He then proceeded to block the doorway with his huge frame. Gus looked admiringly at the book cover in his hands and giggled like a preschooler. "I have to be honest with you Mr. D., when you first mentioned this book to me . . . " He laughed again. "Well, I was skeptical. I said to myself, this meditation stuff might work for Mr. Damon but not for a guy like me. You see I don't really go for all that stuff. I'm not like that. I mean, I've seen those guys in their white dresses hanging out in St. Marks Place. You know the guys with the shaved heads. What do they call them guys again?"

Bud was impatient and barely listening. "I don't know, Gus. What are you talking about now, the Hare Krishna people?"

The doorman's eyes lit up. "That's it—the Hairy Krishna people. You know, Mr. D., I don't really go for that stuff . . . ordinarily. It's too way out for me."

Bud became incensed listening to the doorman's drivel. "That's a book on Buddhist meditation." He chuckled with an irascible edge. "It's not the Bhagavad-Gita. It has nothing to do with Krishna."

"Oh I know. I know," Gus quickly placated. He attempted to ameliorate his statements. "I was just using Krishna as an example."

Bud shook his head, perplexed. "As an example of what? Oh, it doesn't matter. I've got to go."

The doorman smiled but did not budge. "Please Mr. Damon, I'm trying to tell you how you helped me out."

Bud sighed and looked at his watch. "I'll give you one minute Gus. I have an appointment you see and . . . "

"O.K. O.K. This is the thing, Mr. Damon. Up until the time I read this book I was confused and lost in my way. I never really knew happiness. I was suffering even when I wasn't really cogzignant of it."

"Cognizant," Bud corrected.

"Right, even when I wasn't *cogzignant*," Gus continued. "You know I read that whole Eight Fold Path thing in the first chapter and that really blew me away. That bit about how all life is suffering!"

"I'm sorry, Gus, but I really do have to leave." Bud attempted to step around the doorman.

Gus obligingly allowed him to pass. "O.K., Mr. Damon. I'm sorry for holding you up. Thanks for recommending this to me for my anger management. Ever since I beat up that bastard on the subway and I got arrested, management here has been on my back about controlling my temper. But hey, now with this—I have the key!" He shook the book at Bud and suddenly became excited. "Hey, I got a great idea! Maybe we can meditate together, sometime! What do you think of that, Mr. Damon?"

"I don't meditate anymore, Gus. That's why I gave you the book." Bud waited for a response. He had a response of his own all ready to go.

"But you said it helped your creativity," the doorman reminded him.

Bud shrugged his shoulders. "I masturbate now, instead."

On that note, Gus walked away abruptly and Bud exited the lobby.

As he walked toward the park, Bud remembered that he was supposed to e-mail Stan the finished Elvis/UFO story in the morning, which didn't give him much time. He was distracted from that thought by the sight of the redhead sitting on the park bench. Coincidentally, she too had a pen and pad in hand; busily writing away on the wings of an inspired thought. Bud sat down on the park bench, about two feet from the redhead. He wished to sit even closer, but did not want to make his intensions transparent to the lady. Bud yawned loudly hoping to draw her attention. When this did not have the desired effect, he stretched out his arms ostentatiously and yawned again. The lady barely noticed. She was too consumed in her writing. Bud gazed at his muse, admiring her beautiful hair. It fell from her head in waves, resting on her shoulders and down her back. It was not as red as Bud initially thought. It looked more strawberry blonde now. The lady was whispering something to herself as she wrote on her pad. Bud reluctantly pulled his eyes from her and nervously cleared his throat. Suddenly, the lady stopped writing and stared over at him.

"Oh, I'm sorry," she apologized. "You must think I'm *crazy* talking to myself."

"Not at all," Bud bashfully answered. He was overjoyed she had broken the ice. Bud struggled to find something clever to say in response but was dazzled by her captivating smile and gorgeous green eyes. "I often talk to myself," he laughed.

The lady laughed herself. "I guess I was just getting carried away with one of the characters in my story . . . I'm a writer."

"Oh I see," Bud acknowledged, nodding his head politely. "I understand completely, because . . ."

"The character in my story is also a writer," the lady continued, "I was writing a scene in which he's sitting on a park bench, writing. The funny thing is he's talking out loud to himself, getting carried away with a character from one of his stories."

"What a trip," Bud said, admiringly. "That's very cool."

"You think so?" the lady asked, surprised.

"I'm a writer too," Bud boasted. He held up his pad excitedly. "You see? I came out here to do a little writing myself."

The lady smiled. "Well, since you're a writer you understand how easy it is to lose yourself in one of your stories."

"Of course, I understand," Bud empathized. "As a matter of fact, I came out here yesterday . . ." Bud couldn't finish his thought. He was suddenly dumbstruck by the woman's striking resemblance to Ann-Margret. From the moment he'd first seen her face, Bud recognized something familiar about it, but what that something was had been elusive to him, until now.

"Is something wrong?" the woman asked him.

"Oh no, I'm sorry to stare. It's just that you look exactly like . . . " Bud didn't finish his sentence. He did not need to. He could see by the woman's smile and the nod of her head that she knew what he was thinking.

"Everyone says that I look like her," the woman admitted. "I get that all the time."

Bud was dumbstruck again, remembering how Ann-Margret had figured into his story. "I can't get over it," he finally managed to say. I'm sorry but if I only told you the irony of meeting someone that looks like Ann-

Margret. I was only just thinking of Ann-Margret like ten minutes ago."

"Really?" the woman asked. "Isn't that a strange co-incidence?" she added.

Bud's eyes widened. "YES! It is a strange coincidence!" he emphasized.

The woman asked him, "Have you ever heard of Jung's theory of synchronicity?"

Bud's eyes bugged out again. "Heard about it? *My dear*, I'm living it!"

"Well aren't you sweet, calling me *dear*," The woman declared. She offered her hand to Bud and introduced herself. "My name is Mariana."

"Pleased to meet you, Mariana," Bud replied with affected poise. He took her hand and introduced himself. "I'm Bud."

"Bud," the woman echoed.

The name sounded more mellifluous when she said it. Bud thought of a flower blooming.

"Bud," she said again, pronouncing it with care. "Why that's such a nice name. It's a real man's name, isn't it?"

"Oh I don't know," Bud replied. "That's nice of you to say." He humbly shrugged his shoulders, seemingly unaffected by her compliment. But inwardly, Bud was thrilled. As he stared at Mariana's red lips he thought of rose petals.

Mariana was charmed by Bud's longing stare, but also abashed. "Tell me about your writing, Bud. I bet you're a biographer," she guessed. Her words had not broken the spell, so she added some more. "And I bet I know who you're writing about," she teased.

Bud smiled foolishly, like a lovesick schoolboy. "Well, you're half right. Only I have to tell you, I'm not a biographer. You see, I write for the *Examiner*."

"Oh," Mariana snickered. She tried to hide the laugh with her delicate, well-manicured hand. "I see why you hesitated telling me."

"I'm not embarrassed at all," Bud said unapologetically. "It's how I earn my living. I have a great time writing those stories. How many people can honestly say that they enjoy what they do? Not too many. Also, I get to work from home, an added bonus."

Mariana nodded. "Well, good for you," she said.

"I love my work," Bud told her. "It makes me happy. I'm not the only one. People tell me all the time that they love my stories. It's all bologna, but I'm not hurting anyone."

"You're sure about that?" Mariana asked with a wry smile.

"I'm positive, Ann." Bud corrected himself, "*Mariana*. I'm sorry. I meant Mariana."

Mariana chuckled. "That's all right. Don't worry about it," she reassured him, doodling on her pad. "Well, so long as no one gets hurt by your tall tales, Bud, there'll never be anything to regret." She looked up at him to gauge his reaction.

"I don't worry about it," Bud dismissed. He conveniently changed the subject. "So anyway, what do you write about?"

"Oh . . . *stuff*," Mariana replied, evasively. "Lots of . . . ." She searched herself for the right word.

"*Stuff?*" Bud helped out.

They shared a laugh, as children on the playground might after an imaginative game. They each stared longingly into the other's eyes and saw themselves reflected. They each said the things they thought the other might like to hear or would be intrigued to hear and grew closer with their exchange of words for ideas. It wasn't long before Bud worked up the nerve to ask Mariana on a date and to his surprise the lovely lady appeared no less anxious than he to plan a meeting for some not too distant evening when they could again enjoy each other's company. Bud was simply delighted. After the two exchanged their numbers and promised to get in touch, Bud went back up to his apartment so that he could finally write an ending to his story. As planned, Ann-Margret featured prominently in that story's ending and whenever Bud wrote of Ann he would naturally think of Mariana and how very much she resembled the famous entertainer. This association only helped to create a kind of obsession with Mariana in Bud's mind. He simply couldn't stop thinking about her. All night long he had dreams that played out like Hollywood musicals from the 1960's. In some instances, Mariana was singing and dancing as Ann-Margret. In other instances, Ann-Margret was singing and dancing as Mariana. In the very last dream sequence Elvis showed up with a guitar and the two of them did a duet of "You're the Devil in Disguise." Immediately following that number the credits rolled and the two strolled off the stage and went to a clambake. Bud woke up in a cold sweat fearing that Elvis had left the stage, the building, the movie and the dream with Mariana and not Ann-Margret. He imagined calling Mariana's number at that ungodly hour (4:15 a.m.) and hearing Elvis' voice! After a few minutes, he finally managed to calm down and reassured himself that it had all been a nightmare. Shortly thereafter, he fell back to sleep.

The next day Bud e-mailed his story to the *Examiner*. It was entitled, *US Under Attack by Uranus*. It was subtitled, *How Ann-Margret Will Save Us From Elvis!* Bud had a good laugh and suddenly wanted to share it with Mariana. He left his desk to find the little piece of paper she'd written her phone number on. The last thing he wanted was to accidentally throw it out or lose it. He recalled leaving it on the night table by the bedside just before he'd undressed the night before. Bud found the scrap of paper beside his wallet and keys. He read aloud the name written in blue ink, Mariana Webcott. "Mariana Webcott," he repeated, this time carefully pronouncing each syllable. "What an interesting name," he said to himself, thoughtfully. He said it again and again, like it was a mantra. The spell was broken when Bud looked down at the scrap of paper and read Mariana's phone number, 212-548-9208. Bud couldn't believe his eyes. That was his old number, the one he'd just changed because of the annoyance calls that had plagued his line and his life for days. He rubbed his eyes and looked at the number again, 212-548-9208. No doubt about it, it was definitely his old number.

"How could that be?" Bud wondered. What were the odds he'd meet a woman in a park and that she would have his old phone number? It seemed to Bud that those odds were incredible, too incredible to be possible.

Bud scratched his head and asked himself, "Could it be a joke?" He reconsidered, "How could it be a joke? After all, you only just met the woman. She couldn't know your old phone number."

He thought about it from a different angle. "Could someone have put her up to it, one of your old friends perhaps? She was conveniently parked right outside your building." He dismissed that possibility. "Bud, you don't know anyone sick enough to pull off a joke like that. Talk about crazy. It's too contrived!"

No matter how he reasoned it, the event transcended the realm of coincidence. He was getting a headache just thinking about it. When the phone rang he quickly picked it up, hoping it was Mariana.

"Hello?"

"Yes. Hello sir," a man's voice drawled.

Bud was disappointed. "Who is this?" he asked impatiently.

"I was hoping you could help me, sir," the voice on the other end of the line explained. "I'm trying to reach a woman who goes by the name of . . . *Mara?*" The caller said the name with a lack of confidence, as if such a name was new to him and he was unsure that he had it correct.

Bud sighed heavily. "Are you kidding me?" he asked, talking more to himself than the caller.

"No I'm not kidding. That's the name I have on this piece of paper, Mara," the caller answered.

Bud laughed deprecatingly. "I hate to be the bearer of

bad news," he said evenly, concentrating to affect a degree of equanimity, "but you have the wrong number, Charlie."

"The wrong number?" the caller repeated. He then asked, "Is this 212-432-1071?"

"Yes, it is," Bud acknowledged, "but there is no one here by that name." He drew a deep breath and decided to calmly explain the situation to the hapless caller, hoping that if for once he did not lose his temper it might give him the chance to reduce the misdirected calls by one. "You see, I only just received this phone number. I'm assuming that this Mara person changed her number around the same time that I changed mine."

"Well, I'm sorry to bother you, sir," the caller told Bud. "I didn't mean to . . . "

"No bother," Bud insisted. "No bother at all," he lied further. He laughed like a man at his wit's end. "It's no bother," he continued, ". . . so long as you *remember* NOT to call here again, so long as you remember that there is no one named Mara at 212-548 . . . I mean, 212-432-1071. O.K.?"

"O.K. But may I ask one more question, sir?" the caller queried.

"You may!" Bud replied, waxing short.

The caller hesitated, but then boldly posed his question, "Sir, do you, by any chance, know how I can get a hold of Mara? Are you a friend of hers?"

Bud gritted his teeth, but answered calmly, "*Sir*, haven't you heard one word that I just said?"

There was silence on the other end of the line. Bud clearly heard an Elvis Presley song playing low in the background. He could not recall the name of the song but it was on the tip of his tongue. The song was the only reason he did not disconnect the line.

"Are you still there?" the caller's voice asked.

"Yes, I'm still here," Bud answered, in a saccharine tone.

The caller chuckled like a good-natured fool. "I'm sorry, sir, I didn't hear what you said earlier because I dropped the phone. I was asking if you knew Mara, or perhaps knew how I could get a hold of her."

Bud did not answer the question immediately. He was listening to the lyrics of the Elvis song in the background. It was *Don't Be Cruel*. Don't be cruel, to a heart that's true, bla bla,bla. "No I don't know Mara," he finally responded. His voice was deliberately dulled, in a further attempt to suppress his anger. "I believe I mentioned earlier that I only just received this number," Bud sniggered, stifling the madness swelling in his breast.

"Alright, sir," the caller drawled, "If you don't know Mara, you don't know Mara. I didn't mean to bother you any. Have a good day, sir."

Bud was amazed that the caller finally understood. "Huh? Oh right. You too," he said. When he heard the line go dead he shut the phone off and tossed it aside.

Bud was trying to recollect the name of the second Elvis song he heard playing in the background just before the conversation ended. Was it, *"A Fool Such As I?"* he asked, testing his memory. He quickly dismissed the question, recalling his phone problems. "I swear to God, if I get just one more call for Mara I'm going to call the phone company. I don't care if I do have to pay another fifty dollars."

He examined the scrap of paper still in his hands and shook his head disbelievingly, then picked up the cordless again. "Let's see if she's home," he said to himself, dialing the phone number that he knew by heart. "I'll see if she's busy tonight. I wonder if she likes Indian? I'll take her to that new place on 6th Street," he said, thinking out loud. The line began to ring. Bud looked at the scrap of paper in his hand one last time before putting it down again on the night table. He reminded himself, "I'll have to find a tactful way of bringing up the whole phone number thing. I'd like to get to the bottom of that—"

After five rings a man answered the phone. Bud was taken aback. A man's voice was not what he expected to hear. Nevertheless, he greeted the person in a convivial manner and inquired, "Is Mariana there?"

"Mariana?" the man repeated. "There's no Mariana here."

"Oh I must have misdialed. I'm sorry," Bud apologized. He abruptly disconnected the line and redialed. As the line began to ring again, Bud checked the number on the scrap of paper Mariana had given him. Beyond a doubt he had dialed correctly. A moment later, Bud heard the same man's voice answer the telephone.

"Hello?"

"Hello," Bud responded. He wondered if this man could possibly be Mariana's father or brother. "Is Mariana Webcott there?" he asked.

"No you have the wrong number," the man replied, irritably. "Didn't you just call here?"

Bud ignored the question and asked his own, "Have I reached 212-548-9208?"

"Yes," the man confirmed, "that's the number. But there's no Mariana here."

Bud stared down at the number written in blue ink on the scrap of paper. "Are you sure you don't know a Mariana Webcott?" he questioned.

"Quite positive!" the man answered, angrily. "You'd better check the number you're dialing."

A second later the line was disconnected. Bud rehashed the conversation in his head. Whether the man did or didn't know Mariana was no longer an issue for him. What was an issue was the man's voice. It raised more questions than the coincidence of phone numbers, because in every respect the voice resembled Bud's own.

He collapsed on the bed and stared at the ceiling. For the first time in Bud's life, he questioned the self-destructive capability of his imagination. Until he'd heard that voice on the telephone, Bud believed his imagination to be a source of pride. It had brought him good fortune and happiness. But all of that changed in a single phone call. Now, Bud feared his imagination. Because what he heard on the phone betrayed an irrational mind. He debated calling back. He told himself if he dialed his old phone number again he might recognize some aspect of the man's voice that was disparate from his own. On the other hand, calling back might only reinforce his conviction that he had indeed heard his own voice on the other end of the line. The prospect of calling the number back frightened Bud for this very reason. There was no doubt in Bud's mind he would have to be insane to hear his own voice again. As he sat up and found the phone, Bud told himself he had no choice but to call. He dialed the number again, resigned to the outcome.

After the third ring, Bud heard the same man's voice answer the phone, "Hello?"

"Hello," Bud replied. "Have I reached 212-548-9208?"

"Yes," the voice answered, impatiently. "Who is this?"

Bud was afraid to answer. "Well, I'm . . . " He knew that he had to say something but the only thing he could think to say was, "I'm looking for Mariana. Is she there?"

"Mariana?" the voice repeated. "Are you calling here *AGAIN?"*

Bud hesitated, "I uh . . . "

The voice cut him off, "Look, whoever you are stop calling here. There's no Mariana here. Do you understand me? STOP CALLING!"

After the man shouted into the receiver, he disconnected the line.

Bud sat at the end of the bed thinking. He was not confident the man's voice was identical to his own. Their exchange had been too brief. Bud realized he would have to call back and keep the man on the phone at least for a few minutes, in order to satisfactorily assess the voice as having or not having a quality like his own. The question was what could he say to keep the man talking on the phone for a few minutes?

Bud had an idea. He realized that because the man had his old phone number, it was a new phone number for him. It might be possible to then claim he was calling on behalf of the phone company on some matter relating to the man's number. After recognizing this pretext as his best bet, Bud dialed the number for the fourth time that day.

On the fourth ring, the party in question irritably answered the phone, "HELLO?"

Bud fell into character quickly, "Hello. Sorry to bother you. I'm calling on behalf of the phone company, in regards to your new number."

"My new number?" the man questioned, suspiciously.

"Yes, you received this phone number recently, didn't you?" Bud asked.

"No," the man responded, lowering his guard slightly. The hostility in his voice was replaced with an air of mild amusement. "No this is not a new number," he laughed. "I've had this number for years, ever since I moved to New York. That was oh . . . about ten years ago."

Bud gasped. Something about the man's laugh reminded him of his own. If that was not enough to confirm his nightmare suspicion that he was talking with himself, the man's claim was. Indeed, Bud used this same phone number for about ten years, from the time he moved to New York until recently, when he had it changed.

"Are you still there?" the voice asked. *"Hello?"*

Bud gathered himself, "Um, yes, hello. Excuse me, but I have reached 212-548-9208, haven't I?"

"Yes, you have the right number, but your information about its history is incorrect. Perhaps, you meant to call a different number?"

"Yes, that must be it," Bud agreed. He was too numb to say much else. "I'm very sorry to have disturbed you."

"Yeah. Whatever," the man replied, irritably.

When Bud heard a dial tone, he regretted not confirming the man's name. He knew that he needed that name for closure. Reluctantly, he dialed again. After five rings he heard an answering machine kick in, *"Hello, you've reached Bud Damon. I'm not in right now but if you leave a message I'll be sure to call you back as soon as possible. Thank you."*

Bud hung up the phone and sat on the end of the bed, thinking. He told himself that if he was not insane, the only rational explanation was that somebody had stolen his identity. Realizing that many of his freelance contacts were still without his new phone number, Bud grew paranoid. He imagined them dialing his old phone number and consequently hearing the specious message. They would then naturally assume that they'd reached his answering machine and leave a message. If this happened, the impersonator could then call these contacts back and carry on the ruse further; potentially stealing Bud's work out from under his nose. Hypothetically, the thief might even have the resources available to usurp his personal life as well. This kind of appropriation had unlimited potential. Bud decided the only self-respecting thing to do was to confront the impersonator and threaten him with a lawsuit, unless he ceased forthwith from impersonating his character in this fallacious manner.

Bud reached for the cordless, but before he could pick it up, the phone began to ring. 'Perhaps the son-of-a-bitch is calling me back,' he guessed.

Bud answered the phone, prepared for a showdown. "HELLO?"

A warm, woman's voice greeted him back, *"Hello . . . "*

Bud thought he recognized the voice. "Mariana? *Is that you?"*

Before the caller had a chance to reply, Bud told her, "I've been waiting to hear from you. I'm glad you called. You know I dialed the phone number that you gave me and I noticed—well, you're not going to believe this—but ah—"

"Excuse me," the caller interrupted. "I don't mean to cut you off, but I think there's been some mistake." The caller laughed mockingly. "My name is not Mariana!"

Bud was baffled for a moment. "Huh? Wha?"

The caller repeated herself, *"My name is not Mariana."* Again, she laughed.

After Bud realized his mistake, he felt silly for making such an assumption. "Oh my . . . Oh I'm sorry," he apologized. "I thought you were someone else."

"Oh, it's not a problem!" The caller explained, "Actually, co-in-cid-en-tally, I'm also looking for a Mariana. I was told I could find one at this number."

"What?" Bud could not believe his ears. *"You're looking for Mariana?"*

"If she's not there, I can try back another time," the caller replied.

Bud was afraid she might hang up and tried to keep her on the line, "Wait! What's this about? You didn't give me your name!"

"It's not a big deal," the caller replied, dismissively. "I'll try Mariana back later. Goodbye."

Before he could say another word, the caller hung up. Bud's imagination spun out of control. He suspected Mariana of somehow being complicit in the theft of his identity. He couldn't escape the notion that all of his troubles and confusion stemmed from a futile attempt to contact her that morning. Paranoid, he briefly entertained the thought that there was an organized scheme not only to steal his identity but also to drive him insane. He reasoned, why would someone call his number and ask to speak with Mariana, unless Mariana herself had provided the number and given the instructions to do so? Bud swiftly changed gears, reinterpreting the event, "The other possibility is that the impersonator has caller ID and had his wife call back here . . . either to get even with me for bothering him . . . or as part of the plot to drive me insane." Bud found himself in deep conspiratorial thoughts, weighed down with the prospect that someone was out to get him, to destroy him. "It has to be something like that," he told himself, shaking his head. "I just can't get over that answering machine. It's like something out of the *Twilight—*"

As if on cue, the phone rang. Bud decided not to answer it. He had had quite enough aggravation for one morning, for any morning . . . for a lifetime. After the fifth ring, Bud's machine answered the call: *Hello you've reached Bud Damon. I'm not in right now but if you leave a message I'll be sure to call you back as soon as possible. Thank you."*

The caller did not leave a message. Bud stood up from the bed and reached for his wallet and keys on the night table. The clock read twelve o'clock, Noon. That was an O.K. time to get a drink Bud fatefully decided. Drinking was something that Bud was not supposed to do, so that was about as fateful a decision as Bud could make. He locked up his apartment, took the elevator down to the lobby, scurried past Gus out the door and walked around the corner to his favorite pub, O'Reilly's. Once inside, the owner greeted him at the bar. Bud took his favorite seat and ordered a pint of this and a shot of that, to calm the raging storm in his mind. That was always how a binge started for Bud. Predictably, the rest of that afternoon and that evening were a blur to him.

The next day he awoke with a horrible hangover. Lying in his bed, Bud recounted a weird dream that was like a movie. In the dream, he played Elvis Presley and Mariana played Ann-Margret. The two of them performed a song and dance number on one of the moons of Uranus. They both wore space suits, as did the backing band. For some reason they didn't need space helmets, which was just as well for the sake of perform-ing. The song wasn't one Bud remembered ever hearing. It had an impromptu quality about it and reminded him of songs prevalent in beach movies of the 1960's. Bud still remembered some of the words, "You're caught in a web and you can't get out . . . Mara's going to get you, don't you ball and shout!" It was hard to forget a song that mentioned an arch-nemesis, even if that song had no basis in reality.

Bud took a shower and then made some coffee. He wasn't hungry, because his stomach was still shot from the enormous amount of alcohol consumed. His stomach wasn't ready for coffee either, but Bud needed the coffee to snap out of his malaise. Over coffee in the kitchen, he recalled the events leading up to his drinking. He wondered if he could have dreamt dialing his old phone number and speaking to himself. Didn't it make more sense that such an experience would follow the drinking, instead of precede it? It was impossible that he could have dialed his old phone number and spoken to himself, or heard his answering machine—impossible! To prove it, Bud set his coffee cup down, stood up from the table and walked into the bedroom. Without hesitation and brimming with confidence, he picked up the cordless and dialed his old number. What Bud heard was a welcome relief, *"The number you have reached 548-9208 is no longer in service . . . No further information is available."* Bud had a confident smile that nearly cracked his face. He hung up the phone feeling satisfied. But before he had the chance to go back to the kitchen and finish his coffee, the phone rang.

Bud was going to let the machine get it but was nervous it might be Stan, calling to account for his whereabouts yesterday. Bud decided that as an excuse he'd tell Stan his aunt had fallen severely ill and that he had to visit her to deliver food and medication. It was a lie, of course. Bud did not have family relations in New York City. They were all in Boston. By the fourth ring, Bud finally answered the phone. He tried to sound chipper, "Hello?"

"Hello, is Mara there?"

Bud cringed when he heard the name but struggled to answer the caller respectfully, "No, there's no Mara here." He suddenly had the impulsive idea to pretend that he knew Mara in order to obtain some helpful information. He figured if he could find a forwarding address or perhaps a business phone number, he might then be able to direct the unwanted callers elsewhere. "Mara's out right now," he said, correcting himself. "Who shall I say is calling?"

The man didn't answer.

Bud repeated the question, "Hello? Who shall I say is calling?"

"Are you a friend of Mara's?" the caller asked Bud. The man sounded official.

"Yes, I'm a friend," Bud responded jovially. "Did Mara by any chance give you her daytime number? Maybe you could reach her at work . . . Let me just make sure you have that number . . . "

"I don't have her work number," the caller replied, "but that could be helpful to me, if you have it handy."

"Oh!" Bud exclaimed. "I thought I had it handy, but I don't. I thought maybe if you had it—never mind," he dismissed. "Just forget it."

The caller sounded confused. "You don't have another number?"

Bud changed the subject, "I'm sorry, but what did you say your name was?"

"My name is Worthy," the caller told Bud. He sounded impatient. "Detective Worthy, actually. I'm with the New York City Police Department."

"Oh. Is everything alright, detective?" Bud asked. He suddenly felt regretful for pretending that he knew this Mara person, but now felt more obliged than ever to continue pretending. "I do hope everything is alright."

"May I ask what your relationship to Mara is?" the detective inquired.

"I'm her um, boyfriend. We live together," Bud answered. He knew that he was probably getting himself deeper into trouble by fabricating such stories, but he couldn't help himself anymore. He was dying of curiosity and had to find out what this was all about.

"Oh, you're a boyfriend?" the detective confirmed. "Is Mara a nickname?"

Bud laughed, nervously, "Yes, it's a nickname."

"Her real name is Mariana Webcott, correct?"

Bud had a lump in his throat when he heard the name. His mind was racing as well as his heart, but he tried not to let on. "That's correct," he confirmed.

"I'll tell you how I know that, later," the detective told Bud.

Suddenly, Bud's suspicions got the best of him. What if this person was not a detective, but another conspirator in the plot to drive him insane? It was strange that the police would conduct official business over the phone in this way. It occurred to Bud he had no way of confirming that he was talking with a detective.

As if the caller could read Bud's mind, the subject was addressed. "The reason I am calling is because we found this phone number in a dead man's pocket. It was written, along with your girlfriend's name, on a scrap of paper. Aside from this number, we had no other means of getting in touch with your girlfriend. We would normally have tried to reach her in person, but we didn't have an address. For the record, may I have your name?"

Bud gave the first name that popped into his head. "Elvis."

"Elvis?" The caller was taken aback. "Did you say, Elvis?"

"Yes, it's Elvis, like Elvis Presley."

The caller paused, presumably to write that down. "Could I get your last name?"

"Yes, it's um, Margret."

"Elvis Margret?" the caller confirmed. "That's your name?"

"Uh-huh." Bud snickered into his sleeve, laughing at the ridiculous name.

"What is your address?" the detective asked.

"It's 133 Canal Street," Bud lied.

"Great. Now, as I mentioned, I'd like to stop by to talk with you and Mariana. What time does she get home from work, Mr. Margret?"

"Oh about midnight," Bud answered, still taking all of this as a joke.

"Midnight?" The caller sounded displeased. "Well, that's rather late. I'd like to get in touch with her sooner than that. Maybe you could give me her work address? This is very serious stuff, Mr. Margret. As I said, her name and number were found in a dead man's pocket. The death appears to be a murder or a suicide, but there doesn't seem to be a note indicating the latter. Your girl-friend may be the only lead we have in this case. We also have the man's address book but that won't be of much help right now. Most of his family and friends live in Boston. Some colleagues of mine in the depart-ment have already contacted the next of kin and so forth. But Mariana may be able to give us some real information."

Bud listened patiently, still unsure what to make of the call itself. When it came time for him to comment, he did so with some reservation. "Well, we'd like to help out if we can. Though I don't know how we could."

"I'm curious to know if you know the dead man," the detective confided. "You've not asked me his name."

"Oh well, I'm sure it's . . . " Bud did not finish. He asked himself what he was sure of.

The detective persisted in his train of thought. "I mean, if my girlfriend's name and number was found on a dead man, I'd like to know that man's name."

Bud sighed with a deep sense of foreboding. "O.K., so what's his name?"

"It's *Bud. Bud Damon*," the detective replied. "Did you ever hear Mariana mention that name to you? *Bud Damon*?"

"Why no, I don't believe so," Bud answered. He was more frightened and confused than he'd ever been in his life. If this was a joke, it had been taken too far.

"Well, anyway," the detective persisted, "if you could just give me Mariana's work number and address I could stop by there to talk with her."

Bud abruptly hung up the phone, stood up from the bed and walked across the bedroom. When he reached the dresser, he opened the top drawer and found a thirty-eight pistol that he kept handy in case of a break-in. He checked to make sure the gun was loaded and then pointed it to his aching head and pulled the trigger, emptying the barrel. Bud's next-door neighbor heard the shot and immediately called the police. An hour later Detective Worthy was in the room, standing over Bud's body, dialing a phone number found on a piece of paper in Bud's pocket.

The Ivory
Leather Pumps

It had been a long, hard day at the shoe repair shop. Guy and his wife, Marge, were exhausted. In the store's seven year history, the two had never had such a busy day. Guy counted one hundred and two pairs of shoes that were brought into the shop. From eight in the morning until seven that night, the two of them did not stop working. They left the shop after reaching the halfway mark with the shoes, figuring to leave the rest for the next day. By the time they got home to their little apartment on the other side of town, Marge made the announcement that she was not going to cook "a goddamn thing," so Guy ordered a pizza, which they ate while watching TV. The two turned in earlier than usual, knowing the workload they faced in the morning. At ten o'clock, before he turned out the light, Guy set the alarm clock for six. It did not take them long to fall asleep. Though neither one realized it, they were snoring in synchronicity by 10:58.

Guy dreamt that he found a pair of men's loafers that were missing heels. Marge dreamt that she found a pair of heels that were missing shoes. Unbeknownst to both, the heels in Marge's dream belonged to the loafers in Guy's dream. This fact might not have been lost, if only they remembered their respective dreams the next morning and shared their recollections with each other. But such was not the case, as both dreams were completely forgotten in the confusion that roused them out of their sleep at 3:32 a.m.

Guy was the first to awake. He heard someone walking back and forth in the upstairs apartment. The sound was impossible to ignore, because the guilty party wore heels and they were striking a hardwood surface. The longer the noise continued the angrier Guy became. Eventually, he rose out of bed and walked to the hall closet where they kept the broom.

When he returned with it, Marge was awake. "Put a towel on the end of the broom," she advised.

Guy waved her away. "Never mind that," he said.

"I don't want a hole in the ceiling," his wife explained.

"Just be quiet," Guy hushed. He was listening intently for any sign of life upstairs.

"I don't think you should bang on the ceiling," Marge protested.

"I thought you said the Hamiltons moved?" Guy asked his wife.

"That's what Josephine told me in the laundry room," Marge answered with a yawn.

Guy ignored her and stared at the ceiling. "C'mon, you fat Brontosaurus!"

"They moved, Guy. Nobody's up there."

"Somebody's up there, unless we're both hallucinating! Didn't you hear heels?"

"Yes, I heard heels!" Marge admitted, in an exasperated tone. She covered her face with a pillow but pulled it away a second later, adding, "But the sound isn't necessarily coming from upstairs . . . It could be coming from anyplace."

Her husband lowered the broom, "What do you mean, *anyplace?* Our walls don't border any other apartment. That leaves only the upstairs or the downstairs as suspect, my dear! And don't tell me you think the heels came from the downstairs apartment. People don't walk on the ceiling."

"I think the heels came from downstairs," Marge declared boldly. She paused reflectively, before covering her head with the pillow again.

"The heels didn't come from downstairs!" Guy insisted, raising the broom again. He stared at the ceiling expectantly.

Marge took the pillow away from her face. "Come to bed, Guy, for the love of God. WE HAVE TO GET UP AT SIX!"

"Shh!" her husband hushed. His patience had been rewarded. The footsteps recurred, but as he tried to ascertain their point of origin, Guy was forced to agree with his wife; they were not coming from the upstairs apartment. But they were not coming from downstairs either. The footsteps sounded as if they were emanating from within their own bedroom. Guy lowered the broom with one hand while scratching his head with the other. "It can't be," he declared, talking more to himself than to his wife.

"You see, it's from downstairs," Marge argued. "It's William Burroughs."

"It's not Burroughs," Guy objected. "How could it be Burroughs? He would have to be moving the shoes along the ceiling with his hands, Marge. Stop being ridiculous!"

"It's Burroughs," Marge insisted.

"Stop calling him Burroughs!" her husband quarreled.

"I think it stopped," Marge announced.

"What stopped?" Guy asked.

"The footsteps," Marge explained. "The footsteps have stopped . . . Now we can go back to sleep." On that note, she placed the pillow back over her face.

Guy paid little attention to his wife. Instead he waited for the noise to return, holding his defiant stance with broom in hand. After a few minutes, he heard his wife's insufferable voice calling him from beneath her pillow. "Come to bed, Guy," she murmured. "For crying out loud, come to bed."

Tired and beaten, he decided to follow his wife's advice. Before retiring, however, Guy placed the broom where he could easily access it should the footsteps resume at any point during the night. He leaned it against the armoire, which was right next to his side of the bed. As he climbed into bed, he heard his wife complaining beneath the pillow. "What are you saying?" he asked her.

In response the murmuring became louder, but not more distinguishable. Guy ignored it and fell back to sleep.

When the alarm clock rang at six the next morning, Guy awoke in a cold sweat. In an agitated, tired stupor he shut off the alarm, rose out of bed and made his way to the bathroom. When he returned to the bedroom, twenty five minutes later, he roused his wife with a kiss on the head and a pat on the behind then he switched on the clock radio by her bedside, so that she could hear the day's weather report. Before leaving the bedroom to prepare breakfast in the kitchen, Guy heard a rapid shuffling of shoe heels coming from an indeterminate location. The sound came and went, but served as a reminder of the aggravation he had endured the night before.

Later, in the kitchen, Guy heard the heels again. But as he listened this time, the sound seemed to emanate from behind a wall shared with their elderly neighbor, Ms. Jenkins. Guy heard the heels climbing up and down the wall as he toasted, buttered and ate his English muffin. For a while the sound ceased, but resumed as he drank his coffee. Guy paused to reflect on the implausibility of Ms. Jenkins walking up and down the wall. He also reflected on the improbability of Ms. Jenkins moving her shoes up and down the wall by hand. Such behavior was quite out of character for his reserved neighbor.

By the time Marge finished up in the bathroom and came out to give him his morning kiss in the kitchen, the heels had stopped. Guy could then only relate the story to his wife without the benefit of proof. He feared his wife might suspect an overactive imagination. Of course, under the circumstances, Marge had little choice but to accept Guy's story as the product of an overactive imagination and told him as much, in not so many words:

"You're nuts!" she laughed.

"I wouldn't make something like that up," Guy protested. "I heard heels walking up and down this wall," he insisted, pointing at the wall in question.

"Yeah, well, I suppose there is a reasonable explanation for that kind of thing," Marge offered, while pouring honey nut cereal into a plastic bowl. "Maybe the mice are wearing stilettos or something."

"Ha, ha. That's very funny, Margie. So witty—and first thing in the morning too!" Guy quipped, shaking his head.

Marge added milk into the cereal and then a spoon. She looked away from the bowl for a minute to have a good look at her husband, then admonished him, "We're going to miss the bus again, if you keep standing around like that . . . Are you going to work in your pajamas?"

Disgusted, Guy threw up his hands and headed for the bedroom to change.

Marge, meanwhile, carried the cereal bowl over to the kitchen table and began to eat her cereal. After the third spoonful, she suddenly heard loud footsteps. It didn't take her long to realize (it was by the fifth spoonful of honey nuts), that her husband's suspicions had been correct. The noise was coming from the wall that bordered Ms. Jenkins' apartment. Marge dropped her spoon and placed her ear to the wall to further corroborate this. After listening for a few minutes, she decided not to tell Guy about it. She knew, he would insist upon knocking on Ms. Jenkins' door. As if there was anything to get to the bottom of! Ms. Jenkins, as polite as she was, must be a little off her rocker, Marge decided. On that note, she dropped the matter and returned her attention to the consumption of honey nuts. By the tenth spoonful, she was done. She put the bowl in the sink, ran some water into it, then joined her husband in the bedroom.

"Did you hear the heels?" Guy asked her right away.

"No, I did not," Marge lied.

"You heard them, didn't you?" Guy asked, threading a belt through the hoops of his pants.

"No, I didn't!" his wife denied. "You and your little fantasies, Guy!" Marge slipped out of her nightgown and opened a dresser drawer where she kept braziers. She selected one and examined it briefly.

"You don't want me to knock on Ms. Jenkins' door, that's what it is!" Guy declared.

"Well, can you blame me? Marge asked him, fastening her bra. "What on Earth would you ask her, if she's been moving shoes up and down the walls?"

"That's what you implied Burroughs was up to last night," Guy reminded her.

"I never said any such thing!" Marge laughed. "You said that, not I!"

Guy combed his hair in the mirror while his wife stepped into a pair of panties that she selected out of a drawer in the dresser. Guy studied his wife in the reflection of the mirror and then candidly asked her, "You have a thing for him, don't you?"

Marge was incredulous. *"WHAT?"*

Guy laughed at her reaction. "Yeah, you know it's true!" he added.

"You're disgusting," Marge objected.

Guy continued to watch his wife in the mirror. She was putting on a pair of jeans. "When are you going to admit that you'd like a *naked lunch?"* he asked her.

"Just cut it out, O.K., Guy?" Marge pulled a sweater over her head. "He gives me the creeps." She warned her husband, "We're going to miss the bus. You better get ready!"

"I'm ready!" Guy replied, turning away from the mirror to face her. "I'm ready, when you are."

Five minutes later, Marge and Guy were out the door. Twelve minutes after that they were on the bus that brought them to their shoe repair shop. Thirty-seven minutes later they were in their shop starting their workday. Guy initiated the activity by picking up a pair of men's dress shoes that needed black paint on the tip and a shine. It took Guy seventeen minutes to repair and shine the shoes. He then put them in a plastic bag and placed them on a shelf along with other finished shoes. As he did so, Guy noticed a pair of loafers without a corresponding ticket. When he picked them up, he realized they were missing heels. "Where did these come from?" he asked.

"Are you talking to yourself or to me?" Marge inquired.

"I'm talking to the shoes," Guy answered with sarcastic flair.

Marge giggled and without missing a beat said, "I heard if you talk to shoes that will help them to grow." Right after she spoke, Marge paused briefly, smiled and corrected her statement, "No, that's what they say about plants."

Guy turned his back on his wife. As he did so, he spotted a lady just outside the entrance to the shop. He watched her as she opened the door, causing the little bell above it to ring. As she entered, Guy noticed her clothing, which appeared to be sixty years out of date. He imagined her stepping out of an old issue of *Life* magazine. She wore a baby blue blouse with unusually large lapels and prominent shoulder pads. Even more anachronistic, she donned a large green bow at the center-front neckline. Guy thought it gave her a kind of clownish appearance. She approached the counter, proffering a large brown bag. Guy stared at the puffy sleeves decorating her arms, as he accepted the bag.

"I bet there are shoes in here," he joked.

"Yes, shoes," the lady answered, phlegmatically.

Marge looked up from the leather boots she'd been stretching and cheerfully greeted the lady, "Good morning."

"Good morning," the lady replied.

"I love your hat," Marge complimented. It was a black slouch hat made of felt, worn at a rakish angle. In the hat, she reminded Marge of Greta Garbo or Marlene Dietrich.

The lady reached for the hat on her head, as if she had forgotten it was there, and thanked Marge in a low voice.

Guy noticed the label *Best & Co.* as he reached into the lady's bag. "They're out of business, aren't they?" he tried to recall. The shoes were more interesting than the bag. As he pulled them out, Guy couldn't believe his eyes . . . vintage ellemenno style pumps, ivory leather with black patent leather toes, black tips on the strap ends, padded insoles, sculpted heels and flexible outsoles . . . a style popular in the 1940's. Guy remembered his mother wearing a similar pair, many years ago, when he was a child.

As soon as she saw the pumps, the lady began to explain her reason for bringing them into the shop. She called Guy's attention to the strap on the right shoe. Obligingly, Guy responded to her gestures but was distracted by a pungent chemical odor that utterly overwhelmed him. "Wow," he gasped, taking a step back. Guy gaped at the lady, finding it hard to fathom how she could be the source of such a noxious smell. Seeing her close up, he was struck by the heavy makeup applied to her countenance. It looked as if she was trying to hide something horrible about her face, but Guy couldn't determine what that something was. When he stared down at her neckline, however, Guy plainly saw that the skin complexion there had a grayish pallor.

"Is that formaldehyde I smell?" Marge asked looking up from the boots. She sniffed in the air with an air of curiosity. "Yes, that's formaldehyde alright," she affirmed. "I know that smell because my father was a funeral director."

The lady looked embarrassed and brought the subject back to the shoes in Guy's hands, while speaking in a monotone voice, "See what you can do about the strap on the right shoe and importantly, I need the bottom part of both heels replaced. They've been worn down, as you can see."

"No problem," Guy managed to say. "When do you need them by?"

"May I have them back this time tomorrow?" the lady asked.

"Sure, tomorrow," Guy agreed. "Just fill out this ticket, if you wouldn't mind." Across the counter he passed her one of the little yellow tickets used to track shoes in the shop.

The lady reached into a trapezoid shaped leather bag and searched around, presumably for a pen. Guy noticed this and handed her one. "Here you go," he said. "Just fill in your name, address and phone number."

"Thank you," the lady replied, taking the pen. She promptly began to fill out the ticket.

Guy examined the shoes again and told her, "I'm going to charge you ten dollars to replace the bottoms of the heels and another ten for the strap."

"That's fine," the lady replied, handing him back the ticket and pen across the counter.

A big smile passed over Guy's face when he noticed the woman's address. *"Oh, you live at 3220 Oxford Street?"* he inflected.

"Yes," the lady confirmed. "Do you know it?"

Marge looked up from the boots and gasped briefly. "We live there too," she exclaimed.

Guy chuckled and inquired, "What apartment do you live in? I notice that you didn't write down your apartment number."

"I live in 5K," the lady answered.

"5K?" Guy responded, taken aback. "That can't be."

"We live in 5K too," Marge laughed out loud.

Guy rolled his eyes at his wife's futile attempt at humor then returned his attention to the strange woman. He wanted her to leave, having had quite enough of her foul odor and bizarre eccentricities. "Ah look, the apartment number doesn't matter," he dismissed. "I've got everything else." As he looked down at the ticket again, Guy saw that she'd written down a six digit telephone number (some of the characters were letters instead of numbers). He was compelled to say something about it, but realized he'd require a tank of oxygen if she remained in the shop even a minute longer. "S-o-o, we'll see you tomorrow then—"

"I'll see you tomorrow," the lady replied, taking her leave. The little bell above the door rang to confirm her departure.

Guy signaled to his wife with a hand gesture, "Honey, can you open the window? It smells like Hell in here."

Marge looked at him askance. "Oh yes, of course, Guy. I know you couldn't do it yourself."

"Well, you're right there," her husband argued, defensively. "If I was right there, I'd open the window for you."

Marge opened the window. "Satisfied?"

"I thought I was going to puke with her in here," Guy declared.

"Formaldehyde," Marge repeated. "It's a preservative, you know."

"Maybe she sprays it on her clothes," Guy chuckled. "Talk about retro—" he laughed.

"Yes, retro—" Marge replied, half distracted. She'd discovered two men's heels on the floor and reached down to pick them up. "Now where did these come from?" she asked herself, examining them in her hand. The heels weren't new. The bottoms were quite worn. Marge guessed they'd fallen off a pair of shoes brought into the shop and was about to look into the matter further by scrutinizing the group of still unfinished men's shoes, when she was distracted by her husband.

"Hey you know what, Marge? That lady . . . I'm just looking at the ticket she filled out . . ."

Marge looked at Guy and took note of his pensive expression. "What is it?"

Guy laughed to himself. "Oh, it's nothing. Just that uh . . . "

Marge put the heels down on the worktable and inadvertently forgot about them. She stared expectantly at her husband who was never at a loss for words. "What?"

Guy continued to stare at the ticket in his hand. "Her name is familiar to me, in a weird way."

"Well, what's her name?" Marge asked, tired of the suspense.

Guy dramatically turned to his wife and waved the ticket at her. "Ab-er-na-thy," he said, stressing the syllables.

"So, what's so unusual about that name?" Marge asked.

Guy scratched his head. "Well, you recall how she said that she lived in our building?"

"Yes," Marge answered, waving her hand impatiently.

"And you recall how she said she lived in apartment 5K?"

Marge rolled her eyes. "Yes, of course, Guy. That's our apartment. We've been over all of this."

Guy continued, "Well, last night, or early this morning, I had a dream about a woman named Abernathy, who once lived in our apartment."

"Really?" Marge responded, feigning interest. "It's probably just a coincidence." She shook her head, disapprovingly. "Who cares?"

Guy was in a trance, recalling the dream. By the way she was dressed and how the apartment was decorated, he guessed the timeline to be the late '40's, or early '50's. In fact, the actual date of the dream was May 2, 1952, though Guy could not possibly have known that, nor could he have known that the dream began at 5:52 a.m. and ended precisely at 6 a.m. when the alarm clock rang. While the timing of the dream might seem irrelevant, it was significant in that Mrs. Abernathy came home to her apartment at 5:52 p.m. in the dream, after a long day at the shoe factory. Soon after, at 6 p.m. in the dream, she was murdered by her husband. Guy didn't actually get a chance to visualize her death on account of the alarm clock. Had he been unfortunate enough to sleep in as late as 6:01, he would have seen Mr. Abernathy surprising his wife with a blow to the head, while she was busy (and distracted) washing the dishes in the sink. His weapon of choice was a baseball bat. Mr. Abernathy had no good reason for committing the heinous crime. It was pure wrath (he suspected his wife, incorrectly, of an extramarital affair).

Mr. Abernathy's actions in Guy's dream mirrored Mr. Abernathy's actions in real life, six decades earlier. At that time, there actually was a Mr. And Mrs. Abernathy living in Apartment 5K, at 3220 Oxford Street and Mr. Abernathy really did murder his wife. In the end, he was caught and paid for his evil deed by serving the remainder of his life in prison. With infinite sadness, Mrs. Abernathy paid for the faith and love she'd given her husband by forever haunting their apartment; endlessly pacing the floors, the walls and the ceiling, always wearing the same ivory leather pumps, a gift from Mr. Abernathy.

The End
Never Means
THE END

I was sitting next to J.P. Vondel in the *Lizard Lounge*, sipping a vodka martini and listening as he described the opening scene of our film project. Suddenly, as if on the flight his fancy, I was transplanted into the very shot he was describing, running frantically down the avenue of a bustling Metropolis. I could hear the great director's words in my head, as if they were my own, "HURRY UP, STEVE! You must get home to finish your book!" I was too cold to care about the book. As I realized as much, a caramel colored overcoat miraculously appeared over my gray flannel suit. I also felt a hat on my head. Incredulous of this, I reached up and touched the brim. "NO! Don't worry about your ensemble," the director decried. "Your thoughts should only be on the book. You've finally thought of an ending. You must get home to write it!"

Ahead, I saw a gaggle of people impeding my path on the pavement. Vondel warned me not to slow down, "Breaking your pace could destroy the momentum of the shot." I screamed out to the loiterers, "GET OUT OF MY WAY!" Thankfully, they heeded my caveat. I was like a runaway freight train at that moment. When I passed the pedestrians, I realized that they were nuns. I left them in the dust, nonplussed, pondering my eccentric behavior. I heard Vondel scream out enthusiastically, lauding my rude and callous demeanor, "HOORAY! Well done. They're plebeians, anyway." I turned my head in the direction of those words and upon doing so, discovered the great director's location. He and his camera crew were following me down the avenue on a dolly, pulled by a strange animal that resembled a galloping ground sloth or an unknown species of giant bear running on all fours. I took a double take at the creature and noticed one of Vondel's cameramen waving at me in a mocking fashion. He flashed a broad grin that irritated me for its sarcastic quality. I tried my best to ignore him and focused on the great director's words, "The only thing that matters is the book. You must get home to finish the book. For inspiration, you need music!"

It was then that I heard music, vibes and a very cool jazzy rhythm. Where it came from I didn't know but it moved me, as did Vondel's words, "Keep pace to the rhythm. Feel the music. Live the music. Run with it, kid! Fly like the wind!" The vibes were playing like mad, as I imagined myself a superhero, leaping incredible distances, transcending all records for human speed. I don't know how fast I ran, but I was at the doorstep of my brownstone in no time. I heard Vondel's mad laughter echoing down the street, as I reached into my trouser pocket. "Find the key!" he ordered. "Open the door! Don't lose any time. Get inside, Steve!" After fumbling briefly, I managed to open the door. I left it ajar for the crew to follow, as I followed Vondel's direction to hang my coat and hat on the coat rack in the living room. Obediently, I then scurried down the hall to the bedroom and settled at my writing desk. "Good boy!" Vondel lauded. "Now, take some paper and put it in the typewriter." I did as instructed and proceeded to write the beginning of the last story in my short story collection, *Roots & Seeds*. I entitled that last story, *The End Will Never End*. As I wrote, Vondel's cameras rolled.

I tried not to let the crew distract me from my work. Occasionally, I was aware of their presence, but mostly they were considerate of the concentration that a writer requires. But whenever Vondel stepped away on one of his numerous smoking breaks, one of the cameramen would inevitably approach me with an attempt to strike up a conversation (the same one that smiled and waved to me on the dolly outside). The narrative thread in my mind would then be interrupted by a stupid question like, "Do you have a bathroom in this place?" or "Have you got anything to eat around here?" or "Don't you have any pets for company?" This cameraman introduced himself to me as either Bron or Brahm. At first, I thought Bron was only trying to be friendly. But upon further speculation, I now believe he was trying to subtly let me know that I should not be writing while the director was on break. Because, if I was writing while the cameras weren't rolling (and the cameras never rolled without the director), that meant the writing process was not being recorded in its entirety for posterity. And apparently that was the whole point of the film, to record me in the process of writing. When Vondel returned from his break he would also occasionally interrupt me, if he saw that I was writing, despite his solemn promise to be, 'respectful of the quiet required by a writer'. What he said at these moments, as he stood over me, always seemed inane: "Wow! I can see you're on a roll now. What a gift you have. I love it! Keep typing, kid. Some day it will all pay off." It was completely unnecessary and counterproductive. On several of these occasions, I totally lost my train of thought. At such moments, the premise of the film seemed utterly absurd to me.

After all, where was the drama in watching me write? How was Vondel going to make a movie out of such boring material? Why not make a film about the subject matter of my book, instead? I shared my opinion with Vondel, after about the tenth hour of filming. I will never forget his extreme reaction to my suggestion. He screamed something in Dutch, then scowling and enraged, growled. "You dare to tell me, J.P. Vondel, the great director, what to film?" I could see he was insulted. I was about to explain my position to him further, when he shook his finger at me menacingly and released a volley of expletives. I was flabbergasted by his reaction. I feared losing my own temper as a result and not knowing what else to do sat back down at the typewriter and picked up where I'd left off. My compliancy obviously pleased the director, because I saw him smile with a satisfied air as he crouched down again in his 'director's position' (for some reason, he designated the area behind a chest of drawers as his director's position).

Then an unexpected thing happened. When Vondel motioned for Bron to begin filming again, the cameraman refused. "I don't think so," he said, shaking his head. "This isn't going to work, J.P. Can't you see that?"

Vondel was speechless. His jaw fell in a simulated fit of apoplexy.

Bron heightened the director's surprise, by defending my position on the film. "In my opinion, Steve's suggestion is a good one. We should base the film around some of his stories, instead of filming him writing the book!"

Vondel grew impatient, "We are way behind schedule, Bronny!" he pressed.

Suddenly, a lighting technician moved away from my corner bookcase where he had been toying with a lamp. He butted into the argument. "Oh God, Bron, please don't start this again!" he begged. "No one cares about your stupid opinions and personally, I'm sick of hearing them. Why don't you know your place?"

Vondel hushed the technician up. "Be quiet, Lagg. Don't intervene. Let me handle this. You worry about the lighting and let me worry about Bron."

"But, he does this all the time!" Lagg protested. "I don't know how you put up with it, J.P."

'I SAID, LET ME HANDLE IT!" Vondel hollered. On that note, Lagg disappeared again behind the bookcase. The director quickly composed himself and addressed

Bron with an even tone. "Bron, come on. Don't do this to me again. We've been through this before. I'm the director . . . You're my assistant. Do you understand?"

Bron still did not budge. He draped his arms around the top of the camera and stared down at his feet and the legs of the tripod. "But it's pointless to film Steven typing. Don't you see that? It's boring to watch some guy typing for ten hours straight."

"It's not boring!" Vondel argued. "We are witnessing an act of creation." He pointed at me. "This man is creating a world with his writing. I want to see that world being made!"

"But wouldn't it be better to show *what* he is writing? Bron reasoned.

The director threw his hands up and looked away. A groan bellowed from behind the bookcase, presumably from Lagg. Vondel silenced him by throwing an ashtray that he grabbed from my desk. "BE QUIET OVER THERE!" he hollered.

"I would never sit through a movie about a guy writing a book," Bron continued. "I mean, I give you credit, J.P. The opening of the film, it has a lot of promise. It was exciting to see Steve running down the street and funny to see him scare the nuns. But from the time that he arrived at the apartment I've been bored to tears. The whole premise is ridiculous, a guy sitting at a typewriter typing a collection of stories and we don't even know what he's typing." He shook his head, disgusted. "There's no action! This is just a big waste of time *and money!* I mean, how many hours do we really need to film Steven typing? We could have done that in a ten second shot."

Vondel looked like he was about to explode, but held himself in check. In a voice uncharacteristic of his displeasure he made an appeal to his cameraman, "Bronny, please try to understand what I'm doing here."

"I don't understand at all," Bron admitted. He looked at Vondel and crossed his arms, assuming a challenging pose. "You said I could have some creative input on this picture," he reminded the director. "You gave *Sky* the opportunity, I remember one time you let him . . . "

Vondel became visibly vexed at the mention of the name Sky and he interrupted Bron, "I told you never to mention that son-of-a-bitch to me again! You know what he did to me."

"I'm sorry," Bron replied, contritely. "It's just that the other night, when we were in the sauna, you told me . . . "

Vondel laughed out loud in a sustained manner, effectively drowning Bron out. He appeared to be embarrassed by the cameraman's words. I believe Vondel was gauging my reaction to these words, because he stared at me for a sustained period of time immediately afterwards. Since I was as equally embarrassed, I excused myself on the pretense of going to the lavatory. I promptly stood up from my desk and headed in that direction. Before I closed the door behind me, I could hear them whispering down the hall.

Alone in the lavatory, I breathed a sigh of relief. I looked at my watch. It was late. I wondered when and if they would ever finish filming. Certainly, Vondel would eventually let me sleep. He couldn't expect me to write the book continually in an unbroken fashion, right through to its finish! Then it occurred to me, what if Vondel did allow for a break from the writing/filming? Would he expect me to invite them to stay, as my guests? That thought was unsettling. I did have an extra bed and a couch, but there were three of them. One thing was definite. I was not going to give up my bed, not for these unwelcome guests. In the event of their crashing with me, I decided, two would have to share a bed or alternatively, one would have to take the floor. Of course, I was hoping Vondel would have the good sense to rent a hotel room, instead. Hopefully, that hotel would be far enough away to allow me some much needed space. Honestly, they were driving me crazy. I had never written anything before with people standing around me, over me, watching me, scrutinizing me, no less.

I looked at my tired face in the mirror and gave myself a pep talk, "You can do this, Steven. You can put up with Vondel and his crew a little while longer. Before you know it, they will be out of your life and you can write a new book and it need not be filmed either. Who ever heard of writing a book on film?" I asked myself this pertinent question and looked into my reflected eyes in the mirror, expecting an answer. Do you know what happened? Before I tell you, you must promise that you'll not think I am crazy, because I am not crazy. The reflection of my face in the mirror changed, completely. That is to say, my face became another; a face I did not recognize. As I registered this face in my mind, the image changed again. I saw yet another face, one altogether different from my face or the countenance I had seen a moment earlier. Then it happened again. I had a fourth vision of a face in the mirror. Again, it was a stranger's face. These visions occurred several more times in rapid succession, so that in the end I beheld fifteen or sixteen faces, maybe more. I can't say for sure. It all happened so fast. If I had to guess, the experience lasted a minute. I admit that in that minute I seriously thought I had lost my mind, but also realized that I could not have imagined those faces, not with the degree of detail revealed to me.

I ran the water in the sink and splashed my face. I stared hard at my dripping face in the mirror, trying to understand what had happened, when I heard a knocking at the lavatory door and Lagg's voice informing me that my 'guests' had arrived. "Guests? What guests?" I asked.

As I came out of the lavatory, I saw that my apartment was crowded with strangers. A great party was underway, one that I had not been informed of. A few people greeted me in the hall near the vestibule that led into the den. I nearly dropped dead. These were the same faces that I'd seen earlier in the lavatory mirror. I immediately recognized one of them for its scarecrowlike quality. Of all the faces that appeared to me in the mirror, there was one most memorable, because that face did not appear to support a spark of life. Apart from the eyes being wide open, there was no other quality that made it seem sentient. As I took note of the said entity again now in my hallway, I realized it was standing upright only because one of the uninvited guests supported it in an erect posture. This uninvited guest, in an assuming manner, winked at me, as if letting me in on a joke. I don't recall my reaction, but I must have sneered or scowled, because I was outraged by this effrontery. I had to squeeze by this person to enter my den. He barely relented to let me through.

Lagg greeted me holding two martinis, one of which he handed me. "STEVE IS BACK, J.P!" he hollered above the din, announcing my presence to Vondel, who did not seem to care. He was too busy confabulating with all the colorful guests that had obsequiously crowded around him; one wore a blue dog costume that resembled a cartoon character. "I have some good news," Lagg confided. "J.P. has agreed to edit down the actual writing of the book in the film. Now, you won't have to type the whole thing up." He rolled his eyes at me. "You'll want to thank Bron for that. He likes you." Lagg paused from his drivel to sip his martini. I was about to say something again when he interrupted me, "You know he sleeps with the big guy," he said, maneuvering his eyes in Vondel's direction. "He's the new *Sky*, the new lover man, the new assistant cameraman, all-around-up-and-coming superstar," he shared, sounding slightly jealous. His tone of voice (and actually everything he said to me at that moment) made me want to vomit. I excused myself from his company in a manner best described as curt.

"Pardon me! It's impolite to walk away from someone when they're speaking to you," I heard Lagg say, as I took my leave. I paid him no mind. My focus was Vondel.

I was furious at the director for inviting so many strangers into my home without first obtaining my consent. It was obvious to me that they were all his friends. He egregiously played the host, mingling among them, nodding, waving, smiling, raising his glass, shouting salutations across the room. Watching him, I wanted to scream. It was difficult to suppress the impulse to do so, but I made the effort to uphold my dignity under these trying circumstances. I told myself it was more befitting for a man of my position to approach the guilty party and embarrass him for his outrageous conduct. I had every intension of doing just that when I was accosted by a queer looking fellow with long hair and no hands! He blocked my path to Vondel by walking right in front of me and absurdly gesturing with his mutilated limbs. Because of this, I could not see anything but his nauseating countenance.

"My name is Yelch," he said, introducing himself. "I'd shake your hand," he laughed, "but as you can see that would be physically impossible for me."

"Nice to meet you," I said, taking a step back.

"Say, are you going to drink that martini?" he asked me. "If not, I sure would like to have it."

"Take it," I said, offering him the drink. Then I realized the full measure of my folly. He could not accept the martini because of his handicap. "Oh," I gasped. "I'm sorry about that. You can't . . ."

The freak winced and tried to smile. "It's O.K.," he said reassuringly. "You do see my problem though? How am I to have a martini, if I can't hold it? And I'm so thirsty." He stared at me imploringly.

I didn't know what to say.

"Maybe I could ask a favor of you?" he questioned, with anticipation in his eyes. Before I could answer him, he second-guessed himself. "NO! I could NOT ask you to do that," he said, shaking his head. "I don't even know you," he insisted, shaking his head again with an expression of shame. "How could I ask you, a stranger, to bring the martini glass to my lips and nurse me?"

In order to prevent an emotional outburst (he looked about to cry), I obliged him with the martini and brought it to his lips. He slurped at the libation like it might be his last. In the process, he gulped down the olives in the glass whole, pits and all. I tried to be indulgent with him and show some kindness, but this became increasingly difficult for me as he had the nasty habit of finishing each sip from the glass with an exaggerated swallowing noise. I hated this sound effect. On two insufferable occasions, he also moved his lips away from the glass and uttered a satisfied, "Ahhh," before returning his attention to the martini again. This ahhhing made me want to kill him and I might have done so, had it not been for my determination to limit the spectacle we had already created. Lucky for him, I had also spotted Vondel again which drew all of my attention.

The director was now talking to a rumpled looking character sporting a gray fedora hat and a tan colored trench coat. An unlit cigarette was hanging from this man's lips. From time to time, when making a point, the man took it out of his mouth and gestured with it. Whoever this character was, he must have been very important, because Vondel appeared to hang on his every word. I also noticed a redheaded young lady standing beside both men, wearing a long black sequence gown that nearly touched the floor. She was most elegant. Occasionally this lady would impart a message to both men and whenever she did they appeared to stifle themselves and defer to her. I was frustrated that I could not make out her face or the face of the man in the trench coat, though I strained to do so. Either I saw their profiles or they were blocked by someone in the crowd.

"You're not listening to me at all, are you?" Yelch asked. He pushed the martini glass away with his stumpy arm. As I looked at him, I saw martini drops dribbling from his chin. "You haven't heard one word I said. What is so interesting over there, anyway, *the movie stars?*"

"What?" I asked.

"THE MOVIE STARS!" Yelch laughed out loud, "That's what it is! You're star struck!"

"Movie stars?" I said. "Are they . . . Do you know those people talking to the director?"

"I don't know anyone here," was his reply. He wiped his mouth and chin with the stubby end of his arm. "Thanks for the drink," he said, turning to walk away.

"You're welcome," I replied, although by that point he couldn't have heard me. He was halfway across the room by the time I said it and the noise level was such that you practically had to shout in order to be heard. I shook my head as I watched him bumping into people and knocking some of them down in his determined effort to leave the room. He swore at one strange fellow that had his arm draped around a nude mannequin! The man shouted something back but what he said escaped me. I was distracted then by someone tapping on my shoulder. When I turned to investigate the matter, I saw a waiter standing in front of me holding up a full tray of cocktails. I asked myself, 'What is a waiter doing in my den, holding a tray of cocktails?'

"Are you finished with that?" the waiter asked, referring to the empty martini glass in my hand.

"Why, yes." I told him, passing him the glass.

The waiter took the receptacle from me and placed it on his tray. "Would you like another one, sir?" he asked. Before I had the chance to respond, he had already taken a full martini glass off of his tray and handed it to me.

"Thank you," I said, accepting the cocktail. "I'm sure I'll need it," I added.

The waiter smiled indulgently and moved on. I was stunned that Vondel had hired service of this kind—and a little angry about it. This was something else he had not consulted me on. While I was on his payroll, this was still my home and it was presumptuous of him to assume not only that he could arrange a party in my home but that he could have it catered. On top of that, he invited people I didn't even know. I turned to look for the great director. After searching for a few minutes, I finally spotted him again. He was standing on the other side of the den, near the vestibule. His back was to me, but I saw the distinctive gray ponytail that he wore. The man in the trench coat and the redhead were no longer at his side. Now, he was arguing with a strange person wearing a giant cape.

"That's Sky!" a woman's voice exclaimed.

"That's his old assistant," I heard someone else say.

"Vondel will never let him in," a woman told her girlfriend.

This prediction proved to be correct. A moment later, the director had the caped man summarily removed from the premises. This caused quite a scene, because the man vociferously protested as he was escorted outside. In the middle of this scene and on my way over to Vondel, I bumped into and very nearly knocked over a man in a clown costume holding a white rat in his arms. He was stroking it while chatting with a bunch of misfit teens with greasy hair and rumpled clothes. One of these delinquents reached out to grab the clown, to prevent him from falling, and in the process managed to knock down a waiter holding a tray of drinks. I watched helplessly as a punch-like fluid spilled all over my velvet couch. The delinquent fell on the couch, but quickly sprang back up again. In all the excitement, he howled like a wolf. For some reason, this antic brought the house down. The clown and his retinue raised the roof in a burst of laughter that frightened the white rat in the clown's arms. As a consequence, the rodent leaped into the air. For one fleeting moment, the rat was directly over my head. Where it landed I don't know, but I have the sneaking suspicion it met with a certain young lady that I saw not long afterwards, shrieking and flapping her arms. I carefully maneuvered around this young lady to get to Vondel on the other side of the room. When I finally caught up with him, he seemed pleased to see me.

He even welcomed me with a hardy pat on the back and a big smile, which came as a surprise. He said something to me that I could not understand, amid all of the noise.

"WHAT DID YOU SAY?" I asked, in a loud but polite tone of voice.

"WHAT A FABULOUS PARTY!" Vondel lauded. Then, he said something else that I didn't understand. It sounded like, "I'VE BEEN LOOKING FOR A LOVER, FOR YOU!"

"A LOVER?" I laughed. "WHAT DO YOU MEAN *A LOVER?"*

"HUH?" Vondel's expression read like a question mark.

"WHAT DID YOU JUST SAY?" I demanded.

Vondel took a deep breath and with a serious voice replied, "I SAID, *I'VE BEEN LOOKING ALL OVER FOR YOU!* I WANTED TO TELL YOU . . . YOU'RE A TERRIFIC HOST!"

"Oh," I think I replied, half embarrassed by the confusion of my own thoughts and the unexpected cordiality of the director. "Well, I have got to talk to you about a couple of things, J.P." I insisted, suddenly recalling then how very upset I was with him for . . . well, for everything. There must have been a hundred people or more in my apartment and they were making a complete mess of the place! The bastards had long since drifted out of the den and were loitering around in the hallway, smoking cigarettes and stomping them out on the hardwood floor! I had little doubt they were also in my kitchen eating all of my food and heaven forbid, maybe even in my bedroom doing god knows what! A disturbing image appeared in my mind at that moment. Needing to reassure myself about it, I asked Vondel, "Where are Bron and Lagg?"

"Bron is standing on your couch with the shoulder camera over there—" The director pointed him out to me obligingly. "And Lagg is just behind him adjusting the lighting for this shot," he further indulged. "We're on film right now," Vondel told me. "All of this is being filmed."

"Well, you know, you should have told me that you were going to film a party in my apartment," I complained. "You didn't tell me anything about that and well, frankly, I'm a little *cantankerous* about the whole thing."

"You mean you're *angry*," Vondel said disapprovingly, waving his finger at me.

I was offended by his condescension and let him know it. "You have a nerve!" I declared. "How dare you correct me like a schoolmaster!"

"If you're *angry* you should just say you're *angry!*" he countered. "Not *cantankerous!*" he said, shaking his head back and forth. "What is that, *cantankerous?*"

"If I say *cantankerous,* that's what I mean!" I insisted. "I'm the writer here!"

"Exactly, you are the writer and you should know better," Vondel instructed me. "Be respectful of your audience. If you mean, *angry*—say *angry. Cantankerous!*" he mocked.

"It means *bad tempered!*" I said, defending my choice of words. "Why split hairs over something so stupid?" I demanded to know.

"It's not stupid," Vondel argued. "*Angry* is *angry*. Compared to *cantankerous*, *angry* is easier to say. It's less pretentious. Once more, *cantankerous* doesn't sound very *angry* at all. It's more visceral to tell me that you're *angry* with me."

"Alright," I said evenly, "I am *ANGRY* with you. I am very, very *ANGRY* with you."

"That's better," he replied, shaking his head up and down approvingly. "Now, I know where you are coming from!"

"I'll tell you where I'm coming from," I said, throwing my arms up in exasperation. "My home is a total disaster, because of *you!*"

Vondel nodded his head, but said nothing to defend himself.

"It will take me years to clean up this place," I complained. I could feel my blood pressure rising, but made a conscious effort to keep my voice down. "I don't even know any of these people—people that you invited! They could be robbing me blind, as we speak, while you serve them drinks!"

"*And hors d'oeuvres*"*!*" Vondel reminded me. "*GARCON!*" he suddenly called out, soliciting the attention of one of the red-jacketed attendants then making the rounds. The waiter that he summoned came right over to us and lowered his silver tray so that Vondel and I could better see the variety of appetizers he was making available to us.

"Shrimp cocktail!" Vondel announced, taking a napkin and a sample of the offerings. "I just love shrimp cocktail!" he declared boldly—as if I, or the waiter, cared.

"Sir, would you like one?" the waiter asked me, moving the tray closer for my inspection.

"No thank you," I answered, without giving the tray a second glance. I was distracted by the sight of a man sitting on my coffee table. He appeared to be leafing through the pages of a very large scrapbook. I didn't recognize it as one of my own scrapbooks but that was not the issue. The issue was the coffee table. Why was he sitting on it? My impulse was to go over to the stranger and move him to some other place, by force if necessary. Then I recalled just how difficult it was to get Vondel's ear and realized that I could not afford to leave his side without first telling him that I wanted everyone to leave.

"Mm. I love shrimp cocktail," the director shared. He was obviously enjoying himself.

"Can we get back to what we were talking about before, J.P.?" I implored.

"I'm sorry, Steven," Vondel apologized. He lowered his head briefly but brought it back up again so that he could look me in the eyes. He placed his hand on my shoulder and said, "I'd describe the party as an impromptu event." Vondel considered that description thoughtfully, as he relished the last of the shrimp cocktail and wiped his mouth with the napkin in his hand. "It was suggested by one of my assistants, while you were in the lavatory . . . I thought it was a good idea," he added.

"A good idea?" I laughed, derisively.

Vondel clarified his statement, "It was a good idea, comparatively. That is to say, the party was a better idea than filming you at the typewriter for hours and hours. According to Bron, audiences would be more interested in seeing your creations come to life, rather than watching you in the act of creating. After careful consideration, I realized he was right and more importantly, I knew why he was right. An audience needs something to relate to, the action of a drama or the humor of a comedy. They want to be entertained. If they only see you writing, they're left to wonder what you're writing about. It's this guessing that Bron said wasn't much fun—and he was right, by Jove."

Vondel seemed thunderstruck by this revelation. I was thunderstruck by how he had completely forgotten it was I who had originally proposed the idea he had given Bron credit for. As vexed as I was, I struggled to stay focused on what mattered to me most. I wanted Vondel to explain why he had invited all these strangers into my home, so I asked, "How have you brought my book to life by throwing a party for *your friends* in *my apartment?*"

Vondel raised his eyebrows and snickered. "They are not *my friends* in *your apartment.* They are *your friends* in *your apartment.*" He contradicted.

'I don't know any of these people," I argued. I took a quick glance around to make sure. There was a man dressed as a swami waving a sword around. I couldn't be sure if it was real, but it made me uneasy to know that someone might be wielding such an intimidating weapon. The swami made a quick swipe at the air with the blade, fighting off an unseen enemy. There was a woman standing not far from him dressed in the most appalling garment, moth eaten in appearance. She had a worn face, the color of clay. The second the swami moved within striking range of this woman, she hit him over the head with a shoebox she'd been carrying. The swami dropped the sword, grabbed his head and turned around to face his attacker. Before he had the chance to say anything to her, the woman brought the shoebox down onto his head again. "DON'T PLAY WITH KNIVES, MORON," she yelled. The swami said nothing in reply. He simply backed away from her. While continuing to hold his head, I saw him make for the door.

I returned my attention to Vondel. "I don't know any of these people," I reaffirmed.

Vondel shook his head impatiently. "Yes, you do. You know all these people," he told me. "You not only know these people, you invented every single one of them."

"What are you talking about?" I demanded.

Vondel continued, "They're characters from your book. This party is in celebration of your book. What better guests to invite than the characters themselves?"

"Ridiculous!" I scoffed.

"They're from your imagination!" Vondel insisted.

I shook my head, "No, I don't think so."

"How can I convince him?" Vondel asked rhetorically, searching himself. After briefly reflecting on the matter, the director snapped his fingers. He stepped closer to me and stared into my eyes. "Do you remember that short story you told me about in the Lizard Lounge? *The Scholar and the . . .* What was the name again, Steven?"

The Scholar and the Cadaver," I told him.

"That's right. Who was the main character in that story?" Vondel asked.

"Mr. Low," I answered.

"He's standing right over there," Vondel pointed out, "talking to those two nerds in the back of the room. See them? They look like they work for NASA."

I searched the room. "You mean those two guys with the crew cuts?" I asked.

"With the short sleeve shirts and black ties," Vondel elaborated.

"O.K. I see them," I said, "And so who is Mr. Low, the kid talking with them?"

"YES!" Vondel hollered. "THAT'S MR. LOW!"

"That kid?" I laughed out loud. "C'mon!"

"It's the truth, I swear!" Vondel declared. He exhaled, like he was exhausted with me. "Let me try and explain this to you," he said. "Bronny wanted to depict each of the short stories from your book within the film, and I was willing to go along with that, but Lagg had a minor temper tantrum and complained that he had no input on the picture." He threw his arms up in the air so as to display his exasperation with Lagg. "And so, I had to placate him as well. Now, his bright idea was that we should have a party in the film and invite all of the characters from your book, as guests. He pointed out it would be easier and cheaper to film, because it would reduce the necessity of location shots, sets, etcetera. He also pointed out to me it would be more fun. Bron was alright with that idea, as a compromise. As long as he didn't have to film you for hours and hours at your type-writer, he was happy. So, it all worked out in the end and here we are—at the party!"

"This is how the film ends? " I wondered aloud.

"Not quite." Vondel waved his hand dismissively. "This is a *Wunder Haus Picture,* an art house film and an art house film ending this film will have! I'm think-ing about something avant-garde, something eccentric. Now, let me think for a moment." The director placed his hand to his chin thoughtfully and grew quiet. A second later, he jumped. "I know what we'll do! First, we'll con-struct an *Altar to Art* . . . then we will place your book *and this film* on that altar . . . AND WE'LL SET THEM ON FIRE!" Vondel's face grew animated.

"You *can't* destroy my book," I insisted. "I won't allow it! It has too much value . . . and not just for me. It's a good book!"

The director was indignant and dismissive. "The book has no value apart from the film! It is a prop . . . and that's all it was ever meant to be . . . Now, I must de-cide where to build that altar," he said, talking to himself.

"The movie would never have been made, had it not been for my book," I defended.

"Nah ah," Vondel corrected, waving his finger at me. "The book would never have been, had it not been for my movie—it's not the other way around. That is the Devil's logic you are using there, boy, and it will get you in trouble with me."

"What? What are you talking about?" I couldn't be-lieve my ears.

"Where are Bronny and Lagg?" Vondel asked, changing the subject. "I have to tell them we're breaking this party up. It has served its purpose."

I searched through the lingering crowd for Vondel's two assistants and found them chatting with a man wearing pajamas. "They're over there, by the bookcase," I said, pointing in their direction.

Vondel followed with his eyes. "Oh, yes. Thanks, Steven," he said gratefully. "I'm going to tell them about the altar. I'll catch up with you in a bit, alright? Oh, and by the way," he added, "I saw your manuscript on the coffee table, over there. Grab it for me, will you?"

I told myself, 'I'll get the manuscript, but I'm not giving it to you!'

When I went over to the coffee table I saw the same man I'd seen earlier still sitting on top of it, leafing through his scrapbook. I said hello to the man but otherwise ignored him as I rummaged around, searching for my book. I was turning over cups and saucers in my urgent quest and accidentally knocked over one of the cups. It rolled off the table and fell into the crease of the scrapbook. The man looked up and when he did his eyes nearly popped out of his head. *"My God!"* he cried. "You're this man!" he said, pointing at the scrapbook, which as I noticed was actually a photo album.

"What are you talking about?" I gasped, straining my neck to see.

"You're this guy, aren't you?" he pointed at a snapshot. It must have been pasted in the album a very long time ago, because the pages of the album were yellowed and the glue holding the photos in place had long since lost its efficacy. As I came closer to him and was able to make out the photo in question I saw that it did indeed feature an image of me.

"Why yes," I admitted, "That does seem to be me, alright." I tried to recall when the photo could have been taken. It looked very recent. Had the snapshot not appeared so deteriorated I might have thought it had been taken that very night, at the party.

"Hey look at this one, check this one out," the stranger said, pointing at another snapshot on the adjacent page. "This is you *and me.*"

I took a closer look at this other photo. As I did, I saw within its frame an image of me with the stranger at the coffee table. The photo looked like it had just been taken, at that exact moment. We were wearing the same clothes and the stranger was holding the same photo album in his hands. "Well, I'll be damned," I laughed. *"How the hell . . . "*

"Ooh, and hey—here's another one, over here! Look at this one!" The stranger excitedly stabbed at the page with his index finger. "There's another person with us in this snapshot."

I came around to his other side and bent my knees so that I could get a better look. Sure enough, I saw in the photograph an image of me, the stranger—still sitting at the table holding the photo album—and yet a third face that I did not recognize.

"Who is that other guy?" the stranger asked me, as if I had a clue.

Suddenly, a man approached us with an extended hand. I realized that he expected me to shake it. So as not to be impolite, I did. It was then I recognized his face as the third face in the photo. In his other hand he held a manuscript, which interested me very much. He said, "It's a pleasure and an honor to meet you, Mr. Orion. Allow me to introduce myself. My name is Moigle. I am a main character in one of your stories, *Acting on Meditations . . .* " At that point, he handed me the manuscript. "This is yours," he said. "I only meant to borrow it." He elbowed me in a kidding manner. "Wanted to make sure you spelled Moigle correctly."

I thanked him for returning the manuscript.

"I had a conversation with Vondel earlier," Moigle confessed. "He informed me that you're the reason I am here, Mr. Orion; the reason why everyone is here. While most of your guests probably don't realize or appreciate this fact, I wanted you to know that I do." Moigle cocked his head and stared at me. "Forgive me, it's not every day a man gets to meets his maker," he chuckled. "Well, if there's anything I can ever do for you . . . just let me know. I'll be taking my leave of you now and getting on with my life. I'm not sure what I want to do with this life you've given me, but I know one thing: The sky is the limit." He placed his hand over his mouth as if he'd uttered a foul word. "Damn, I forgot! Lagg told me to never mention the 'sky' in Vondel's presence. Well so long, Mr. Orion." I nodded to Moigle and watched as he walked toward the door. He helped himself to a cocktail from one of the passing waiters, before he exited the room.

The photo album guy tapped my shoulder. "That's the other guy in this photo," he said.

"Yes, I know," I said. "Will you excuse me?" Following Moigle's example, I headed for the door.

On my way out, I saw Vondel talking with his two cronies. Lagg tried to make eye contact with me. I avoided his gaze, of course. I quickly ran down the hall and hurried for the front door. The moment I stepped outside, I heard someone call my name. I ignored it and proceeded down the street in a nonchalant, carefree fashion. When I heard my name again I turned around to confirm my suspicion and sure enough I spotted the director and his two assistants charging on my heels. With the preservation of my book as the motivating factor, I ran down the block as fast as I could. I was nearly run over by a garbage truck, when I darted across the street in an effort to lose them. I had seen an entrance to the park and had the idea to hide out in there. Why I selected the park as a place to hide, I don't know. I suppose I had the crazy impression I could camouflage myself more easily in a natural setting, surrounded by trees. In retrospect, anyplace else would have been better . . . an abandoned building, or a garbage can in an alleyway. The park was too open and revealing a place to hide.

At that odd hour I was surprised to see people walking their dogs. I saw one young lady walking a German Shepherd; she was leaving the park as I was running in. I also spotted a clubfooted man walking a Doberman Pinscher. Both the German Shepherd and the Doberman Pinscher went berserk when I passed them. Their owners somehow managed to calm and retrain the dogs, but after a pause I again heard them barking in a frenzied manner. I recognized this as confirmation that the director and his cohorts were still on my trail. I was wishing that I knew the park more intimately at that stressful moment, then I might have formulated a plan of action: 'If I run in that direction, I can find sanctuary by the benches that run between the river and the bike path,' or 'If I run up that hill, past the abandoned vending booth, I can hide out in the public restroom, in one of the stalls. Sometimes, they're open during the winter.' But I had no plan to speak of, aside from following the moon in the sky. I was practically out of breath, as I frantically approached a tall, dark figure that appeared from a wooded clearing.

"Help me, you've got to help me," I pleaded. "Three men are chasing me. They're trying to kill me!" Why I said men were trying to kill me, I don't know. I suppose in the back of my mind, I thought it would increase the likelihood of the stranger assisting my escape. It wasn't until I approached him that I realized he was wearing a top hat. Just the sight of a top hat had an unusual effect on me. I felt as if I had been transported to another time. The second I thought about this, I saw another stranger emerge from the wooded clearing. Like the first stranger, he was dressed in black and sporting a top hat. "Oh, thank God you're here too," I said. "You've got to help me, both of you. There are three men chasing me, trying to kill me!"

The two strangers looked at each other, then at me and said nothing. I could see their pale faces outlined in the moonlight, with strong jaw lines and deep furrows. Not a trace of human emotion could be found in these works of stone. Two things occurred to me, as I stared at them. First, their top hats might be irremovable and second, they might not understand English. Why else would they not respond to a plea as desperate as mine? Even though they didn't reply to me in an expected, sympathetic way, I still hoped for their assistance in the event of a confrontation with Vondel and his men. I hesitated leaving them, for this reason. Three men were better than one, especially since Vondel and Company also added up to three.

"Do you speak English?" I asked, growing desperate.

"English?" the taller of the two questioned.

"Do you speak English?" I asked again.

Both men shook their heads no.

"Wir sprechen Deutsch," the taller one replied.

"You're German?" I gasped.

Both nodded yes.

"Wir sind Deutsche," the shorter of the two confirmed.

Fortunately, I knew a little German. *"Konnen Sie mir bitte helfen?"* I pleaded.

"Was ist los?" the taller of the two men asked, eyeing me skeptically.

Before I had the chance to say another word, I was interrupted by a desperate cry from across the park, "HEY!" I instantly recognized the voice as belonging to Vondel. I had heard him scream before like that many times over the years. Our history together went back a long way and now I had a profound sense of foreboding that this history was about to come to an abrupt end in an ugly expression of self indulgence.

"It's too late," I said, lapsing back into English, talking more to myself than to my company. "The end is upon us."

It really wasn't a great surprise to me that Vondel closed the gap between us in such an immediate fashion. I'd lingered with these two ignorant fools much longer than I should have. In short, I had gambled on the two of them and lost. It was a poor choice of judgment on my part. After thirty-six years of trials and tribulations in this wicked world I should know better than to gamble on anyone but myself. A perverse sort of theory took hold of me at that depressing moment. What if Vondel knew these two men and what if they were all involved in the plot to prevent me from escaping with the book?

I turned around to face the inevitable and quickly spotted Vondel sprinting in the moonlight. He was just ahead of his two assistants who were lugging the equipment. As I studied the director, I made out what I perceived to be an infernal, satisfied smirk upon his face. That smirk made my blood boil but it did not infuriate me nearly as much as the gay, at times hysterical, laughter of Bron and Lagg. Those two were obviously overjoyed to see me in such a compromised position.

"Now, we face the end," Bron laughed, focusing his camera on my face. Lagg was holding up a light for him. It was clear that they wanted to capture the expression on my face as they caught up to me. "You're on *Candid Camera*," Lagg laughed.

A second later, Vondel was standing right beside me. "You shouldn't have taken the book, Steven. You had no right," he scolded.

I ignored him and appealed to the two men in top hats. *"BOSE!"* I said, pointing at Vondel. *"Er ist sehr bose!"*

The two men looked at each other and for the first time I saw them smile. *"Bose!"* they mocked.

"Bozo," I heard one say. They stared at me with contempt.

Vondel chuckled and addressed me again, "Why would you call me evil, Steven. I just want what belongs to me." I felt a push from behind and I stumbled. At that point, Vondel grabbed the book out of my hands.

"Mein buch!" I declared, appealing to the two strangers one last time.

"MEIN BUCH!" the taller of the two repeated, scathingly denouncing me with his eyes. His penetrating gaze frightened me, but I was quickly distracted by Lagg's voice:

"You've been a bad boy," he said to me.

I told him to shut up.

Vondel laughed. "Put the light down on the ground, Lagg, and take hold of him," he instructed.

It did of course occur to me that I could run away from them at this point, but it seemed easier to resign myself to my fate. After all, where was I going to run? There were five of them and one of me. No matter where I went they would catch up in the end. There was nowhere to hide in the park, except for the wooded clearing. The second that I glanced in that direction I felt

Lagg take hold of my arm. "You're not going anyplace," he said, "except where WE want you to go."

Bron placed the camera about two inches from my face and added, "You're in trouble, wise guy. You shouldn't have run off with the book. Now, you're going to share the same fate as the book. You're going to burn—BURN!" he screamed.

"Shut up, Bronny!" Vondel ordered. He had been talking to the two strangers in Dutch, Flemish or whatever that other language was he occasionally used. After chastising Bron, Vondel resumed speaking in his native tongue. It sounded like German at times and shared some common words, but for the most part it was incomprehensible to me. The two strangers certainly knew the language. While Vondel spoke, both of them nodded obediently. From time to time they stared at me ominously, which gave me the chills.

Bron's words also carried a burden for me. What did he mean when he said that I would share the same fate as the book? That I would burn? I reflected on those words and recalled Vondel's proposed *Altar to Art* and his plan to burn the book and the film on such an altar. I asked myself, was this altar our ultimate destination? It was a logical conclusion, but was it built yet? I had the distinct impression from the director that it had not.

I watched the two men in top hats, as Vondel's voice commanded their attention. I was trying to read their expressions, to get an indication of the subject matter. It seemed as if Vondel was sharing a joke, because the two men were giggling like impish children, but then that giggling developed into a laughter best described as diabolical. Each new laugh brought with it something more ominous and threatening than the last. With an increased frequency their menacing glances came to rest on me and I had a foreboding that they were planning my demise. My suspicions were confirmed, when one of the two strangers announced, *"Die Kunst ist todt,"* or, 'Art is dead.' In response to this, the other stranger replied, *"Der man ist todt."*

Vondel laughed at their black humor, but it was obvious that something serious had taken hold of him, because the director solicited their attention again in Dutch and broke up their levity with a demand of some sort.

As if in response to this demand, Lagg tightened his forearm's hold on my neck. I heard him say to Bron, "Vondel is telling them to hand over the knife. This is it."

Bron giggled, "Boy, are you gonna get it, Steve-O! Boy, are you gonna get it!" He briefly paused from adjusting the camera on the tripod to punch me in the arm. He punched me with all of his might, so I would not mistake his actions as playful. I would have stumbled from the blow, had Lagg not been holding me firmly.

"Check this out!" Lagg said. He shifted my position so that my attention was directed at the two strangers with Vondel. The taller of the two opened his frock coat and removed a long, thin, double-edged butcher knife from a sheath at his side. He held the dagger up to the moonlight, so that it gleamed.

"A beautiful thing!" Bron exclaimed, punching me again.

"It is beautiful, isn't it?" Vondel asked, looking my way.

"Why are you doing this?" I asked him. "You have my book. Burn it with the film, if you want. Just please let me go!" I begged him. *"You don't have to kill me!"*

"I don't have to kill you, eh?" Vondel mocked. "I need an ending for the film before I burn it," he declared, with a determined and ruthless expression. "Every great movie deserves a great ending, no?" He stared at me, waiting for my response.

"But you don't have to kill me!" I pleaded.

The director ignored me and turned to the man with the knife. *"Gibt es mir!"* he ordered.

The man handed the dagger over to Vondel. *"Hier,"* he said. *"Viel gluck!"*

From the smile on Vondel's face I could see that he was most grateful to have the dagger in his possession. He admired it with a kind of awe, as if the knife was a special treasure. *"Danke,"* he replied, seemingly beside himself at the prospect of holding it. "Tell me, do you recognize this knife?" the director asked me.

"No," I replied.

"That is a pity," he pronounced, raising the dagger to the moonlight himself. "I hope you noticed, Steven, that this is not *a silver dagger . . .*"

Bron and Lagg laughed at this joke. I thought it was tasteless.

"It is a steel dagger," Vondel explained, "with more weight than a swami's knife, greater significance, more profundity!"

"I don't understand," I admitted, then looked at Bron and Lagg stifling their laughter. "What is so funny?" I demanded to know.

"Funny?" Vondel repeated. "We are not trying to be funny," he told me. On that note, he turned to the two strangers in top hats and shook their hands. The three exchanged some words in German and it became evident to me that they were leaving:

"Guten Nacht, Vondel."

"Auf Wiedersehen. Bis bald!"

Vondel said something else to them in Dutch, as they departed. The two strangers turned around briefly to give a last wave goodbye before disappearing into the wooded clearing from which they had first emerged.

When they were gone, the director returned his attention to me. "And now, my dear boy," he said, pointing the butcher knife at my throat, "Behold the *Altar to Art!*" The director made a slight gesture with the blade, indicating a reference point behind my back. Obligingly, Lagg turned me around. Repositioned, I beheld a magnificent golden light. This luminescence had arisen out of nowhere and overwhelmed us all. As my eyes adjusted to the light, I was able to discern a golden spire and recognized it as the source of the light. How the spire appeared on the scene, I do not know. For sure, I hadn't noticed it until that point and it was not something easily overlooked. The spire stretched endlessly upwards, so that the peak disappeared into the clouds lingering over the park.

"What do you think of it?" Vondel asked me, as he approached the base of the spire.

"Where did it come from?" I asked, in response. "It wasn't here a minute ago."

Bron and Lagg laughed at me. Vondel laughed with them.

"What?" I asked. "How did it get here?"

They continued to laugh at me. I felt more humiliated with each passing second, as their laughing became a sustained jag that I thought would never end.

"ALRIGHT, ALRIGHT," Vondel finally cried, catching his breath. "This is serious business," he announced, hushing the other two up. "There will be time for gaiety and celebration later, *once our work is finished*." At the completion of these words, he raised his hand to show me the book in his possession and stared at me.

I returned Vondel's stare defiantly, but my eyes soon drifted to the base of the spire behind him. I saw a ceremonial altar made of the same brilliant golden material as the spire. The golden altar was shaped like a table, only there was smoke rising from it. Noting my keen interest, Vondel smiled at me then turned around and faced the altar himself, pausing briefly and dramatically before it, in what could be interpreted as a moment of prayer. Then, with a stoic resolve he said, "Goodbye!" and dropped my book into the pyre burning on the altar. I wanted to scream my lungs out at the rotten bastard as I saw the book catch fire, the book that I had slaved over, sacrificed for. But I did not want to give Vondel the satisfaction of knowing he had defeated my spirit. Instead, I stood there like a catatonic and gave him nothing.

"How do you like that, Steve?" Bron asked me, focusing the camera on my face as he waited for my reaction. "There goes your book!" he added, maliciously antagonizing me. "There it goes!"

"Yeah, there goes your book!" Lagg mimicked, tightening his grip on my throat. "It's up in flames now."

Within seconds the book was reduced to ashes. Vondel said nothing the whole time. He just stood over the altar, watching it burn. At a certain point, he broke away from the altar and approached me. Lagg tightened his grip of me at Vondel's approach. Until then, he'd been holding me from behind with his left arm around my throat. As the director stepped toward us, Lagg also brought his right arm around my waist and secured it there tightly, bracing me, as if in preparation for something. When Vondel raised the knife I knew what that something was. I heard a scream as the director plunged the knife into me, into the middle of my chest. I was braced all the tighter by Lagg as I absorbed the blade, but I did not actually feel any pain as a result of the director's thrust. This lack of pain made me question whether I had actually been stabbed. I wondered about this, even as I saw the dagger sticking out of me and saw that I was soaking in my own blood. What washed away all lingering doubt in my mind that I had been severely wounded, nay mortally wounded, was the dimming of the golden haze, the dimming of everything. Before the entire scene faded to black, I saw a sinister smile widen across Vondel's face. After that my eyes closed, but I clearly heard Lagg whisper the words, *"Like a God!"* into my ear.

When I opened my eyes again, I found myself alone in a darkened movie theater, staring at the scene I have just described projected onto a giant movie screen. I saw myself being murdered, basically. To my surprise, I was not disturbed by this morbid tableau, probably because I knew it didn't mean the end of me; as it did not mean the end of me when I saw Vondel and Lagg take my lifeless body and lay it across the *Altar to Art*. Not even when Bron's camera lens zoomed in for a close-up shot of my burning skeleton was I the least bit disturbed or shaken. How could these images mean anything to me, if I knew they were not real? After all, I was sitting in a movie theater watching the whole thing happen as if it was an out of body experience.

Likewise, I was not disturbed when the film ended with a sudden explosion and the movie screen caught fire. I knew it didn't really mean the end of the film. Just because I couldn't enjoy the footage didn't mean that the action wasn't still taking place somewhere. The fact that the movie screen was ablaze was a testament to that belief. It was ablaze because Bron or Vondel removed the film from the camera and tossed it onto the altar to burn. I didn't have to see that happen to know that it happened. Why else would a movie screen suddenly catch fire? But this is the important point: despite its implied destruction, the spirit of the film lived on.

Now you may ask, did I get nervous and run out of the theater because the screen was on fire and I was afraid for my life? No, I did not. I was confident that if I died there and then it would only mean that I would be reconstituted elsewhere, perhaps *in another movie the-ater* watching an image of my lifeless body burning *in this movie theater.* I felt a kind of immortality, for lack of a more inventive word. Do you want to know what I did do then? I sat there calmly in my seat, reached into my package of popcorn, found some kernels that had never popped and tossed them at the burning movie screen in a disinterested way. Then I ate what remained of my chocolate-coated nuts and raisins and sucked the final traces of my soda through the crazy straw that I brought from home.

I hear you ask the question, "But why, Steven, should these actions of all possible actions be the last actions that we perceive for you as a character that couldn't die in a film that couldn't burn, in a book that couldn't burn?' I knew you would ask that question. Here is my reply: you've perceived me throwing popcorn kernels at the burning movie screen, eating chocolate covered nuts and raisins and drinking soda through a crazy straw, because this has allowed me something amusing to do while I wisely reflect on the immortality of words. I said . . . *the immorality of words.* After all, my book—this book—could not really have been destroyed on the *Altar to Art* if you're still reading it, still reading my train of thoughts. As you are reading my train of thoughts, allow me to share a single defining idea:

The end never means THE END.